The Bride Experiment:

What Happens When

Single Women Get Fed Up?

The Bride Experiment:

What Happens When

Single Women Get Fed Up?

Mimi Jefferson

www.urbanchristianonline.com

Urban Books, LLC
78 East Industry Court
Deer Park, NY 11729

The Bride Experiment: What Happens When Single Women Get Fed Up? Copyright © 2011 Mimi Jefferson

ISBN 13: 978-1-60162-869-5
ISBN 10: 1-60162-869-2

First Printing September 2011
Printed in the United States of America

10 9 8 7 6 5 4 3 2 1

This is a work of fiction. Any references or similarities to actual events, real people, living, or dead, or to real locales are intended to give the novel a sense of reality. Any similarity in other names, characters, places, and incidents is entirely coincidental.

Distributed by Kensington Corp.
Submit Wholesale Orders to:
Kensington Publishing Corp.
C/O Penguin Group (USA) Inc.
Attention: Order Processing
405 Murray Hill Parkway
East Rutherford, NJ 07073-2316
Phone: 1-800-526-0275
Fax: 1-800-227-9604

Mr. Lee

The Big Relentless

Ladybug

~For exemplifying sacrificial love~

Acknowledgments

I had the pleasure of meeting so many wonderful people with my first novel, *The Single Sister Experiment: What Happens When Single Women Stop Having Sex?* We had some unforgettable discussions. Thank you all for encouraging me to write this new novel.

I am very thankful to everybody who e-mailed me. It brought joy to my heart that you would take the time to connect with me. Each time I turned on my computer, I could hear all of you rooting for me: *"Go, Mimi! Go, Mimi!"*

Congratulations to all of you who have decided to join the "Experiment." What a fabulous journey it will be! I am praying with you. *Go, ladies! Go, ladies!*

Thanks to the members of *The Single Sister Experiment* Yahoo Online Group for inspiring me to continue despite the obstacles.

My family and friends have been a constant source of strength in more ways than I can count. Thank you!

Mom, I couldn't do this without you. You are my second biggest supporter.

Reda, our work together was truly a divine connection. Thanks for answering all of my questions.

Clifford and Ollie, our Monday evening dinners were delicious. You two take such good care of us!

Dr. Dryden, every woman needs to know a woman like you.

Acknowledgments

Nicole, the terrible twos have nothing on you. Thanks for blowing bubbles, baking pizza, and watching way too much *Caillou*.

Thanks, Pastor Jones and Pastor Lovelady, for laying the foundation.

Thank you, Mrs. Jossel-Ross and Mr. Weber, for allowing me the opportunity to share what God has given me.

Love is an action. My husband proves that to me every day. I am eternally grateful.

I pray this novel was written to the glory of God. I can do nothing without Him.

Chapter 1

James could taste the sweat as it trickled past his eyebrows and down his lips. He pulled the string to open the wooden blinds, looked around outside, then closed the blinds in less than two seconds. The street was empty just as he had hoped. Once again, his timing was perfect.

He had his neighbors' schedules memorized. Mrs. Edison and the twins left for their walk at approximately seven forty-five each morning and returned fifteen minutes later. The retired couple across the street tilled their garden each day, rain or shine, starting at seven and finishing forty-five minutes later. By seven-fifty, the school buses and car pools all arrived and departed. To be sure to avoid all of them, he needed to pull his Tahoe into the garage at eight-ten sharp, each morning.

The tension in his body eased a bit as he took a long gulp of his fourth cup of coffee in less than two hours. He needed to relax; he had made it through another morning. James had not seen anyone, and it appeared as if no one had seen him.

His hideout was a convenience store with a restaurant attached to it. He waited there each day until he was sure Raquel and the kids had left and his neighbors had dispersed for the morning.

He practiced his speech again. "Baby, I don't want you to worry, but I kinda lost my job." He tried to prepare himself for Raquel's objections. "Of course, I know it is less than a month before our wedding. Yes, I know we just purchased our dream home. Yes, I did say I was finally going to do right by you and our kids."

James had been having imaginary conversations, sneaking into his own house, and consuming obscene amounts of coffee for the last week. He didn't like the way the words were leaving his mouth today. Instead of coming out soft, like satin, they seemed explosive, like bullets. He was growing more terrified that he would make things worse by rambling incoherently. He couldn't remember the last time he felt the need to write a letter. But he suddenly recalled hearing on a talk show that writing was the best way to deliver bad news. This way, he could take his time and word things carefully.

James's hands trembled as he wrote,

Dear Raquel, You know I love you and the kids with all my heart. But my love has caused me to keep something from you. I am very sorry. It has been so hard to keep up this lie.

James slammed his cup on the counter. He wanted nothing more than to be able to concentrate on Raquel and write this letter. But then a silhouette of another woman appeared in his mind, interrupting his thoughts. He tried to stop thinking about Joan Dallas, but the closer he drew to his wedding, the more he couldn't help but wonder if he had made the right decision choosing Raquel over her. It hurt him to do it, but he finally stopped dating Joan, the perpetual other woman in his life, and mother to one of his children. He wanted to prove to Raquel that he was finally serious about being a responsible father and husband.

James's mother once told him he needed to pick one woman and settle down, because as much as he would like it, he was never going to be able to create a "Joquel." Raquel was beautiful. Joan was ordinary-looking. Raquel graduated from beauty school. When James met Joan, she was managing several professional offices. Joan also held a college degree. Raquel was loud and could be embarrassing, but she was also spontaneous, with a fiery streak that ignited passion in James. Joan was more reserved, well spoken, and fit in perfectly when James needed a date for an upscale function.

In regard to physique, Raquel couldn't compete with Joan. The bad thing was, she didn't seem to realize it. James asked Raquel repeatedly to wear clothes that complemented her plus-sized frame. Raquel just ignored him, continuing to dress as if she still had the body she had in high school. On the other hand, Joan had the body Raquel had in high school, which is why he couldn't stop meditating on her curvaceous silhouette in his head.

What brought Raquel to the finish line was the fact that she had been fully committed to James; no man had ever touched her, but him. James certainly couldn't say that about Joan. James smiled. Raquel was pure, lovely, and faithful. That's why she won him over. He started to work on his apology letter again, with a new enthusiasm.

Days ago, all James could think about was how he was going to surprise Raquel. He had planned and paid for an over-the-top honeymoon orchestrated to leave her speechless. Instead of shopping for their beach attire, he needed to figure out how he was going to tell Raquel the truth without losing her forever.

James told everybody he was finished with his lying, manipulative, and womanizing ways. He was finally going to be the man his family needed. At their engagement party, he tore his little black book to pieces to the delight of all 200 of their guests.

The poster-sized high-school picture of Raquel on the wall in their den caught James's attention. It was his favorite photo of her. It wasn't the type of photo a person hung up and never noticed again. He took a good long look at it every time he had the chance.

He meditated on her honey brown skin, slightly slanted eyes, and thick wavy hair. She had her majorette leotard on, with those legendary white high-heeled boots. Her figure was svelte back then, 140 pounds of hourglass perfection. James walked into Mrs. Hunter's eleventh-grade history class and knew he had to have Raquel. She was the most beautiful girl he had ever seen.

Raquel could have married anybody, but she chose the guy who did not know how to appreciate her; the guy who cheated on her consistently for over a decade; the guy who made her feel inferior, because after having his two children, she no longer looked like the shapely majorette in the picture.

He thought back to his first apartment, nestled right in the middle of the wrong side of Houston. He used to joke about how the rats were as big as cats. Now he was living in a five-bedroom luxury home located in a suburb, miles outside of Houston. Everything was finally going to be perfect. That was until he lost his job of over fifteen years. James had been a constable ever since he graduated from college with a degree in criminal justice.

Kenny G's saxophone buzzed from James's cell phone. His first thought was to not answer it, but a quick check of his caller ID made him change his mind. He paused a moment, then swallowed hard before taking a deep breath. "What's up?" James hoped he sounded like himself.

"Hey, it's Miles."

James instantly knew something was wrong. His younger brother never identified himself when he called. "Hey, bro, what's up? Why are you calling so early?"

"I need to talk to you," Miles said. "What time do you get off duty?"

Lies were accustomed to flowing effortlessly from James's mouth. "I took off today. I needed a break. I'm at home."

"Are Raquel and the kids gone?"

"Yeah, why?" James tried to sound calm. He didn't like the fact that he couldn't read anything in his brother's monotone voice.

"Good, I'm on my way over. I'm about fifteen minutes away."

James wanted to ask another question. He glanced down at his phone. He would have to wait. Miles ended the call without the words that had ended all of his phone conversations since he read *The Autobiography of Malcolm X* in middle school. James wondered why his brother chose this morning not to end their conversation with the words he always said, "Peace be with you."

When Miles wasn't golfing, he was obsessed with finding the one thing that would allow him to be alongside the founders of Google, Myspace, and Facebook. He and one of his law school dropout buddies had gone through several ideas, each failed. Their latest venture was to form an Internet-based company where men could discreetly get paternity tests on their alleged children. He said they were seeing case after case where men were paying child support for children who did not belong to them.

A man just could not ask the woman in his life for such a test, without causing a major catastrophe. He needed to be able to get results discreetly, and the discretion was what their mail-order DNA business provided.

James had no doubts he had fathered James Jr., his son by Joan, and Morris and Alexis, his children by Raquel. He was only trying to help his brother when he gathered his children one weekend and met Miles and his associate at a restaurant. They secured the swabs they needed from the children without them realizing they had been tested.

James remembered something Miles had whispered to him as they were leaving the restaurant that day.

"The results will be back in two weeks."

James glanced at the date on his cell phone. It had been exactly two weeks.

Chapter 2

Raquel pulled up to her favorite restaurant, stepped out of her Mercedes, and posed for the women getting into the car next to her. She could see them staring at her and she wanted to make sure they didn't miss one delectable detail.

The Mercedes was black, with matching leather and customized rims. Her stilettos were Jimmy Choo. The jeans hugging her frame were tailored to fit her every curve. The forest green Versace handbag on her arm was one of the largest and most expensive in their collection. The ring sparkling from her left hand was a specially designed creation of Henry Vu, jeweler to the stars. Her look was completed with flawless bone-straight hair, Versace shades—the same hue as her handbag—and makeup so perfect it looked like the work of a professional.

James went ballistic when she came home with her engagement ring. He couldn't believe she went and purchased a piece of jewelry that cost as much as a car. Raquel was quiet during his tantrum. She wasn't about to sell it. It made complete strangers shamelessly stop, stare, and gasp. Of course, nobody suspected she had bought it herself, and that was just the way she liked it.

Raquel strategically planned the engagement. It was going to be a breakfast James would never forget. She made his favorite foods and gathered their children, Morris and Alexis, around the table. She called James to the table, and with all of them in a circle holding hands, preparing to say grace, she asked, "Will you marry us?"

Stunned, James hesitated, and then he took a few moments to look at each individual member of his young family and said, "Yes."

Raquel had only three weeks left before her wedding. Everything had gone perfectly until Karen, her maid of honor, was sitting in a coffee shop after a long night at the club. A young woman walked up to her and shared the Gospel of Jesus Christ. In less than a month, Karen moved out of the house she had shared with her longtime boyfriend, stopped stripping, and joined the church. She sold her beloved BMW because she knew she would no longer be able to pay for it, moved back home with her mom, and did something she said she would never do—no matter what. She went back to working a nine-to-five gig, answering phones, at a delivery service.

Raquel knew her friend had officially lost her mind when she exchanged her stilettos and designer clothing for no-name flats and mom jeans. Raquel had been avoiding the issue, but now she had to make sure that Karen's new born-again status was not going to cause her to reveal the secret they both shared. That is why she scheduled this lunch date to make sure she and Karen were on the same page.

Raquel tried to appear calm as she followed the hostess to her seat. The fact was, though, she had never been more nervous. She used to feel like she had known Karen all of her life, now she felt like she did not know her at all.

They met when Raquel was new to the beauty business and was still hustling for clients. She would stand outside of grocery stores and hand out flyers showing pictures of her makeovers.

Karen had recently moved to Houston from Dallas and had tried several stylists, but none she really liked. She agreed to give Raquel a try. When Karen saw how natural and gorgeous her weave looked under Raquel's care, she was so grateful that she asked Raquel to be her guest on an all-expense-paid cruise. Raquel had never met anyone like Karen. Raquel was used to women hating her because of her looks, but Karen wasn't like that. She was generous and always had an upbeat attitude. Compared to the grumbling and complaining people in Raquel's life, Karen was a breath of fresh air. She didn't sit around waiting for something to happen; she made it happen.

If she wanted a $5,000 dress, she bought it. If she wanted a man's number, she asked for it. If she wanted the chef to make something off the menu, she had him summoned so she could instruct him on how to make it.

It wasn't until years later that Raquel fully understood how Karen supported her lavish lifestyle. She told everyone she sold real estate, but what she really did was show expensive homes for a real-estate agent. The agent thought her striking appearance would make the homes look better, especially to his single male clients.

Her full-time job was being "Allure," the only black stripper at the exclusive gentlemen's club, The Serpent. Karen did not make a habit of selling her body. However, every now and then she would get an offer so lucrative, she would find herself taking it.

Raquel perused the menu out of habit; she already knew what she was going to order. She ate at Fontenot's almost daily since it was near her salon, and she could grab a quick bite in between her clients.

She got to the restaurant early to make sure she would have all of Karen's favorite dishes hot and at the table upon her arrival. Before Karen became a Christian, she used to eat all her meals out, but Raquel knew now that Karen was answering phones for a living, days like these were reserved for paydays and special occasions.

Raquel usually ordered the spicy chicken tenders, mustard greens, and a side of sweet potato fries. But since today was about Karen, she ordered from the more expensive side of the menu: jumbo lump crab cakes, seafood gumbo, filet mignon, Parmesan risotto, and peach sangria.

Raquel thumped her French-manicured nails on the table and got angrier with each thump. Karen made it clear during their phone conversation two days ago that she no longer approved of Raquel's lifestyle. Who was Karen to tell her how to live? So what there had been other men over the years besides James? It wasn't like he was innocent. Karen must have forgotten James had a baby on her with that ugly baboon, Joan Dallas. He had a longtime thing with Joan, and she had a long-time thing with Randall. Only, James knew nothing about Randall. As a matter of fact, James thought he was the only one with whom she had ever slept.

"Hey, girl," Karen said, abruptly interrupting Raquel's thumping.

Raquel faked a smile while wondering why Karen felt it was okay to come outside looking like a dirty mop. "I will do your hair for free if you promise to never come out in public looking like that again."

"What?" Karen patted her weave down.

"What do you mean 'what'? You look like you got your weave done by somebody's thirteen-year-old cousin in the back of a truck going a hundred miles per hour. Patting it is not going to help. You need to pull that stuff out and start all over again. And what's wrong with your outfit? It's the summer, way past time for warm-up suits." Raquel looked around the restaurant, then back at Karen. "Hurry up and sit down."

Karen meekly took her seat across from Raquel.

Raquel suddenly noticed the sullen expression on Karen's face and remembered she needed to be nice to her. She tried to redirect the conversation.

"I'm sorry. I was tripping. It's just that you usually are so pulled together." Raquel motioned to her stylish ensemble. "I mean, look at me. You taught me a lot of what I know, and look how good I look."

Karen looked down at the table, unable to focus on Raquel's eyes.

Raquel continued. "It's okay, girl. We are going to get you fixed up just as soon as we leave. I have a client coming, but she can wait until I'm finished with you."

Karen mumbled something.

"I'm sorry, I can't hear you, Karen."

Karen wiggled back and forth in her seat. She still refused to look at Raquel.

Raquel could feel her temperature rising. The Karen she knew didn't wiggle, and she certainly didn't mumble. Whatever she said, she spoke it fearlessly. Raquel moved in closer and in a whisper said, "You are making me nervous . . . very . . . very nervous. What's up with you?"

Karen said nothing. Raquel took a deep breath when the food arrived. Surely, Karen would be excited about the spread she had ordered. Raquel said in a voice that sounded like a kindergarten teacher, "Look, Karen, I got all your favorite things."

Karen stared blankly at the steak and risotto the waitress had set in front of her. Raquel went on. "I even got a small bowl of gumbo and a few of those crab cakes you like so much. I know it's a lot, but I was thinking you could take some of it home . . . you know."

Raquel could feel the beads of sweat forming on her forehead.

Karen waited until the waitress left, then pushed her food away. She finally looked up at Raquel. "I've decided to fast today."

"What!"

Raquel caught herself and then said in a softer tone, "I mean, I don't understand."

"Now that I'm a Christian, I find it necessary to get closer to the Lord. I have found that I can hear God's voice better during a period of fasting." Karen waited for Raquel to say something; when she didn't, Karen went on. "I know why you have brought me here, and I want you to know I have been thinking and praying about your situation."

"Really?" Raquel resisted the urge to squeeze Karen's neck and watch the life stream out of her. "What are you going to do about my situation, Karen?"

"I'm going to pray that you tell James that there is a possibility that Morris and Alexis are not his because you have been sleeping with Randall from day one."

"I knew I should have never told you. What in the world was I thinking?"

"You never meant to tell me, remember? I found you and Randall in the back of his van at Lacey's housewarming party."

Raquel sneered at Karen. For years, she had kept her secret, then one slipup and she spilled her guts to Karen. Of course, she thought that Karen could be trusted with this information. For a long time, she could. Only Karen knew about Raquel's secret obsession, a so-called rapper/producer she had known since high school. He was an overall mess-up, in and out of jail, no ambition, still living at home with his mom, but he could satisfy Raquel in bed like no man could. He was an addiction. As much as she tried to leave him for good, the hours of ecstasy he supplied her body with had her running back for more. It was their little secret, and it had to stay that way. It was weeks before her dream wedding. She was too close to spending the rest of her life with James to blow it.

Raquel tried to sound like she was calm. "James thinks he's the only man I have ever slept with. That's the one thing I have on that baboon, Joan. If the information is revealed, don't you know what it would mean?"

"Well, it is about time he found out the truth. Do you really want to start your new lives together with a pile of lies?"

The nervousness in Raquel was quickly turning to rage. Last night on *48 Hours Mystery* the reporter interviewed a man who had killed his wife with rat poisoning by injecting it into her food and water. The last interview was with a woman who had hired a hit man to kill her husband's mistress in what appeared to be a drug deal. Raquel wondered how she could do what needed to be done to Karen, only *without* getting caught.

"I thought we were better than this," Raquel said.

"This is not about me and you. This is about you and God."

Raquel shifted the conversation. "Are you still going to be my maid of honor?"

"I have been meaning to talk to you about that. I know I should have told you earlier, but no. I'm sorry, Raquel. I love you like you are my own sister, but I cannot participate in this mockery of God's holy covenant of marriage."

Raquel wanted to slap her, good and hard. How many married men had she serviced dishonoring God's holy covenant?

Karen seemed to read her mind. "I know my new life is confusing to you. It is confusing to me too. I'm so different now. Everything has changed. Especially now that I have my diagnosis. All that hard living got the best of me." Karen paused; then she looked around to make sure no one was listening to their conversation. "I'm HIV positive, Raquel."

Raquel felt sick. Karen didn't have anything to lose. Now that she had an incurable disease, she could tell James the truth and not have any regrets.

Karen started to weep. "I'm sorry, Raquel, for leading you astray the way that I did. I know that my past life was beyond evil. I'm trying to make amends and give back what I have taken. I know Jesus has forgiven me of my sins. He is giving me the strength to apologize to those I hurt. That includes you. I'm so sorry, Raquel."

Raquel stared at her and waited for the sympathy, which she knew she was supposed to be feeling, to rise up inside her. But nothing came. All she could feel was anger. She knew she needed to choose her words wisely; so she paused momentarily and then said, "I'm sorry to hear that."

Raquel handed her a tissue to wipe her eyes. Karen seemed to believe she was genuine. "I found out a few weeks ago. I wanted to tell you, but I didn't know how you would respond." Karen paused. "All I've ever wanted was a family, but now it seems like I'm not going to have one, huh?"

Raquel couldn't help herself as she blurted out, "Are you going to tell James about Randall?"

Karen looked repulsed. "Did you just hear what I said? And that's all you have to say to me? Shoot, are you even human? Can you show no compassion?"

Raquel held her breath, then exhaled slowly before she launched into a monologue: "Do you know I have spent my whole life planning this wedding? Do you know I'm having my reception at the Oakley in the grand ballroom, with a full band and orchestra? Do you know I am having orchids flown in from two different countries to make up my towering centerpieces? Do you know that I joined some stupid church and went to weeks of Premarital classes so I could have a thrilling two-story glass altar in my wedding photos? Do you know I spent over seven thousand dollars for a dress I'm only going to wear one day? Do you know that I'm a ghetto girl from the hood and for once in my life I get to be the princess? I have worked hard and saved harder. I have spent many days in the streets pounding the pavement getting clients. I have been on my feet to the wee hours of the morning, day after day, month after month, and year after year. I finally got the man, the house, and the kids, and now everything will go down the drain if poor, sick little Karen decides to blow it all away."

Karen looked at Raquel, desperately searching for a glimmer of compassion. When she didn't find any, she stood up from the table. "You don't have to worry about me telling your beloved James the truth. The two of you deserve each other. Both of you are sick, material- istic, egotistic heathens." With that, Karen walked out.

Raquel watched the back of Karen as she moved closer to the exit. Raquel was surer than ever Karen could not be trusted. If only she had paid more atten- tion to that rat-poisoning story.

Chapter 3

"There's a time when it's okay to be one of many—you know, the one woman of many." Joan resisted the urge to look up at her best friend, Tisha, for a reaction. She continued to read. "It's okay to pretend, as if he's not lying to you. It's okay and even desirable to be the woman he glides into, supplying your body with pleasure. And then one day, it will be over. It does not matter if you have been with him hour after hour, day after day, or year after year.

"He'll get up, and in that moment, what used to be good enough will not be good enough anymore. It won't matter where he's going and who he's going to be with next. All you know is that's the last time he'll be with you. You could have spent the last ten, fifteen, twenty years desperately trying to hold on to him, and then you just let him go. The feelings that you seemed destined to carry around forever just disappear.

"My whole life has changed since I got James out and let Jesus in. I have been celibate and walking with the Lord strong for a while now, and the sight of James just makes me think about the past and all that time I wasted holding on to a dream, or maybe I should call it a nightmare. I hold no conversations with him. He is my ex for a reason. And yes, I have vowed to allow him full access to our son, but he has absolutely no access to me . . . at least not anymore.

"His biceps, triceps, and perfectly chiseled body screaming with temptation used to haunt me." Joan's voice cracked. "'The gym has always been his very special friend. He had me on lockdown while he cheated on me and abused me for eight years and fifty-seven days. He didn't just have my body. He had my mind too. In the beginning, we would take walks and talk about politics. We could go on and on for hours. He would take me on his motorcycle and we would make love in the park. He would sing me songs, even though he couldn't sing. He even wrote poems. They didn't make sense, but do you think I cared? I was like a little girl caught up in a fairy tale. I had found somebody to complete me.

"Just to think, I would have drunk his bathwater, sucked his toes, and ate his boogers, if I had thought it would make him stay with me instead of her. Okay, so maybe I would not have done all that . . . but to think of all I did do. If it wasn't for the almost ten-year-old boy we share, I promise you I would never lay eyes on him again.

"Don't get me wrong. I don't blame James alone. He was only one act in the drama-filled existence that used to be my life. He was only one of the men I'd slept with. Bed-hopping was not my only vice. When I got tired of that, I island-hopped, and while I was there I did a little bed-hopping too. Sometimes I didn't know one room from the other. I was in pain. I was searching for something. I'm here to tell you I found it. Or maybe I should say Him, the Him I had always been looking for.

"I was reborn. No, I didn't travel through my mother's birth canal again. But I was reborn nevertheless. I was set free. In what seemed like an instant, my world came together. My Mercedes-Benz SUV, my handbags that cost small fortunes, and extensive designer wardrobe didn't matter to me. Nothing mattered, except being filled with His presence and walking in His ways."

Joan looked away from the paper and looked directly at Tisha. She tried to look calm, despite the knots that were forming in her shoulders. Joan got jittery every time she had to speak for Woman's Day Wednesday at their church, even though this was her fourth time being selected.

Joan chose to read the beginning of the address to Tisha because her friend could be blunt, to the point of humiliation, if necessary. Tisha smiled and then started to cry. Joan shuffled her papers and wondered where she went wrong, or if she went wrong.

It was Monday afternoon; the bakery Joan owned was practically empty. Tisha and Joan sat on wooden stools behind the counter. They would not have a rush again until this evening when the college students from the community college came by with their laptops, earphones, and oversized books.

For now, Lindsey, the author who came by every day, was busy pecking on her laptop, sipping a latte. She was pushing out a best seller, Joan and Tisha often joked. She had sat there almost every day since the bakery officially opened, two years ago. Rebecca and Shamar, the interracial newlyweds, were sitting on the stools by the window, staring at each other, sharing a piece of chocolate cake and a deluxe café mocha, with two straws.

Tisha walked away from her stool and faced the assortment of stainless-steel coffee equipment so she could hide her tears. Joan could only watch her as "To God Be the Glory" played on the sound system. It was important for Joan to have a spiritual theme in her bakery. She wanted it to be a place where people could pray, read the Bible, and talk about Jesus freely.

Sometimes they would have a Christian band, praise dancers, or spoken-word artists come out and perform on the weekends. Multiple verses of scripture were printed on the walls and the portable coffee containers.

"It's just that . . ." Tisha tried to speak.

"It's just what?" Joan asked nervously as she stared at Tisha's back. Part of her wanted to see Tisha's face, but she was afraid she would see the truth in Tisha's eyes. Joan had spent two weeks preparing the speech and didn't know if she had the heart to start all over from scratch.

Joan looked around and made sure the counter was clear of customers. Tisha quietly wept. Frustrated, Joan asked, "Is it that bad, Tisha?"

Tisha turned around instantly. "That bad? That bad? No, Joan, it is not bad at all. It's perfect, absolutely perfect. It's different from any of your other lessons. You are so vulnerable, so exposed. You are really going to help a lot of women with that one."

Joan looked confused and relieved at the same time. "Well, then, why are you crying?"

Tisha walked to the end of the counter, which was lined with freshly made chocolate, lemon, and peach croissants. "Joan, look around. Look at us. . . . Look at all of this. . . ."

Joan exhaled; she knew exactly why Tisha was crying now. It really was remarkable. They had gone from club-hopping to Bible Study, from having sex to being celibate, from unbelievers to being Christians, from not going to church to speaking at church functions. Everything about them seemed to have changed.

"Who would have thought," Tisha added, "I would be able to live without Marcus? And that you would have finally gotten James Sr. out of your system? That we would have put our talents and money together to start up this bakery? And then, with all that, God is still doing more!"

Tisha pointed to the first review the *Houston Tribune* had posted about the bakery. It read:

Happy Endings, the newest chic bakery, promises just that. The hardwood floor, inviting music, and perfectly brewed South American coffee would have been enough. But the owner, Joan Dallas, and her assistant, Tisha Lewis, added lemon scones, chai, and raspberry truffles so good they will make you scream. The sweet potato pecan pie should be against the law. It is more savory than sweet, and so succulent! This is no ordinary dessert shop, but an elegant way to end a meal. Or if you like dessert as much as I do, begin one.

Joan looked around like she was taking it all in for the first time. Tisha was right. God had moved and moved mightily in their lives.

The phone rang. Tisha walked over to answer it. "It makes you wonder, huh? I mean, what is going to happen next?"

Joan smiled and grabbed a towel to clean the already spotless counter. "You never know what the day will bring."

Chapter 4

James admired the determined click of his favorite pair of Italian dress shoes. He hurriedly made it down the hall of Coolwater Church. His ringing cell phone stopped his stride midstep. "It's about time you called me back. What's up with you?"

"What's up with me? What's up with you?" Miles retorted. "Some lady claiming to be your wedding planner called. She said something about not forgetting to go get the final alterations on my tux. Since there is not going to be a wedding, why do I need to be worried about a tux?"

James looked around to make sure he was alone. "That's what I needed to talk to you about. I haven't told Raquel a thing. As a matter of fact, I'm about to meet with her now so that we can speak with the preacher about the final rundown for our wedding."

"What! You are going to actually marry this woman after finding out that both Morris and Alexis belong to another man? She's been cheating on you for as long as you have been together."

"Exactly, that's why I'm going to pay her back in a way she will never forget. Last night I came up with a plan."

"Tell me more."

"I can't give you the details right now. Just don't let on that you know something is up. Do whatever the wedding planner tells you."

"I can't wait to see what you have planned for that lying trick."

"Just think—I was tripping about this. I actually threw out my numbers, started going to these lame church meetings, trying to live right by this woman, and she did this to me for all these years. She is going to pay for this."

"When is this meeting over? I got to hear this."

"Well, I don't know, about an hour or so, but I was thinking about going by Joan's afterward."

Miles laughed. "I knew you were going to make your way back to that. You always do. She would be a fool to take you back. Besides, I heard her and Tisha are some Holy Rollers now, going to church all through the week, and they stopped giving it up."

"Haven't we heard that before?"

"So many times. Well, call me when you leave Joan's."

"Sure, bro, but don't be surprised if you don't get that call until tomorrow morning."

James hung up the phone and made his way down the hall. Moments before he stepped through the door, he paused and took a deep breath. He slowly walked into the room, with a confident smile on his face.

Just like all six of their other Premarital sessions, Raquel beat him to the meeting. She was so busy with the wedding that he had hardly laid eyes on her since finding out he was not the father of her children.

He kissed her on the cheek, out of habit. She barely noticed. She was too busy telling the preacher assigned to perform their ceremony where he should stand, what he should wear, and what he should say.

James always hated these sessions. He hated he had to pretend he believed the mumbo jumbo that Christians believed. Raquel took one look at Coolwater Church years before they were ever engaged and decided this place would be the perfect spot for her wedding. The only problem was that the church required all couples that wanted to get married in their facility attend seven Premarital sessions, in addition to the hefty fee.

The minister, overwhelmed with Raquel's directions, turned toward James. "Praise the Lord, here's our groom. It's good to see you, James."

"Praise the Lord." James paused but couldn't remember the minister's name. He looked around awkwardly, but he didn't see the minister's name anywhere.

Raquel looked like she wanted to crawl under a rug. "Minister Tyler, remember James."

"I'm sorry, sir. It's just that . . . I'm so excited about making this lovely woman my bride."

Raquel and Minister Tyler were both appeased.

During their first session, the preacher had asked them all kinds of questions. Did they believe in Jesus? How would they raise their children? What church did they belong to? Did they know God created marriage?

They answered all the questions perfectly, because one of Raquel's stylists had tried to have her wedding at Coolwater Church, only to be turned down because she and her fiancé didn't answer the questions correctly. The minister had told them they needed to join a church and learn about God's design for marriage before he could recommend that they get married. They ended up getting married somewhere else, but their failure allowed for Raquel's success. She knew all the questions the minister was going to ask beforehand. She had spent three days drilling James, until he gave the right answers. They even joined a church in their neighborhood. They only went for about two months straight, long enough for the church secretary to sign a paper saying they were active members. Since they got the paper signed, they had yet to return to the church.

Church people made James itch. They seemed uptight, fearful, and hypocritical. James's father and uncle were deacons. They ministered to all the women in the congregation. Looking over at Raquel made James remember something his Dad had told him and Miles repeatedly. "A man ain't supposed to have just one woman. It just ain't natural. Try to stick with one of these old ladies without having another on the side and watch yourself go crazy."

James's father died on top of a woman. Shot dead by the daddy of the sixteen-year-old who lay unharmed underneath him.

Raquel's thighs were hanging off the sides of the chair. James shook his head in disgust. He was about to settle for that for the rest of his life. His daddy was right; men will go crazy with just one woman.

Joan had a nice, tight body, with firm thighs and smooth skin.

"James."

Startled, James looked up to find Raquel and Minister Tyler looking at him.

"James, the minister says we are all set." Raquel clapped her hands like a five-year-old. Their seventh and final session was over.

Minister Tyler stood up and extended his hand to James. James did the same.

"I'll see you on the seventeenth, young man," Minister Tyler stated. "Don't be late for your own wedding."

"I'll be there with bells on." James grinned at Raquel.

Minister Tyler hurried out of the office.

Raquel shuffled through her papers. "Okay, I think I have almost everything done. I need to go and check on Alexis's flower girl dress. Then I have to get back to work. I have a client coming at eight. I'm going to get the wedding planner to call and remind everybody about the rehearsal dinner and make sure the flowers are on schedule to arrive. I want to make sure nothing is late."

Raquel put her papers in her handbag. "I hope Charlene can still get into her dress. I can't believe that girl went and got herself pregnant for my wedding. I don't know what we're going to do if she can't get into that dress."

"I made the final arrangements for our honeymoon." James played his role. "Everything is a go. You just make sure you are packed and ready to go."

"I'll be home late tonight. I'll probably be up half the night trying to put Debra's weave in. She gets on my nerves. She is so hard to please, but her money is still green, and right about now, I can't turn it down." Raquel sheepishly looked down at her shoes, and then said really quickly, "Especially since I just spent fifteen hundred dollars on our custom-made aisle runner."

"No! Raquel, I thought we agreed not to spend any more money on this wedding. You know we have to live afterward."

"I know, boo, but I couldn't help it. When you see it, you will understand. It is hand painted with our monogram. The same monogram that is on our cake, our wedding and reception programs, and embroidered on my dress. And besides, that's why I'm taking on additional clients. I'm not going to tap into our savings."

James made a mental note to withdraw all the money from their accounts on the morning of the wedding. He and Raquel decided to combine accounts when they purchased their home three years ago.

James remembered Joan. "Um . . . well, I'll be working tonight too. Frank called and asked if I would help him guard the all-white party they're having at Club Jazzy tonight."

Raquel looked concerned. James knew what to say. "Baby, don't worry. We can't afford to miss out on this easy money. Since I'm a constable, they are paying me two hundred an hour to stand around and pretend to patrol something."

"All right, just don't get yourself in trouble with those young girls."

"Of course not, baby." James walked Raquel to her car, kissed her on the lips and watched her drive away.

With Raquel out of sight, he pulled out his cell phone and started to dial Joan's phone number. Before the call went through, he hung up the phone. Joan could wait. He needed to make sure his plan to destroy Raquel was foolproof. James walked back inside the church.

Chapter 5

Pecan-crusted tilapia always made Joan feel like a chef. She pulled the fish out of the oven and plated it with wild rice and a balsamic vinegar glaze, like she was preparing to present it at a five-star restaurant. She then poured herself a glass of champagne before taking her seat at the table. It was celebration time, because Tisha had moved out of her condo and into her own apartment. She loved Tisha like a sister, but living with her was starting to be too much.

Just one more month, and she feared she would have stopped liking her altogether. Everything that came out of Tisha's mouth was a Bible verse. She was always walking around with a ton of scripture cards, ready to hit somebody over the head with one of them.

Joan hated to have to pretend in front of Tisha, since she thought Joan was some sort of super Christian. When Joan joined the Singles Ministry at church, Tisha followed her. When Joan started going to Bible Study each week, so did Tisha. When Joan started taking a Bible class at a local Christian school, Tisha signed up the following semester. And now that Joan was regularly teaching at the women's meeting at church, Tisha arrived early and stayed late. She always told Joan she was the best Bible teacher she had ever heard. The compliments were sincere and constant.

Joan enjoyed these compliments, but she just wished Tisha could turn it off sometimes. She missed having a best friend she could be herself with, and she was starting to feel like a stranger in her own home. Every once in a while, Joan wanted to watch a soap opera, crime drama, or have a glass of wine with dinner, but she knew she would have to explain herself to Tisha, so she didn't bother. Tisha didn't believe Christians should watch anything with murder, sex, or violence.

She would not have understood how Joan could teach a Sunday School lesson, pray out of her heart, read the Bible every day, worship God regularly, and drink a glass of wine with dinner, occasionally.

In Tisha's world, people that drank were lumped into one big category: drunks who needed to run to the next AA meeting. Joan looked down at her perfectly plated fish on her thirty-dollar plate, and her fifty-dollar champagne in her hundred-dollar Austrian crystal glass. She stood up from her $7,000 table, leaving her meal untouched.

This elegant dinner for one was not making the anxiety she started feeling this morning go away. As she was going through her son's things, she had found James's wedding invitation. She read it, over and over, touching the engraved writing and admiring the texture of the expensive paper. How many times had she imagined her name on a wedding invitation with his? Twenty-four hours ago, Joan was so sure of herself; now she could feel the tears forming in her eyes. Joan plopped down on her sofa, buried herself underneath the oversized pillows, and grabbed her journal from off the end table:

God, why does it still hurt? So many blessings have come into my life since meeting you, but I still find myself longing for something more. Just when I thought I was over him, I had to come face-to-face with this wedding. I could go days or even weeks without having lingering thoughts about him. But now he is constantly floating through my mind. I thought I was over him. I know I'm crazy. I can't admit this to anybody but you.

God, I know I shouldn't care that James Sr. is getting married, but the closer it gets, the more I do care. It pains me to admit it, but I care. I care so much. But why now, Lord? I guess it was all the time I spent believing that one day I would be his wife.

Lord, when is it going to be my turn? How long will I have to wait? Some of those ladies in the Singles Ministry scare me. I know that you know what's best for me, but, God, many of those ladies have been waiting for a long time. You don't want me to wait that long, do you? Please don't tell me I have to wait that long.

I want somebody to share myself with or let me get real. It's not like you don't know me. God, I need to be touched. I guess it wouldn't be so bad if I saw a glimmer of hope; you know if I had a prospect or maybe a date in the last six months. But nothing. All the men I meet don't know you, so they can't know me. But, God, it is getting difficult out here. Sometimes I feel like I'm wasting away. Like I'm waiting for my life to begin. I love my son, but he's already getting so independent. In a little while, he'll be a teenager and where does that leave me? I want to be somebody's wife, maybe have another child or two.

"Mama."

Joan turned to look at her son and closed her journal in the process.

"Yes." Joan tried to sound upbeat.

"Is it time to go yet? Mama, did you forget?" Joan wished she could forget. Today was the day the children in James and Raquel's wedding were supposed to go to Cyclone to play and have pizza and then attend the rehearsal afterward.

James Jr. did a little dance. "Come on, Mama, let's go. Last time I went to Cyclone, I got two thousand tickets."

Joan had the overstuffed red teddy bear on her bed to prove it. Her son, who couldn't remember his homework or when to take out the trash, remembered this statistic.

Joan went to her bedroom and changed clothes. As much as she hated to admit it, James was getting married to Raquel, and her son was in the wedding. It was time to face the truth.

In less than twenty-five minutes, the time it was going to take to drive to Cyclone, she was going to be face-to-face with the happy couple.

As soon as she turned off the ignition in front of their destination, James Jr. blurted out, "Mama, you gotta come see me jump off the dive board into the bubbles." James Jr. jumped out of the car and waited for his mother on the driver's side. Joan had barely stepped out before James Jr. continued his pitch. "If you get into the bubbles right on target, you get fifty tokens."

"Really?" His enthusiasm was contagious. Joan looked around for any sign of James Sr. or Raquel. Not seeing anybody, she walked to the colorful door behind her son. The entire building was silver and red and looked like a spaceship ready to take off.

Joan was opening her wallet so she could purchase a game card when Raquel walked up and handed James Jr. one. He didn't say goodbye before he took off running, joining the other children and leaving Joan and Raquel alone.

"My fiancé is in the playroom with Alexis, since she's too little to play with the big kids." Raquel never missed the opportunity to let Joan know that she had a daughter by James. James had always wanted a daughter, and Raquel had given him one.

Joan looked around to see if she could find her son in the large game room. She knew Raquel wanted to get her angry, and she refused to allow her the satisfaction. Instead of playing any of the games, her son was stuffing his face with pizza at a table in the back of the building. James Sr.'s mother, Agnes, was seated next to him. She smiled and waved at Joan.

Raquel handed Joan a piece of metallic gold paper, with silver italic writing. "This is our itinerary for this weekend and next weekend, our wedding weekend. After we leave Cyclone, we are going to take the kids to the church for rehearsal. Only the children will rehearse this weekend. We wanted them to have extra practice before the wedding.

"James Jr. and the other children will be staying with Agnes for the rest of the weekend. So call her if you need to speak with him."

Joan knew she could trust Agnes with her child. She grabbed the paper and turned to leave. Raquel went on, "Tomorrow they'll have breakfast, play a bit, then take a nap before having lunch. After lunch we'll have another rehearsal. You can pick him up from my mother-in-law's that evening."

Joan had enough and started to walk faster. Raquel kept talking. "I'm having Chick-fil-A cater for the children. Does James Jr. like nuggets? Our children certainly do, especially Alexis."

Joan nodded, trying to hold in her emotions. Raquel continued talking. "Next Friday, they will meet the adults in the wedding party for our official rehearsal. Then—"

Joan stopped walking right before she reached the door and spoke. "Thank you, I see you have everything under control."

Joan remembered she had forgotten to say good-bye to her son and yelled out for him. James Jr. came and gave her a kiss on the cheek. "I'll see you on Sunday." She kissed him on his forehead, and he ran off to join the other children.

Joan walked out the door. Raquel walked out right behind her. "You didn't think this was going to happen, did you? You thought James would never make me his wife."

Raquel lifted up her hand to show Joan her engagement ring. "Now look at me, and look at you. I got James for life. All that free nooky you gave up, and now you don't have nothing to show for it. I've got the house, the car, the kids, and the husband. You should have known better than to mess with my man."

"I know where and when you are getting married, my dear. Don't make me watch you eat your words." Joan opened her car door, got inside, and started her vehicle.

Raquel looked confused. Joan rolled her window down and said, "Maybe I should come. . . . You know the part where the preacher says, 'If anybody knows why these two people should not be married, speak now or forever hold your peace?' Right then, I could stand up and say, 'Yes, I know a reason. She is a manipulative, insecure, fat, overdressed, made-up freak who couldn't keep her man happy, so he kept coming to me.'"

Joan drove off, surprised at how easily those ugly words spewed from her mouth. She felt the tears fall as soon as Raquel was no longer in sight. Who the heck did Raquel think she was talking to like that? She could have just smacked her in the face.

Joan picked up her cell to call Tisha, but before she pressed her speed dial, she hung up the phone. Tisha would not be any help. In the past, she would have offered to slash Raquel's tires or put sugar in her gas tank. But the new Tisha would insist they pray for her and wish her well. Joan was in no mood for that.

Spotting her favorite spot for ice cream, she stopped and purchased a pint of double chocolate fudge brownie ice cream and drove home, thinking of the ways she could hurt Raquel.

As Joan drove up to her condo, she saw someone standing in her designated parking spot. *It couldn't be,* she thought. This man was over six feet tall, slender, dressed well, and looked just like James Sr.

Why would he be waiting for her? Wasn't he supposed to be at Cyclone playing with Alexis? Joan pulled up to where he was standing. He smiled, and she smiled back. Joan grabbed her ice cream from the backseat. She saw her favorite Bible lying next to it. She needed to pick it up so she could prepare for the Bible Study that she and her friends had each week at one of their homes. When she got out of the car, all she was carrying was the ice cream.

Joan had a million questions. Instead of asking any of them, she walked to her front door, with James walking beside her. She could smell his cologne and hear the clanging of his watch as he walked. She was so glad Tisha had moved out. Joan would not have been able to explain this one to her.

Joan closed the door behind James and they stood in the foyer looking at each other awkwardly. They had not been this close in a few years. Their short conversations were always over the phone, and mostly about their son. When they dropped their son off or picked him up, neither of them bothered to get out of the car.

"How are you?" James broke the silence.

"I'm good."

James sniffed the air. "Something smells good and familiar." James walked to the kitchen and saw the dirty dishes from Joan's unfinished meal. "This looks like the remnants of your pecan-crusted tilapia."

"Yes, it is." Putting away the carton of ice cream, Joan felt herself smiling. "I was going to take the extra piece for lunch tomorrow, but I guess I'll give it to you."

Joan made his plate. She was glad she hadn't had the chance to eat all her food. Now they could sit and eat together.

The champagne was on the table, still cold from the ice in the chiller. James poured himself a glass, then took a small bite of fish, reminding Joan how refined his palate was. James loved fine food and had taken Joan to the best restaurants in Houston when they were together.

Joan eagerly awaited his response.

"Joan, you have the gift. I haven't had fish this delicious in a minute." James complained to her many times that Raquel could not cook, and he tried to take her to nice restaurants, but she only picked over the food. She would rather have a fried pork chop sandwich and strawberry soda than braised lamb and merlot.

The feelings that were springing up through Joan were exciting and frightening, all at the same time. James looked so innocent, so sweet. She loved the way his mustache was curling up around his face as he chewed his fish.

"You remember the time James Jr. came running in like he had found the cure for cancer?" James asked.

Joan started laughing, recalling the memory. Joan mocked their son's voice, "Mama . . . Daddy . . . Daddy . . . Mama . . . Did you know I was born on my birthday?"

James laughed so hard, he had tears in his eyes. "It just wasn't what he said, it was how he said it—the expression on his face. He was so excited. I didn't have the heart to tell him everybody was born on their birthday."

James took another bite of his food; then he turned to look at Joan. Something in his eyes made Joan warm all over. His lips were right there and perfectly kissable. Joan had taught and listened to Bible Study after Bible Study about not putting herself in compromising positions. She knew one hundred different reasons why she shouldn't have allowed James Sr. in her condo, with the scripture to back up her reasons.

After they finished their dinner, Joan picked up their plates and took them to the kitchen. James got up behind her. He was way too close. "I know you have some homemade dessert somewhere in this house. I read about your bakery in the *Tribune*. I'm really proud of you."

Joan blushed. James always loved her desserts; he'd even inspired a few. "Well, I have a little something."

James got much closer. Joan stepped back slowly. She opened the refrigerator and pulled out a sweet potato pecan pie. She created the recipe years ago because James's favorite pies were sweet potato and pecan.

James looked like the wind had been taken out of him. He pretended to cry and wipe away tears. "You don't know how much I missed this. You just happened to have one."

Joan put the pie on the counter and proceeded to cut it. With Joan facing the counter, James came up behind her and wrapped his arms around her waist. Joan couldn't believe he had the nerve to get this close to her after all this time. She knew she needed to move, but instead she kept cutting the pie, like she didn't feel James Sr. breathing down her neck.

James started to nibble softly on her neck. Joan dropped the knife, took a deep breath, and turned to face James. She turned around to tell him to stop, that she was a new woman now, and having premarital sex was out of the question. Instead of saying anything, Joan sank into the delicate kiss James planted on her lips. She felt like she was watching herself interact with James. She had not kissed a man in years. When James went for her pants, she protested. James unsnapped her bra and pulled off her shirt before she realized how he had done it. Before long, James was all over her, and she lost all means to protest.

James picked her up and placed her on the sofa in her living room. Joan was pulling off his shirt, when she heard a noise she recognized. She bolted to the door, fearing it was Tisha. When she didn't see anyone through the peephole, she got confused. Then she heard the noise again. Embarrassed, she hadn't recognized it the first time. She walked over to her buzzing cell phone.

"Hello." Joan tried to sound normal when she answered.

"Hey, girl," Tisha responded. "You are not going to believe this, but my ex bought his lanky self to my place. I don't even know how he found out where I lived. Anyway, here he comes trying to sweet-talk me and rub up against me. That fool actually thought I was about to give in. As if! I ain't about to go there. I have gotten off that fornication crack for a while now and I ain't trying to go back. What! And get my heart broken again or, even worse, lose fellowship with the Lord. And for what? A few minutes of 'ooooh' and 'ahhhh, baby,' please! I got better things to do, like finding out what the Lord has for me. And a cheap roll in the hay is not on my growth plan. The devil is always busy sending distractions, but he is going to have to do better than that. Marcus is my past and I have come too far to turn back now. It reminds me of that Proverb, you know . . ." Tisha's words trailed off as she tried to recall the scripture.

Joan said, "Proverbs 26:11. 'As a dog returns to his vomit, so a fool repeats his foolishness.'"

"Girl, I promise you are like a Bible concordance, but don't fear I'm going to be like you when I grow up. I'm on my way over there. I left my iPod there somewhere, and you know I am not right when I don't get my worship on. I just have to go by my dad's for a second first. Is that cool?"

Joan remained silent.

"Joan, are you okay? You seem kind of out of it."

"Oh no, girl, I am just tired." Joan hoped Tisha was ready to end this conversation.

"All right, well, I'll let you rest. See you in about an hour."

Joan hung up the phone. James walked to her, ready to resume things where they had left off. Joan walked away and began putting on her clothing.

James looked defeated as he watched her. "You know I will always love you."

Joan didn't look up at him. If he loved her, why was he marrying Raquel?

As if reading her mind, James said, "It's complicated. You will see. I wish I could tell you, but just wait. You will find out. This situation with Raquel—we aren't what we appear to be, and soon enough everything is going to be out."

Joan looked at James. "I don't know what the crap you are talking about and I am frankly too tired to attempt to read between the lines. Will you just put on your clothes and leave? Your fiancée is probably looking for you. Why did you bother coming over here, anyway?" Joan shook her head. "No, never mind. I don't want to know. Just leave!"

James started to put on his clothes. Joan watched him, angry he had given up so easily. Before James walked out the door, he turned to Joan and said, "I'll leave, but I'll be back."

Chapter 6

James wasn't the only Houstonian who decided to golf in the midst of June and endure the stifling heat. He drove around the parking lot of the West Galleria golf course twice before he found a spot. He got out of the car, grabbed his clubs, then went to meet his brother. Miles was a golf addict. When he wasn't busy pushing one of his get-rich-quick schemes, he could be found trying to become the next Tiger Woods.

Losing his job had caught James completely by surprise. After having been good for almost two years, James thought he needed to reward himself before the wedding. He had been sleeping with two past lovers for a month straight: Pam, one of the stylists in Raquel's salon, and Lauren, a married officer in his department. One day, he and Lauren couldn't contain their lust until the end of the workday. They thought they could slip in and out of a hotel without anyone noticing. Lauren didn't know it, but her estranged husband suspected she was having an affair and hired a private investigator to follow her. The husband promptly mailed to their superior officers pictures of James and Lauren leaving the hotel room when they were supposed to be working. James and Lauren were quickly fired.

James wanted to tell Miles the truth, but James was too cool to get caught slipping. He couldn't believe he had been stupid enough to jeopardize his job. He and his brother had always been close. They had to be with the type of parents they had. If it hadn't been for each other, they would have melted in what they called the two-story house of horrors.

On Sunday mornings, seated in the second pew at church was the only time of the week where their family actually had any peace. Their father would stand at the altar with the rest of the deacons, praying over the offering, singing hymns, and reading scriptures. Their mother would stand up straight, looking up at their father with adoration. Years of dealing with his unfaithfulness had taught her to be a great actress. Saturday evening, she would wash and roll her hair and iron a nice dress. She always wore a hat, black flats, and no makeup. It was as if lipstick and high heels were signs of being unholy. If someone visited the church, he or she probably wouldn't have spotted the charade, but all of the members of Ebenezer Family Church knew it was an illusion.

Their father was wealthy in a small town, due to his successful oil business. Some of the single women in the church and many of the married ones would grow tired of waiting on God to bring about their deliverance. So when the tires went bad on their car, when the light bill needed to be paid, or when the women needed a little extra money to buy a bus ticket, they would go see Mr. Reynolds. A trip to Mr. Reynolds didn't last long, was thoroughly enjoyable, and the women always left with more money than they needed. Otherwise respectable women came from all over town to exchange sexual favors for cash. Mr. Reynolds was tall, attractive, and treated each woman like she was the only woman in the world. When they were finished, Mr. Reynolds never handed money to the women. Instead, he would place the money in a fine linen envelope and spray it with French cologne. Before sealing it, he would place a handwritten note inside, with messages like, *Your eyes are as mesmerizing as your scent.*

While the pastor of Ebenezer Family Church didn't approve of Mr. Reynolds's actions, he didn't do anything to stop him either. He threatened to remove him from the church many times, but then Mr. Reynolds would send a large donation to the church, a designer suit, or even a Cadillac once. The gifts kept the pastor quiet.

The men in the church wouldn't dare get in Mr. Reynolds's way. While they hated him, they secretly wanted to be him. They wanted to walk into a room and own it. They wanted to have beautiful women at their beck and call, as well as what appeared to be unlimited resources. Mr. Reynolds could make one phone call and get someone a job. If they crossed him, he could make one phone call and they would lose their job. He had so much power that men who knew their girlfriends, wives, or daughters had slept with him would garner up the strength to smile in his face.

At home, Mr. Reynolds didn't have much to say to his wife and children. They ate all of their meals around the table while their father read the paper or documents from work. Their mother would attempt to keep the discussion going, asking the boys about school and activities, but Mr. Reynolds hardly ever appeared to be interested. After dinner, he would take a short drive back to his office, where he would work in between taking his female callers. James remembered his mother crying often in the evening.

The people at Mr. Reynolds's funeral pretended to be sad, but many were joyful, glad James's mother was free of a man she wouldn't leave. James and Miles sat near their mother at the funeral and watched her weep. They were frustrated they couldn't make her stop. They sat there silently, embarrassed and humiliated. Their father had been shot and killed by one of the members of Ebenezer Family Church. Mr. Reynolds was having sex with the man's daughter at the time.

Right then, James knew he couldn't tolerate church people. The same people who were talking about his mother behind her back were the same people who were kissing and hugging her at the funeral. The same people who broke out in shouts of praise about the Lord were the same people who would be cursing and yelling before they drove out of the church parking lot. As far as James was concerned, church people were hypocrites and he wanted nothing to do with them.

"Hello, my brother." James stepped up just as Miles was putting the ball.

Miles jumped, surprised to hear his brother's voice. "Brotha, would you roll up on Tiger Woods like that?"

"No," James responded. "But since you are no Tiger Woods, we don't have to worry about that."

Miles flashed his golf bag. "I might as well be. I went and got these Tiger Woods-approved golf clubs."

James looked at the ball Miles had just putted. He completely missed the hole at close range. "Yeah, but buying Tiger Woods golf clubs does not make you Tiger Woods."

Miles looked at his ball and shook his head in agreement. "True, that." He turned to face his brother. "I hope you feel better than you look."

"No, I look like crap, and I feel the same way." James let out a fake laugh. "I need a T-shirt that says, 'If it ain't one thing, it's another' in bold red letters."

"So what are you doing out here?" Miles asked. "Doesn't somebody need to be arrested?"

"I quit."

"What?"

"What do you mean, 'what'?" James asked. "You have been trying to get me to quit the department for years and go into business with you."

"Yeah, and you have been telling me no for years too."

"Well, things have changed."

Miles looked away. "I'm really sorry about that. Man, I would have never guessed. I was just trying to test out the business."

"Don't trip, little brotha, everything happens for a reason. I'm not going to try to lie. I can't believe Raquel. But I'm going to give her something she will never forget."

"You remember that time old girl tried to play me?" Miles asked.

"Yeah, you got her good, didn't you? Getting her girl to tape her admitting she was trying to put a baby on you that wasn't yours?"

"I would have never thought Raquel was like that."

"It's just like our pops used to say," James shouted, "women ain't good but for one thing!"

They laughed and exchanged a closed-fist pound shake.

"You ought to get her back for this. I mean real good." Miles slammed his golf club into the grass. "You have been robbed."

James stood up straight and tilted his sunglasses in Miles's direction. "Believe me, brotha, the plan I got is going to go down in the history books. While I beat you, hole after hole, I'll tell you all about it."

Chapter 7

"Hello, gentlemen." James watched as his class of middle-aged men turned around in their chairs and faced him. Instantly their chattering voices ceased and they sat up straight in their chairs.

James almost felt sorry for them. There isn't anything more pathetic than a grown man who needs help getting a woman. They come in every week, most of them early, hoping to get a seat near the front. They act like if they can get close enough to him, perhaps some of his magic would rub off on them.

The Adult Learning Catalog listed dozens of teachers who thought they could teach everything from "How to Sell a Home" to "How to Write a Book in a Year." James's class was "How to Get Any Woman You Want."

James started teaching the class on a dare. One of his former classmates wanted to see if James was playa enough to teach his skills to a group of losers. At first, James declined, claiming he didn't have time due to graduate school. However, James changed his mind when he started failing one of his courses. He dropped out of graduate school and paid the $250 to have the description of the class, cost, and location placed in *The Adult Learning Catalog*. The catalog, in turn, promised to distribute the information about James's class all over town.

From the first day he started teaching it four years ago, the class had been overbooked each quarter. His ex-students wrote recommendations: *James is a genius*, or *I finally got that blonde at work to need me, like I needed her*, or *This class saved my life. I hadn't been on a date in a year, now I date three or four times a week, with women more beautiful than I could have imagined.*

James had expected to stop teaching after his wedding, but now, as he glanced at his notes, he was glad he had not mentioned getting married to the men in his class. He hadn't even bothered to tell them he was engaged, afraid they might misinterpret it for weakness.

Not only did he need to continue the class, but he needed to have more classes—now that he had lost his day job. He had been holding back, only giving the men nuggets of wisdom, but now he needed to take it to another level. He needed them hungry for more and spreading the word about his classes. Next quarter, not only was he adding several more sessions, but he was going to charge twice as much as he had been.

James cleared his throat as he slowly walked into the middle of the room. He felt like a superhero when he was in this old office building in the southwest side of town. In other suites, on other floors, there were doctor offices, nail salons, and a variety of other businesses. But in this room on the eighth floor, stuck in a corner, was an entirely different type of business, the business of learning to run a woman. Men from all over town flocked to this all-male chat session each Monday evening, hoping to get a piece of wisdom that would ensure that by Friday night beautiful women would be in their beds.

"Gentlemen, I hate to tell you this, but I've been holding back," James admitted to his students. "It has been hard for me to be completely honest with you. I was afraid to reveal the real playa rules. I was afraid to have this valuable information in the wrong hands. But over our time together, I think that you are a very mature group and you are ready to learn this highly delicate information."

James made eye contact with the men. He crossed the room slowly, his gaze transferring from one man to the other until he had sized up all twenty-two of them. He wanted to smile but held it in. They were practically drooling.

"So tonight I will open up my golden rule book. I assure you I have never done this before. These secrets have been tried and tested and virtually are failure proof. If you want her, you can have her. " James paused for effect. "That is, if you can handle it.

"Can you handle it, Mr. Banks?" James went down the roll. "Can you handle it, Mr. Brooks? Can you handle it, Mr. Clay? Can you handle it, Mr. Davidson?"

After James completed the roll and was satisfied that he had sufficiently enticed the men, he sat down on a stool in the middle of the room. The men brought their chairs inward so they wouldn't miss anything. The shuffling of paper and chairs screeching on the floor permeated the room.

James waited for everyone to settle down. "Rule number one, if you want to have sex with a beautiful woman, don't mention sex, ever." The men looked puzzled, but that didn't stop them from feverishly scribbling on their notepads.

"Beautiful women know that they are attractive. They have been told this all of their lives. They know they have bodies that we meditate on, long after they leave the room. They know we want to have sex with them. They feed off it. They have the control and we don't. But there is a way to have her eating out of your hands."

James glanced down at his notes. "You can't walk up to a beautiful woman and say, 'Hey, hottie, you fine as heck, and I want to get with you, no strings attached just pure sex for the fun of it.'" James shook his head. "That wouldn't work, would it?"

"So what does?" one of the men asked.

James took a deep breath, as if he was about to release the greatest hoax ever. "Let's say there's a drop-dead gorgeous woman who sits at the back table at the coffee shop you frequent. She sits back there, day after day, typing on her laptop, completely oblivious to the fact that you want to jump her bones. She's beautiful, unapproachable, and unconcerned about you.

"Beautiful women tend to have few or no real friends, because women hate them, and men are always trying to sleep with them. Beautiful women are just like other women; they love to talk. Only, beautiful women have very few opportunities to *just* talk. They crave the opportunity to have a conversation, where there are no strings attached." James looked at the men and pointed. "That's where you come in.

"You walk into that coffeehouse and you approach this woman. You tell her you need her advice desperately, if she could only spare thirty seconds. You explain that your girlfriend from out of town is coming in a few days and you want to make the weekend extremely special, only you can't figure out what to do. Normally, you wouldn't be this out of sorts, but your girlfriend is a beautiful woman, and frankly she's a bit out of your league. She's been a lot of places and done a lot of things. A simple date just won't work. She's coming all these miles and you need to make an impression. You are so excited to be with her and desperately in love, even considering marriage. Does she have any suggestions?"

James's voice dropped to almost a whisper. He folded his arms and scanned the room again. "What have you done, my friends?"

His normal voice returned. "Your coffee lady is about to put her guard down. You are a simple guy only looking for thirty seconds of her time. Of course, you will use more time, but she appreciates your desire to be brief. You have told her you are desperately in love with another woman. So she doesn't have to worry about you trying to jump her bones. Then you asked her for suggestions, satisfying her need to be heard. Finally she gets to voice her opinion in a comfortable atmosphere. You, my brother, are in! All you have to do is sit back and listen and pretend, as if everything you are hearing rings absolutely true.

"The next week, your coffee lady will be in her exact same spot, waiting for a full report on how everything went with your girlfriend. As the hours went by, you had become more and more intriguing. All weekend long, she wondered about you and how the weekend was going.

"You walk into the coffee shop as happy as can be. You tell her how much your girlfriend enjoyed her suggestions and how grateful you are. You only wish your girlfriend could have stayed in town. Only, she's working on a big project and can't move, and you need to stay close to town, too, because of a job you love too much to leave. Then abruptly end the conversation. Don't make it seem like you are trying to prolong the conversation. She will not want you to leave, but she's not about to admit that. Go back to your side of the coffee shop, sip your coffee as you text or phone your imaginary girlfriend. The coffee shop lady will be watching your every move, even if it seems she never looks up from her keyboard. You are proving to her that you are not the least bit interested in her. This is key." James wanted to smile, but he remained serious. He could tell the men couldn't wait to hear the rest of his lesson.

"Once you finish your coffee, hang up your phone, then get ready to leave. Make it to the door, then turn back. Walk over to the coffee shop lady and say, 'My girlfriend really enjoyed this weekend. She just told me again. I was going to blank-blank restaurant for dinner tonight. I would love to show you my appreciation.' Make sure the restaurant is close by. She will not mind having a quick bite with you, but she needs to be able to do so with little effort. If she can drive her own car and stay in close vicinity to the coffee shop, she maintains her control, or so she thinks.

"But this is all a part of the plan to become her new best friend. Laugh at her jokes and compliment her on her intelligence. Never, and I mean *never,* compliment her on her looks or her body. You need to satisfy the need in her that says she's more than just a pretty face and a nice body. Pay very close attention to her. What does she like to read or eat? Who does she admire? What does she like about her job? What doesn't she like? Who would she most like to meet? Is something big happening in her life? Is she up for a new job? Is her sister having a baby? Is her dad sick? What is it that she admires about the lady who sits in the cubicle next to her? What does she hate about her?

"You need to know these things because this is how you are going to spark new and interesting conversations with her the next time you see her. She will be so surprised that you remembered she was up for a new job or that she was about to become an aunt for the first time. Most men never learn this step. They spend entirely too much time talking about themselves, and not enough time talking to the woman. And what she tells them, they don't bother to remember.

"So with this technique, my friends, you will stand out bigger than the rest. You will have her waiting at the coffeehouse looking for you so she can tell you the next big thing that just happened in her life. And you will be all too interested to hear about everything. Afterward, you will offer follow-up questions about the things you talked about last time.

"So when does the sex come in? With this particular technique, I average about six weeks. By the third week, she's at my place or I'm at hers. By the fourth week, we are touching casually."

"What do you mean 'casually'?" one of the men blurted out.

"I mean, when you briefly grab her hand while you talk to her. Or, as you are watching a movie, you briefly place your hand on her thigh before removing it. It's when you hug when you arrive and when you leave," James explained.

"By the fifth week, you will be kissing. You will not need to mention your girlfriend after this point. The coffee lady has had enough of her by now. On the sixth week, you do something special. Offer to take her to the beach for the weekend to celebrate finishing up that project or completing her classes for the semester. This is the week she will be in a hotel room screaming your name.

"Men, listen to me"—James bent down—"I don't care if you collect garbage for a living and this woman is the CEO of a Fortune 500 company. If you patiently follow my techniques, you will not fail." The students started to clap.

"Women are always complaining about there being no romance in a relationship. Men think romance is expensive dinners and flowers, but real romance is much cheaper than steak and roses. Have you ever seen an ugly, broke man with a beautiful woman?" The men nodded. "Sure, if you have money, power, good looks, you can have your share of women, but when you don't have that, you just have to work a little harder. If you stick with me, I'll give you a step-by-step growth plan. The technique I told you about today is only the beginning."

James's heartbeat suddenly started to race. His hands and face started to sweat and his throat felt dry.

"Are you okay, sir?" one man asked.

James didn't respond.

Another man shouted, "Somebody call 911!"

Of course, James wasn't okay, but how was he supposed to explain to them that their fearless leader was not fearless anymore? And even though he had never had a panic attack in his life, he was almost certain he was having one now.

He needed to find a way to speak. He drank a sip of water and put all of his effort into saying, "Gentlemen, I just remembered something. I have to go. Feel free to e-mail me whatever questions you may have. See you next week."

The men looked at each other, puzzled, but James grabbed his belongings and stumbled for the parking garage before anybody could stop him.

Chapter 8

When Joan saw the silver-embroidered pillows at the furniture store, she gasped. They were so pretty she hoped that by adding them to her sofa, they would make her forget about what she and James had almost done on it. Every time she walked past her sofa, it reminded her of James Sr. She adjusted and readjusted the new pillows, hoping something would stop his muscular silhouette from appearing in her mind.

It was pointless. She gave up after she glanced at the clock. It was only fifteen minutes before her friends would start to arrive for their weekly Bible Study. The salmon canapés were chilling in the refrigerator and the chicken satay was already on the table. When they had their meetings, her friends expected to eat, and eat well. Joan made sure she didn't disappoint them.

She looked around the room again to make sure there were no signs of anything that might offend her friends. There was no wine, or wineglasses, or even a steamy romance novel. Then she put out the vase her friend Lila had bought her. The vase was hideous, but Lila thought it was beautiful, so Joan put it out when Lila was around. Joan then spread her Bibles and Christian literature around. Her friends expected this of her. She had to be strong for them. She had to at least look like she had it together. When they were gone, then she could be herself.

Joan passed her journal on her way to the kitchen. She had yet to talk to God about the incident with James. When she was brushing her teeth, it came up. As she was mindlessly waiting for a traffic light, it came up. While she was ironing her son's shirts, it came up. Yet, Joan pushed it down. She was an excellent Bible student, familiar with all the scriptures related to sexual sin. She knew what God had to say, and right now, she wasn't ready to recall it.

What did God expect her to do? Wasn't it natural for her to have sexual energy? Would one night with James really be that bad? Yes, being a single celibate Christian had worked for a while, but now it was no longer working. What if God wanted her to be single forever? What if there was never going to be a husband?

Not one man had approached her in weeks. No wonder she was such easy prey for James Sr. She thought it would be okay if she filled her days with working in the bakery, and filled her nights with numerous activities. She and her son had a full calendar. On Mondays, they would have their special little date of going to a restaurant and watching a movie together. On Tuesdays, James Jr. had karate and Joan had kickboxing. On Wednesday, they went to Bible Study. Thursdays were spent helping out in the community at the neighborhood recreation center, and on Fridays, James Jr. was off to spend the weekend with his dad or his grandparents. She had recurring appointments at the hair salon and nail shop at the same time.

Weekends were spent with her friends. Joan was so tired of spending every weekend with her friends, she could scream. For once, she wanted to be able to say she had to miss this or that outing because some strong, employed, handsome, well-adjusted, Christian gentleman had asked her out for coffee. But here it was—another Saturday night—and all she had to look forward to was Tisha, Lila, and Janet.

Lila was the first to arrive, as usual. "Hey, girl." Lila walked in the room and turned around in a circle. Joan clapped as Lila did an imaginary catwalk sashay down Joan's hardwood floors. Lila was almost down to her goal weight, and she didn't need anybody to tell her she looked fabulous in her red sundress and strappy black sandals. Her natural hair was in two-strand twists that hung right below her neck. Two years ago, she was overweight, insecure, and jobless, but one certainly couldn't tell by looking at her now.

Joan smiled after Lila stopped pretending to be "America's next top model."

"You look wonderful! Who are those sandals by? I must get myself a pair."

"Sanfrann. They were on sale last week. I got a pair in black and in dark brown."

Joan pointed to her own ensemble of cotton workout pants and an oversized T-shirt. "You look a little over-dressed for Bible Study."

Lila lit up more than she already was and blurted out, "I have a date." The doorbell rang. Joan immediately turned away to answer the door, thinking the entire time, *Lila didn't just say she had a date.*

Tisha came in with two oversized pillows, laptop, and a suitcase full of books. Ever since Tisha started going to the College of Biblical Studies, she carried her schoolbooks everywhere she went. The oversized pillows signaled that Tisha was planning to stay the night. Joan sighed, but Tisha was too busy hauling in her luggage to notice.

"Don't close the door, Joan," Tisha warned. "Janet was pulling up right behind me. I was going to wait for her, but my hands were loaded with too much stuff." Joan sighed again and walked down the hall.

This was going to be a long night. Lila had a date. *How can Lila have a date before me?* Joan walked in the hallway and waited for Janet.

The elevator doors opened. Janet was a pitiful sight at seven and a half months pregnant. She had acne like a teenager, and her face looked several shades darker than the rest of her body. Her hair was in micro braids that should have been taken out weeks ago.

Sonya, Joan's new neighbor, was walking in the elevator as Janet was walking out. "Hi, Joan," Sonya said.

Sonya had on a pretty gold evening gown and was obviously going somewhere special. Joan gave her a quick, fake smile before grabbing the fruit salad Janet was holding.

Joan shook her head. Sonya was going out for a night on the town and she was stuck holding a pregnant woman's fruit salad. Joan told Janet repeatedly that she didn't need to bring anything, but Janet refused to show up each week without a box of gourmet tea, homemade cookies, or some other knickknack Joan didn't need.

Joan said hello, but Janet held her hand to her chest, signaling to Joan she was too out of breath to talk. They silently walked down the hall to Joan's place.

Janet plumped herself on the sofa, where Tisha and Lila were seated. Joan headed to the kitchen to put away the fruit salad.

"Are you okay?" Tisha asked Janet.

Lila smirked. "There is nothing wrong with her except she's pregnant."

After a few moments, Janet gained her composure. "I could slap you, Lila and Joan. Y'all did not tell me it was going to be like this. You made being pregnant look easy. Walking around in heels and wearing stylish clothes." She exhaled loudly. "I cannot breathe. I'm having pains I don't like. Oh, and don't let me tell you about the heartburn and the gas, and I have never been this constipated in my life. I can't find a comfortable position to sleep in, and my feet are disappearing from my vision, more and more each day."

Lila laughed and tapped Janet on the thigh. "Oh dear, just wait until the first contractions start."

Janet rolled her eyes.

Tisha looked worried. "Is it really that bad?"

Joan put the fruit salad in the refrigerator and yelled, "Yes." She turned to Tisha. "Did you forget how much I was moaning and screaming with James Jr.? I felt like somebody was trying to pull my organs out, one by one."

Janet and Tisha gasped.

Lila shook her head. "My water broke at the grocery store. I was too embarrassed. I thought that was the worst thing that could have happened to me. Then I got to the hospital and lost control of my bowels."

Joan teased. "That happened to you too, girl."

"You see why we didn't tell you," Lila said. "There are just some things you don't need to know. It will all be worth it in the end, though. Being pregnant is a beautiful thing. I love my Jasmine."

Tisha started to act like she was itching. "All this baby talk is making me nervous. Let's eat and start talking about something else. Please!"

Tisha grabbed a plate from the table and handed one to the other ladies. "Joan, would you like to say the blessing?"

Joan paused for a moment. "No, I always do it. You go ahead and bless the food." Tisha did, and Joan served the ladies.

"This is delicious," Janet said. "I love when Saturday night comes around and so does my hubby. He reminded me to bring him a plate before he left home to play basketball with his buddies."

"One day, I'm going to have a man I need to bring home a plate to," Tisha said, chomping on a piece of salmon. After Tisha swallowed her food, she got this serious look in her eyes. She put her plate down and said, "Ladies, last night the Lord woke me up. I feel led to talk about some things today."

Joan took a deep breath. She should have known they couldn't have a nice meal together without Tisha preaching.

"Ladies, I want to tell you what each of you mean to me." Lila and Janet put down their plates and turned toward Tisha. Joan continued to eat.

"Janet," Tisha proceeded to say, "you are an inspiration to me. I see how Jesus blessed you when you received Him into your life. I see how He gave you a godly husband when you became a godly woman. I thank you for your prayers. Because you could have just left me, Joan, and Lila in the world, but you didn't. You prayed for God to show us the way. I am eternally grateful for that."

Tisha turned to Joan and Lila. Joan continued to eat. Tisha said, "Ladies, it has been a few years since we joined *The Single Sister Experiment.* We wanted to know what would happen if we gave up sex. Well, it took us a while to be obedient and we went through more drama than a little bit. It seemed as if we would not find our way. But God saw fit for us not only to find our way, but to make it to His side with our friendship in tact.

"Thank you, Lila and Joan, for walking this walk with me. Thank you for listening to me when I couldn't stop talking about my mother's death, or my ex-boyfriend, or my money problems." Tisha laughed. "I know I was getting on your nerves, but instead of telling me to shut up, you let me talk so I could heal."

"You could work a nerve, girl," Lila said.

Tisha grabbed Lila's hand. "As cousins, we have always been a part of each other's lives, but now that we are Christian women, we are a part of each other's spirits. I watched God take you out of the darkness and bring you into the light. You have always been stunning, but now that you have overcome your food addiction, God has revealed a spark that I didn't know existed in you."

Joan had to agree. Not only did Lila look like a new person, she acted like a new person. She was always smiling and energetic. She was like a dose of sunshine. Joan could see why single men would be attracted to her.

Tisha grabbed Joan's hand. Finally Joan put down her plate. "We have been best friends since middle school. What we have is rare, and I do not take it lightly. Thank you for introducing me to Jesus. I watched God change you and that's how I knew He could change me. Thank you for giving me a place to stay when I couldn't afford a place to lay my head. Thank you for being a great example of what a godly single woman should be."

Tears dropped down Tisha's face. "Ladies, I just want you to know that you are the answers to my prayers. I thank Jesus for the changes He has made in all of our lives. I can't help but cry every time I think of what God has brought us through in this short time of rolling with Him."

Lila looked up. "It has only been a short time, but we have made so many positive steps. I didn't think I would ever get over it when Steve kicked my daughter and me out. But that was the best thing that ever happened to me. I surrendered it all to Jesus, and He showed me He is more than sufficient to supply all of my needs.

"Now I have a decent job that allows me to provide for my daughter. I'm finally at a place where I can teach her not to go down the same path I did. And for the cherry on top of the sundae, I have been dating one of Pastor Benjy's elite eight."

"What?" Joan and Tisha cried out in unison.

Tisha said, "You mean *our* Pastor Benjy?"

"You mean Minister Makita's husband, Pastor Benjy," Joan added.

Lila laughed. "Yes, *our* Pastor Benjy. The senior pastor of our church, the Miller Street Church. Yes, the one married to Minister Makita. I am as shocked as you are. "

Joan and Tisha continued to look confused. Janet asked, "What is Pastor Benjy's elite eight?"

"Pastor Benjy is committed to making young men into godly husbands and life-changing Christians," Lila explained. "Every few years, he takes a group of men with exceptional leadership qualities and mentors them personally."

Tisha added, "Janet, it is so clear that you are married, because every single Christian woman in Houston, regardless of where she attends church, knows about Pastor Benjy's elite eight."

"What type of stuff does he teach them?" Janet asked.

"Everything, I heard. They have to be studious Bible students. They need to be able to teach, understand, and live the Word," Joan said.

"They go on missionary trips abroad. They also teach and preach locally in churches, jails, and hospitals," Tisha continued.

"They pray for each other and hold each other accountable for living set apart lives for Christ," Lila said. "Each week, they have accountability meetings. For instance, if they watched a questionable program or had sexually immoral conversations, they have to report that to the group."

"They are also not allowed to ask a woman on a date until they have tested her," Joan said, staring intently at Lila.

"Tested her?" Janet asked. "How so?"

Joan repeated what she overheard from one of the older ladies in church. "First of all, they pray and ask God's guidance about a wife. If they notice someone of interest, they have to watch her first. Some men even talk to the godly people around her, like her pastor, friends, and the other people in ministry with her. They want to make sure she is just not pretending to be a godly woman but *is* a godly woman. They compare her character to what the Bible says about a godly woman."

Janet looked impressed. "Wow! Lila, how did you snag him, and what's his name, anyway?"

Lila blurted out, "Kenneth Harrison."

Joan and Tisha turned toward each other in disbelief. Kenneth Harrison's baritone voice led them into the Spirit every Sunday morning as he opened the church in prayer. It didn't matter that church started fifteen minutes late, or that Sister So-and-So was singing off-key, or that the air conditioner was broken in the middle of the summer—none of that mattered when Kenneth walked to the podium.

He was slim, spoke well, and all of his prayers were permeated with the Word of God. He didn't mind showing his emotions. Some Sunday mornings as he prayed, he would start crying as he thanked Jesus for His goodness.

He was the assistant principal at a local elementary school, where he was committed to molding young boys into strong Christian men. Each week, he had dozens of boys bussed to Miller Street Church for the church's Youth Ministry meeting.

"A few weeks ago, after Wife Prep class, Minister Makita asked me to stay," Lila said. "She told me that a young man from the church had come in asking about me a few times over the course of several weeks. I begged her to tell me who, but she wouldn't. She seemed really happy for me, so I stopped bugging her, even though I wanted to shake her until it came out.

"Right after I left Minister Makita that day, I went to the church's day care to pick up Jasmine. Kenneth was there, and he was reading a Bible story to the handful of children who were still there. Jasmine was right in front and completely engaged in the story. Well, instead of interrupting, I sat in the back, my mind racing with what Minister Makita had just told me."

Tisha blurted out, "Hold on! I got to go pee and can't hold it anymore. Don't say a word until I get back." She ran down the hall.

Joan shuffled around in her seat before getting up to get a glass of water. She was too involved in her thoughts to ask her friends if they needed something. Kenneth was the finest Christian man she had ever seen. He was the complete package. Once, he asked Joan for her phone number when they were working on a project for Minster Makita. Joan had gotten so excited, thinking maybe he was interested in her. But the only time Kenneth called was when he needed to get some information about something church related. He never tried to make the conversation last any longer than necessary. Joan was devastated.

Tisha returned and Lila started again. "Well, the teenage girls who usually work in the day care started talking and giggling. Then they went and got the remaining children and took them to another part of the day care, leaving me, Jasmine, and Kenneth alone."

Tisha prodded, "That's when you knew it was him?"

"That's when I knew Kenneth had arranged for Minister Makita to hold me up, and for the day care workers to take the other children away," Lila answered.

"Well, what happened next?" Janet asked, patting her oversized stomach.

"Next?" Lila paused. "Next he asked if he could take me to lunch. Girls, I could have screamed, 'Thank you, Jesus!' We've been hanging out pretty regularly for two weeks."

Tisha stood up. "Two weeks! How dare you hold on to this kind of information."

"I know, I know. It's just that if things didn't work out, I didn't want to get my hopes up," Lila pleaded.

"And now?" Joan questioned, rejoining the ladies on the sofa.

"Well, it's too late, my hopes are up. Kenneth is wonderful and everything I could want in a husband," Lila paused. "Everything God wants me to have in a husband. I'm telling you now because tonight he asked me to meet his parents."

Tisha started jumping up and down. "I'm going to be in a wedding! I'm going to be in a wedding!"

"You see why I didn't tell you?" Lila laughed. "Kenneth hasn't asked me to marry him."

"He hasn't asked you *yet*," Janet said. "Jerome told me he knew right away I would be his wife. Men know right away if they are going to make you a wife. Meeting the parents? Girl, that means you are in."

Janet waddled up and gave Lila a hug. "I'm so happy for you." Tisha joined the hug. Joan looked around first. Sensing no way to flee, she joined the hug too.

As Joan embraced her friends, her mind wandered to the day Minister Makita announced she was launching a new ministry: Wife Preparation class. She said the women would search and study the scriptures and learn what God said about being a wife. In addition to Bible Study, they would have homemaking and money management classes. They would get training on raising godly children and having a vision for their families.

Joan and Tisha couldn't join the class because it was a six-month commitment, and with their work in the bakery, they wouldn't have time. But Joan wondered if that was what had attracted Kenneth to Lila, and why wouldn't it? A woman who had made the commitment to the extensive schedule Minister Makita had proposed for the class—and the personal one-on-one sessions the minister had planned to have with the women—had to be showing all the single men that she was committed to being a wife. Joan could have slapped herself. She could have figured out how to rearrange her schedule to get into the class. Every Christian man in Houston was probably trying to marry a woman from Minister Makita's Wife Preparation class.

After the group hug, Lila started to gather her things so she could meet Kenneth. Before she walked out the door, Lila nervously looked back. "Would one of you pray for me?"

Joan was glad when Janet stepped up to do it. "I know what you're feeling right now." Janet grabbed Lila's hand. "I remember when Jerome asked me to meet his family. It was such an exciting time."

The ladies held hands in a circle as Janet prayed. "Dear Heavenly Father, Creator of heaven and earth, Lord, how we thank you. We thank you for sending Jesus to pay for our sins. We thank you that we have received Jesus' death as payment for our sins, and therefore when we die, we will spend eternity with you in heaven.

"We thank you for giving us what we need, instead of what we deserve. We thank you for friends and family. We thank you for homes, food, your mercy, and your grace. We thank you for your guidance and the security you provide. Lord, we pray for Lila. Lord, we have watched this woman grow under your attentive care. We thank you for her changed life. We pray, Lord, that you would guide her as she meets Kenneth's parents. Allow her to be calm and free from anxiousness, knowing that she is fearfully and wonderfully made in you. If it is your will for these two to become one, Lord, we pray that you would make that clear. Please give them insight, Father, and direction, in Jesus' name we pray."

After one more group hug, Lila left with a smile on her face and tears in her eyes. Joan looked at Tisha, and Tisha looked at Joan—each knowing what the other was thinking. Bible Study would have to wait. There was no time to waste. Joan dashed to the computer in her home office. Tisha jogged to the sofa and yanked her laptop out of its protective case. They needed to go online and register for Minister Makita's next Wife Preparation class.

Chapter 9

Joan rushed to Minister Makita's office. The last thing she wanted to do was be late. Makita insisted on meeting face-to-face with everyone who applied for the Wife Preparation class. It was only a matter of time before the minister would be telling Joan how pleased she was that she decided to join the class. She probably called her in early because she wanted Joan to take an active role in the class, helping the other single women along. She had only completed her application that Saturday and Minister Makita called her in for a meeting the following Monday evening.

Joan had only been at Miller Street Church for a short while, but everybody knew she was one of Makita's favorite people. Joan had grown quickly and soon started teaching New Members Orientation classes and Women's Bible Studies. When Minister Makita had to have an unplanned surgery in the midst of a women's conference, where she was the keynote speaker, instead of using a more tenured member of the church, she chose Joan. People were surprised, until they heard Joan deliver an outstanding Bible lesson. From that point on, people in the church started to look at Joan in a different light.

Minister Makita was one of the most influential people in Houston, but that's not what Joan admired about her. Joan admired how she could make the scriptures come alive. Minister Makita didn't preach so

that people could be happy; she preached so they could
be changed. Joan was only one of the women whom
Minister Makita's teaching had impacted in such a
huge way. She had throngs of faithful Christian women
who looked to her for guidance.

Joan walked into Makita's opened office door and
tapped on the door. Makita looked up from a stack of
papers, then asked Joan to close the door behind her.

As Joan closed the door, she tried to ignore the worry
she saw on Makita's face. She had expected Makita to
greet her with a smile, like she usually did, but Makita
looked troubled. Surely there wasn't anything wrong
with her application. She had spent hours on it, inserting
relevant scripture and interesting stories about herself.
Besides, Makita loved her, Joan reassured herself as she
sat down in the chair across from Minister Makita.

"Hello, my dear," Makita greeted Joan in her deep
Southern accent.

Joan nodded, wondering why Makita still hadn't
smiled.

"Do you have any idea why I summoned you here
today?"

Joan's mind started to race. If this wasn't about the
Wife Preparation class, what could it be about?

"No, I guess I don't." Joan shrugged her shoulders.

Makita shuffled through the papers on her desk. "I
received your application."

Joan looked alarmed. "Yes, I completed it on Saturday. Is there something wrong? I could do it over."

Makita looked over Joan's paperwork again. "Joan,
you are the best Bible teacher I have come across in
years. I look across the room when you are teaching
and everybody seems engaged and actively learning."
Makita shook her head. "And that three-part lesson

you did on the Book of Ruth, it was wonderful." Makita laughed. "Pastor Benjy kept the CD in our car for two weeks. He was delighted a teacher of your magnitude had been discipled through our ministry."

Joan sat up straighter in her seat and took a deep breath. "Makita, you really had me worried. I thought I had done something wrong. Your mood seemed so somber when I walked in."

"I'm not finished, Joan," Makita said tersely. Joan sank back into her seat.

"Joan, while you are a great Bible teacher, there are some problems. I should have spoken to you sooner, because, well, now things are worse. And when I printed out your application for the Wife Preparation class, it became apparent that it was time for you and your spiritual mother to have a talk."

Makita shoved all her papers to the sides of her desk and made a clear path between her and Joan. Joan avoided Makita's intense eyes and stared at a photo above Makita's head.

"Have you heard about Kenneth and Lila?" Makita looked like she wanted a reaction.

Joan started fiddling with her handbag. "Yes, Lila told us all about her and Kenneth." Makita looked like she wanted something more. "We are all so happy for her," Joan added.

"Joan, I'm up here."

Joan put her gaze on Minister Makita. She had not realized she had started to look down while talking about Lila.

Makita continued speaking. "Last week, Tisha taught her first small group meeting. I don't remember seeing you."

Joan made a point to continue looking up. "James Jr. had a project I was helping him finish."

"I see," Makita said suspiciously. "You remember when Sister Felicia criticized your interpretation of scripture in front of the entire class?"

Joan perked up. "Yes, and I quickly corrected her. She had it all wrong. I studied that passage up and down. I don't know who she thought—" Joan abruptly stopped talking.

"Go on, Joan. Finish what you were saying about Sister Felicia."

"Never mind," Joan responded as she crossed her arms over her chest.

"Let me finish for you, Joan," Makita said. "What you were about to say is 'I don't know who she thought she was talking to. Doesn't she know who I am? I am Joan Dallas. When I teach, there's no need to ask any questions. If you didn't understand, it was because you were not paying attention.'"

Joan said nothing. She only glared back at Minister Makita.

"What you really wanted to say to Sister Felicia was written all over your face that day, as it is today. You can't stand the idea that somebody would criticize you. You were right that day, Sister Felicia did have it wrong. But it was the way that you dealt with the situation that has me concerned. It is the way you respond to anybody when they don't seem to understand who you are."

"What do you mean?" Joan asked.

"When they don't understand that *you* are Joan Dallas, the queen bee in charge," Makita explained. "You didn't come hear Tisha teach because . . . Well, what was the point? I mean, she can't teach like you. She couldn't exegete a passage of scripture to the point where it was worth you coming out to listen. As a matter of fact, you never come to small group when new people are teaching. And then the time your best friend was teaching, you couldn't rearrange your schedule. You knew months ahead of time, and poor Tisha, she didn't even realize what was really going on."

Joan's face was expressionless.

"You see, Tisha is fine as long as she stays in her place. As long as she realizes that Joan is the smart one. Joan is the star. And Joan shines the brightest in every situation. You didn't want to hear Tisha teach because you were scared that maybe she is better than you. Could somebody dare to attempt to dethrone the queen bee?"

Joan remained silent.

"Admit it, Joan, this thing with Lila and Kenneth is making you livid. You sat in my office and just lied to me. You are not at all happy for this couple. You can't believe Lila has a shot at getting married before you. The fact that it is Kenneth is just making it worse. If anybody should be marrying one of Pastor Benjy's bunch, it should be you. Because, after all, Lila does not have anything on you, along with the rest of the single women in the world. Because you are everything a single Christian man would want.

"I could see your desperation all through your answers on the Wife Preparation application. You might as well have said you want to be in the Wife Preparation class because Lila can't possibly get married before you do.

"I am denying you entrance into the Wife Preparation class. Lately you have been hateful, prideful, and hypercritical. No, I do not expect the Wife Preparation class members to be perfect. No one is perfect. But I do expect for them to exhibit a teachable spirit. At one point, you had that, but now you don't. Joan, you are not ready to be anybody's wife."

Joan had enough. She started gathering her things.

"I hope you take the time and spend it with God to find out what is really going on with you. I would hate for your spiritual growth to stop when you started out so promising. Maybe it's my fault. I used you too early and too often. Maybe that's why you are so high, you can't relate to the 'common people.'"

"Are we finished?" Joan stood up.

"Joan, I would be more than happy to schedule a few prayer and counseling sessions with you to help you get to the heart of the issue."

"That won't be necessary," Joan replied.

"Will I see you Sunday?" Minister Makita asked.

"Probably not."

"I know this was a lot to take, but love is telling people the truth whether they want to hear it or not. I'll call you in a few days. Maybe we can have lunch."

"Is that all, Makita?" Joan turned to leave.

"Joan?"

Joan turned around slowly.

"I'm allowing Tisha in the class."

Joan left without saying another word.

Chapter 10

"Daddy sleep. . . . Daddy sleep," Alexis whispered as she kissed James on the face repeatedly. She shook him gently. "Get up, Daddy. Let's play." The moment James felt the first kiss, he smiled. But when the fourth kiss came, he almost pushed Alexis away.

Waking up this way reminded him of weekend mornings. He looked forward to meeting the day with a flutter of tiny three-year-old kisses. Alexis would cuddle up to him, along with her two favorite stuffed animals, Mr. Dinosaur and Major Piggy. They would sing songs before going downstairs to watch cartoons and eat big bowls of cereal in their personalized daddy/daughter bowls. Any other day, this would have been a wonderful way to wake up, but now he felt sick to his stomach, knowing Alexis belonged to another man.

Avoiding Raquel and the kids had been easy the first few weeks after finding out the children were not his. All he had to do was make up a lie about working overtime each night to get the last-minute spending money for the bigger-than-life honeymoon he had planned. But now that there was only one week to go, he knew that would get old.

Raquel had no idea he was really at his brother's house. Tonight, though, Miles was having a business meeting, which was why James went home to watch the game. He had planned to return to Miles's place well before he expected Raquel and the children to arrive home for the evening, but he had ended up falling asleep on the sofa.

James moved past Alexis and looked around the room for Raquel and Morris. He only spotted Raquel's handbag and keys on the table in the foyer. Assuming she was upstairs, he yelled for her. "I gotta go to the bathroom! Come get Lexi!" He heard Raquel's footsteps walking toward them.

"Alexis, bath time," Raquel said.

James started briskly walking toward the downstairs bathroom. Alexis giggled as she ran behind him, thinking they were playing a game of chase.

"Come here, baby girl," Raquel said, leading Alexis upstairs. James paced the bathroom floor, trying to come up with his next move. Like magic, he suddenly remembered something Raquel had said months ago. They needed to sleep apart the days leading up to their wedding. She thought it would make their honeymoon night more special. James thought it was a stupid idea, but he was now glad he had not argued with her.

He stepped into the master bathroom, where Raquel was bathing Alexis and singing "The Alphabet Song."

"Hey, I'm about to pack my stuff and head over to Miles's place. He was cool with the idea of me staying with him this week." He added, "Just like you said he would be." James looked in the mirror to avoid looking in Raquel's eyes.

"Oh . . . I didn't think you thought that was such a great idea. You didn't say anything when I told you about it."

"Yeah, I was thinking about it and decided whatever my bride wants, my bride gets."

Raquel cut her eyes at James. "Well, if that's the case, where are we going for our honeymoon?"

"Except for that. I told you it was a surprise."

James grabbed a brush and started stroking his hair. "All you need to know is what I already told you. You need to pack for somewhere tropical. Our flight leaves at ten the morning after the wedding. I'm going to have you up all night, so don't think you will be in any condition to wake up that morning and pack. You are going to need to sleep in! So whatever you do, don't forget to get everything ready before the wedding."

Raquel smiled. "You know you shouldn't be talking like that in front of the baby."

"Whatever. . . . That's how the baby got here." James got a lump in his throat. He put the brush down and walked off, leaving Raquel with a smile that looked as if it was going to be permanently plastered on her face.

When James walked past Morris's room, he was busy playing a video game. The door was closed, but James could hear Morris pounding on the buttons of his PlayStation. Now that Morris was twelve, it was hard to get him out of his room. On any other evening, James would have been sitting on the bed with him. But at that moment, all James wanted to do was keep walking.

He paused when he reached Alexis's room. Unlike the other rooms in the house, he had painted and decorated this one himself. He decided on a sunny yellow because it fit her personality. She was always happy and smiling and ready to play. It took him four days to individually put up each of the flowers, butterflies, and honeybee stickers that adorned the walls in her room. For a final touch, he put a big picture on the wall of him holding Alexis when she was first born.

He hadn't bothered to make an appearance during the births of Morris and James Jr., which was why he insisted on being there for Alexis's birth. He didn't miss one prenatal appointment and even won the prize for the most supportive husband at their labor and delivery class. When they arrived at the hospital, Raquel demanded an epidural, but the doctor said it was too late because the contractions were too close together. Raquel immediately started to panic, but James was able to calm her down when the nurses and doctor could not. He did the breathing techniques right along with her, keeping her focused as she pushed.

After seeing Raquel give birth to his daughter, he knew he wanted to spend the rest of his life with her. Raquel never looked more beautiful than the moments after the delivery, nursing tiny Alexis, and then the two of them falling into a deep sleep. It was that day that James knew everything had changed, for real this time.

For the first time since finding out the children were not his, James felt tears in his eyes. He didn't want to run into Raquel again, so he pushed himself to walk to the bedroom he shared with her. In less than ten minutes, he had his rolling suitcase stuffed to capacity, headed downstairs and out the door. He had barely opened his truck door before he freely allowed the tears to flow down his face.

Chapter 11

Withdrawing most of the money from their joint account was the last thing James needed to do before heading out to meet Miles and the other groomsmen for the pre-wedding festivities. He noticed Raquel went against their agreement and spent more money on the wedding, but he wasn't about to let that ruin his evening.

Just because he wasn't actually getting married didn't mean he was going to miss out on his long-awaited two-day bachelor party. The wedding was scheduled for Saturday afternoon, and he and his friends planned to party up until then.

It was Thursday night, and James was driving to the barbershop to meet his friends. After getting haircuts, they would head straight to Jazzy Fast Nasty's for dinner and drinks. The waitresses at Jazzy Fast Nasty's wore next to nothing as they sauntered to and fro, serving up huge steaks and the freshest lobster in town.

On Friday, they were checking into the hotel and attending the rehearsal and the rehearsal dinner. After the rehearsal dinner, the official party would begin in the extra large two-bedroom hotel suite he was sharing with Miles.

James could feel his heart racing already. Miles had promised to get "Butter" and "Crème," of the Passion Palace in Las Vegas, to perform at his bachelor party. The two exotic dancers traveled the world and were highly sought after because of their athletic and acrobatic show. James and Miles had seen them for the first time when they were visiting Vegas for Miles's birthday.

James merged onto Highway 59 with a big smile on his face. He couldn't wait to see how Butter and Crème made everything better. His thoughts were interrupted by his ringing cell phone. James glanced at the caller ID. He took a deep breath. It wasn't Raquel; it was Pam—sexy, fun, eager Pam. James met Pam years ago when he went to visit Raquel at work. He ended their eight-month affair years ago. However, when James decided he needed to have a little fun before he officially got married, he reconnected with Pam.

"What's up, sexy?" James smiled as he spoke into his cell phone.

"All I need is one more night."

"Now, you know I told you we had to stop messing around, since I'm getting married."

"I know . . . I know, but you are getting married, not me. I need my James fix."

"You coming to the wedding?" James asked.

"Of course. Your crazy soon-to-be wife has all the girls in the shop working. But at least I don't have to do hair. I'll be doing the makeup for the mothers and grandmothers." Pam sighed. "I'm still mad I'm going to miss a whole Saturday's pay at the freaking wedding. Raquel acts like she does not know that's our biggest appointment day, and besides, you should be marrying me, not her."

"You are sexy as all outdoors."

Pam giggled. "So how are you going to make it up to me? Why don't you come by tonight? Please! Come on, James, all I need is one more night."

"Just one more night?" James teased.

Pam whispered, "Just one more night, Big James."

"I'll see what I can do. But if I can, it will be late . . . real late."

"I'll be up," Pam purred.

"All right, hottie, I'll talk to you later."

As soon as James disconnected the call, the phone rang again. He picked it up quickly. "What's up, Sharonda?"

He should have known she was going to call. Sharonda was only nineteen when they met at a football game. James ended up taking her virginity a month later. Miles told him not to do it, for fear that Sharonda would be exceptionally clingy. Miles was right. Sharonda was clingy, and crazy too. James broke up with her over two and a half years ago, but Sharonda still found a reason to call him, almost weekly.

"Hey, baby, what are you doing?"

"I'm on my way to get a haircut. What about you?"

"I need to tell you something."

"Go ahead, Sharonda."

"I'm in love with you, James. If I can't have you, there is no reason to live. If you go on with this wedding, I'm going to kill myself."

James hung up the phone without saying a word. Sharonda practically threatened to kill herself every other day. He wasn't about to let that ditzy broad ruin his day. James suddenly got a vision of what Joan would look like in the bikini he purchased for her yesterday. She was going to look scrumptious next to him in the villa he had rented for his honeymoon. Nobody could wear a swimsuit quite like her. They would spend their time making love on the beach underneath the stars, in between eating magnificent gourmet meals.

After they came back, he would move in with Joan and James Jr. for a month or so. It would take at least that long for Raquel to move her things and find another place for her and the kids to live.

He had thought about continuing to stay with Miles. However, after being in Joan's place with her delicious food and sexy vibe, the last thing he wanted was to be trapped in that oversized dorm room Miles called an apartment.

James scrolled until he found Joan's number on his cell phone. Before it went through, he stopped the call. He needed to wait until everything was over. Joan wouldn't be able to resist his invitation to Jamaica after discovering the lengths he had gone through to break up with Raquel for good.

He pulled up to the parking lot of the barbershop he had been going to for the last fifteen years. All of his groomsmen were waiting next to a black Hummer limo. James stepped out of his truck and approached them. "My, it looks like you have spared no expense. We're going to be traveling in style."

"Oh, big brother, you have no idea." Miles opened the door. The limo was laid out with champagne, shrimp, and Butter, along with her sidekick, Crème, wearing nothing but their stilettos. James peeked inside and almost jumped for joy. Miles grinned deviously. "This is only the beginning. What I have waiting for you at the hotel tonight will have you screaming for more."

Chapter 12

Joan looked over the financial statements while she lay in bed, drinking peppermint tea. Looking at the excellent numbers should have brought her relief, instead all she felt was numbness. Here she had successfully opened her dream business, but she couldn't celebrate. She had made all the right decisions: spending the money up front to get a top restaurant consulting firm to come in and help her with everything from acquiring the property to hiring the perfect management team.

She had hired a well-known publicist to help get the word out about the bakery. It had worked. The bakery received rave reviews from the local newspaper's food critics. Soon after, a popular Christian radio host decided to broadcast her talk show on Wednesdays at the bakery. That brought people from all over the city. The radio host went on and on about the friendly Christian environment, beautiful décor, and delicious desserts and coffee.

Joan tossed the financial statements on the floor and sank back into the softness of her down comforter. Despite being scared, she had left the corporate world behind to follow her passion, and now it was official. Happy Endings, her bakery, was a success. Ordinarily, Joan would have sent up an audible prayer to God at a time like this, but currently she wasn't speaking to Him.

She hadn't opened a Bible or said a prayer since she
left Makita's office almost a week ago. She had stopped
answering Tisha's phone calls too. Most mornings, she
was at the bakery early, but for the last few days, she
had left Karla, the bakery manager, in charge. Joan
typically managed the back of the house, and Tisha
and her enthusiastic personality worked the front.
Joan didn't want to be around Tisha right now, though.
Maybe later, but right now she wasn't ready for the
questions. She could already hear them in her head:
*"Why did Makita let me in the class and not you? Why
have you been so quiet lately?"*

Joan reached over to the nightstand to retrieve
James Sr.'s wedding invitation from her handbag.
It was gorgeous, embroidered in gold and black and
printed on fine linen. When she found the invitation
in her son's things, she had no interest in going to the
wedding. But after she walked out of Makita's office,
she knew she would go.

It was because of closure, she needed to see the man
of her dreams become eternally wed to someone else.
Maybe then she could let her heart heal. She could be
free of her bondage, the domination that James still
had over her. Nobody would understand, so it was
no point in trying to explain. They had never loved as
deeply as she had. As hard as anyone might try, they
would never be able to identify with the pain.

On one hand, Joan knew that God loved her; but
on the other, she felt as if He hated her. Here she was
alone, with no man to call her own. It seemed as if
everybody's life was moving forward except for hers.
Yes, the bakery was going well, but a successful career
wasn't enough. Joan wanted a man to share it with,
and she craved a chance to have more children. After
talking to Makita, she seemed to feel as if getting mar-

ried was beyond her. A decent man wouldn't want her. She was too prideful, too arrogant, *just too everything*.

Joan bowed her face into her hands. How in the world could she still be a mess? After living for the Lord this long, how could she still have pieces that needed to be put together? Would she ever be whole? If it wasn't one thing, it was another. If it wasn't feeling the urge to have sex, it was using her tongue for evil. If it wasn't her selfishness, it was her pride. If she wasn't constantly complaining, she found herself lying. Now Makita had brought it all home. She was a miserable excuse for a Christian.

Joan decided she needed some snacks for her pity party and headed in the direction of the refrigerator. She had leftover spinach enchiladas and beef queso and chips from the night before. She heated it up and headed back to bed. James Jr. was at the final wedding rehearsal, so she didn't have to worry about him asking her why she could eat in her room and he couldn't eat in his.

Joan loved her son, but he could really work a nerve, especially now that he was regularly attending Sunday School and learning about the Bible. A month ago, she was exhausted, so she told her son to lie to his dad and tell him that she was at work and couldn't drop him off. James Jr. refused. He looked Joan right in her face and said, "God is for truth. The devil is for lies. Whose side are you on?"

Joan took a chip and dipped it into the rich gooiness of the queso. Before she finished chewing, she was already stuffing her mouth with all the spinach enchilada she could get on the fork. Joan felt guilty, but as she labored to chew all the food she had stuffed in her mouth, she wondered what her life would be like if she had never had a child. When she found out she was pregnant with James Jr., she was thrilled. She thought she had James Sr. for sure. It never entered her mind that James Sr. would marry somebody else. She resented having to be both father and mother. James Sr. didn't have to discipline their son, help him with his homework every night, or take off work to be with him when he was sick. He just showed up on the weekends bearing gifts and football tickets, as if he was nothing more than a doting grandparent.

She didn't know how she was going to do it, but now was the time to let it go. She had to release the idea that somehow, someway, she and James would find each other. They were never going to be that family she had envisioned. James had another family, another life, and she would never be a part of it. Raquel was right— she had the man, the house in the suburbs, and the two beautiful kids.

What should a girl do the night before the man of her dreams gets married to another woman? Tisha was too holy for any earthly good. Janet was happily married and pregnant. Joan certainly didn't need to be reminded that Lila had been chosen by an HGM, aka "hot godly man," of the highest magnitude. When was she going to get her hot godly man?

Joan finished off the queso and enchiladas and headed back to the kitchen for an extra big slice of chocolate cake. She heated some chocolate sauce in the microwave and added it to the cake, along with some vanilla ice cream, whipped cream, and chopped pecans.

She climbed back into bed and turned on the television. She flipped channels until she found a talk show featuring three different women of different ages. Joan took large bites of her ice cream as she listened to their discussion.

"I knew God wasn't going to send me a husband until I didn't want one. Yes, He was telling me He needed me content, single," the youngest one said.

"When I got married almost forty years ago," the oldest one stated, "I didn't know the degree of selflessness that would be required. I know why we have a fifty percent divorce rate in the country. Selfish people are getting married. Marriage is not about what you can get out of it. It's about what you can put into it."

"These young girls don't want to hear that," the middle-aged woman chimed in. "They don't want to know the truth. They think it's about flowers and cake. They don't want to hear about sacrifice, forgiveness, and the selflessness it takes to maintain a marriage."

"Hey, Tracy," the youngest one said. "You and your husband counsel engaged couples. Have you ever told a couple they were not ready to get married?"

"Yes, we have. They are easy to spot. They have a hole in their souls and have decided that getting married will fix it. We tell them they need to deal with those issues, but they think walking down the aisle will fix everything. They usually leave our church and go somewhere else, where they will marry anyone with money to spend. Months later, they come back, hoping we can save them from a divorce that seems imminent."

The middle-aged woman started to turn red and firmly said, "People just need to wait, bottom line. Allow God to prune and prepare. He will send that perfect person along in His perfect timing. I mean, would you really want to marry someone if it wasn't God's best?"

"I knew marriage was the most important decision I would ever make, and I wanted God all up in it. You feel me?" the youngest one asked. "I had seen too much destruction. I knew we needed Jesus from the beginning. And now that we have been married for only three years, and have gone through more drama than I could have imagined, I'm so glad I followed the Master's plan. Let's face it—this world does not have a clue about how to be married. Oh, we know how to pick out a big diamond ring and a Vera Wang dress, but we don't have a clue about how to make a marriage thrive."

The oldest one said, "And the funny thing is, it is right in the Bible, but nobody bothers to read it. God created marriage. He's the only one who knows how to work it."

"We are too busy watching celebrities jump in and out of marriage," said the middle-aged lady. "I heard a pregnant, single, twice-divorced celebrity say on a talk show the other day that she and her boyfriend were going to redefine marriage. I guess God didn't get it right the first time, so now he needs her help."

All the women shook their heads. Joan turned off the TV and threw the remote control across the room. "I quit! I quit! I quit!" Joan couldn't believe she was actually yelling out loud. "I don't want to do this anymore. I don't want to be single, celibate, and lonely. I don't want to go to Bible Study anymore. I don't want to go to church. I don't want to have one more conversation with any more church people. They are full of it.

"Am I the only one struggling? Am I the only one who gets up in the morning and doesn't feel like shouting, 'Hallelujah, praise the Lord'? I don't want to have to worry about *if* or *when* I will ever have sex again. I'm tired of seeing all the older married couples hand in hand at church, reminding me of what I may never have. I'm tired of seeing all the swollen bellies of the pregnant married couples reminding me of what I may never have again. When is it going to be my turn?"

Joan turned to look at herself in the mirror across from her bed. "I should have just done it. I should have just had some fun with James last week."

Joan looked at her cell phone on the nightstand. James Sr. wasn't married yet. Maybe she should give him a call. Yes, just maybe she would. . . .

Chapter 13

Raquel looked at the bubbles emerging from her tall chilled glass. After taking a sip, she delicately nibbled on a chocolate-covered strawberry. This was just how she imagined the morning of her wedding: cool, calm, and refreshing.

All of her bridesmaids, minus Karen, were in a hotel suite down the hall getting their hair and makeup done. The children were in another suite with James's mother. Raquel had arranged to have her own private suite. She didn't want the busy chatter of the other people in her wedding party to disturb the best day of her life. There was no way she was going to give anyone the pleasure of preventing her from soaking up every delectable moment.

The masseuse had arrived at six in the morning. After an hour-long massage, Raquel let the masseuse out and let the manicurist in. An hour after that, Raquel's hairdresser and makeup artist arrived.

The bridal suite was exquisite. To her left, Raquel could see the sprawling oak trees through her oversized bay window. It was a serene and peaceful sight. Raquel chose this hotel because it was minutes from Coolwater Church. Both were located in Fordham, Texas, a city less than an hour and a half from Houston.

Raquel and a group of other hairstylists had fallen in love with Coolwater Church over five years ago after a bunch of them had attended a funeral for their longtime supplier. They couldn't believe such a beautiful church existed. Before the funeral was over, Raquel knew she would get married in that church one day. After leaving the funeral, she drove around until she found a suitable hotel for her reception. She fell in love with the Oakley because it was almost as beautiful as the church. She had to drive up a long, winding road to get to it. The road had huge trees on both sides of it, so big they shaded the entire path. It looked like something out of a movie. When she finally arrived at the hotel, she was greeted with a building that looked like a multimillion-dollar mansion. This was no ordinary hotel. It had the "awe" factor that Raquel was looking for.

The four-poster king-sized bed was as soft and supple as Raquel had imagined. After the rehearsal dinner last night, she hurried to wrap herself within the Egyptian cotton sheets. Raquel particularly enjoyed the unique antique furniture and oversized mahogany desk. As Raquel walked through the room, her bare feet walked over a hallway elegantly designed with marble. The hotel provided several large vases of fresh flowers to add the finishing touches to the room.

All the hard work had paid off. She had pounded the pavement for years, even doing hair for free in the beginning just to get clients. It was embarrassing at times, standing outside of grocery stores with flyers and business cards while her old friends passed her, barely acknowledging her presence.

Raquel knew they would never understand her. She would only be wasting her time trying to explain. They wouldn't understand what it was like to grow up with a mother who did not really want a child and with a father who did not stay out of jail long enough to be much use.

***

Raquel was a teenager when her mother looked her in the face and told her she needed to find somewhere else to live. Her mother had a new man in her life and he didn't want to be bothered with Raquel. It didn't surprise Raquel to have those words come out of her mother's mouth. Mothering hadn't been one of Samantha's qualities.

Samantha wanted a job that paid the rent and supplied her with adequate funds to buy all the alcohol and food she wanted, while having enough left over to make sure she kept her man happy. That was it, nothing more, nothing less. Raquel barely knew the rest of her family, because her mother didn't keep in touch with them.

Raquel convinced her mother to let her stay for two more weeks. Her mother agreed. During that time, Raquel took off from school, claiming she had chicken pox, and braided all the hair she could. Each day, she hustled until she found someone willing to pay her at least sixty dollars for micro braids. Mostly, she stopped mothers or single fathers walking around with little girls with unruly hair. They loved the price and the fact that Raquel would do the braiding in the privacy of their own homes.

At the end of the two weeks, Raquel had enough money to furnish and rent a small garage apartment near her high school. Raquel knew she could have stayed with one of her friends, but she didn't want anyone to know about her circumstances. People thought her life was perfect because she was pretty and captain of the majorettes. The illusion was all she had, and she didn't want to risk losing it.

Raquel supported herself by shampooing hair in salons in the evening. After she graduated from high

school, she pursued and received her cosmetology li-
cense and started working to build her clientele. Her
goal was to be one of the most sought-after stylists
in Houston. It was what she would work for in all the
years to come.

Raquel looked around the suite again and smiled.
She had succeeded.

It was time to take her wedding gown out of the
garment bag. She wondered if she had made the right
decision, excluding all of her bridesmaids from the
room. The silence in the room, along with the beautiful gown, was starting to remind her of prom night. All
the other girls had mothers who took them to the mall
or to the seamstress to pull together that perfect prom
ensemble. The hours before prom, mothers and daughters primped and giggled before the mirror.

Raquel remembered fighting back tears as she dressed
and put on her makeup alone in that garage apartment.
She had invited her mother to go shopping with her for
her prom dress, just as she had for her wedding dress.
Both times, her mother had declined.

Raquel had desperately wanted to tell her mother
about the grandeur of her wedding day, but she decided it was best to wait. Her mother would walk into
that wedding and know that Raquel was worthy, that
she was a success. She had worked to make sure every
detail of her wedding made a statement. After today,
everybody would know that Raquel was to be admired.

She would have it all: a wonderful husband, a beautiful family, and a lucrative career. Once she walked
down that aisle, she was going to be Mrs. James Reynolds, and there was nothing anybody could do about
it. James was a good man, and Raquel was thrilled to

have him. Yes, there had been other women in the past, but she was James's future. James was the best thing that had ever happened to her, and the only man she had ever loved. Life simply wasn't worth living if she couldn't have him.

All she ever wanted in her life was a family and nice things to share with them. She couldn't have that with Randall. He was a total loser. He may have been able to supply her body with pleasure, but that was it. In no way did he compare to James.

Raquel smiled. She was only moments away from completing the ultimate dream. Most weddings were attended by *supportive* family and friends, but that was not the case at this ceremony. Today, all of the people who said she was crazy for staying with James after he got Joan pregnant would be there. All of the people who saw her standing on the street corners handing out flyers in the blistering heat would be there. All of the people who said she would never get married, and all of the people who said she couldn't manage her own successful salon, and especially her mother, who thought she would end up like her, would see her shining brightly today, glowing like the star she always knew she could be.

Raquel slipped into her gown and stepped into her shoes. She glanced at the mirror. She wanted to cry at her stunning reflection, but there was no way she was about to ruin a $1,000 makeup job.

Raquel heard a knock at the door. She answered without looking through the peephole. She knew it was her wedding planner, Anna, checking up on her.

"Hello, my dear," Anna gasped. "You are a sight to be seen." Anna handed Raquel her cell phone. "You left this in the other room. Your hubby-to-be is on the line."

Anna walked into the hotel room and stepped away from Raquel to give her some privacy.

"Hi, James." Raquel used her sexiest voice as she answered the phone.

"Hello, my love. Me and my boys are en route. I was a little late because I was making the finishing touches to your surprise. I want to make sure you have no intentions of coming back home until after the wedding, or you will spoil the surprise I have for you."

"Oh, James, you are so sweet. I can't wait to see what you have planned. And no, I wouldn't dare ruin the surprise. We are about to do a final rundown and then the photographer is coming up to take pre-wedding shots of me."

"I can't wait to see you, my love. See you at the altar."

"I can't wait!" Raquel hung up the phone.

Anna appeared next to her with a spiral notebook. "Everything looks great, Raquel. This has got to be one of the smoothest weddings ever. The bridesmaids, children, and parents are ready to go. My assistant at the church tells me all the vendors have arrived and are setting up."

Anna checked her list again. "Aha, there's something I didn't ask you! Where's James's ring?"

Raquel got this scared look in her eyes. "Oh no, I left it at home!"

Anna didn't miss a beat. She got on her cell phone and started dialing. "Where did you leave it? I'll get one of my people to go by your place and pick it up."

"Anna, I have to get it. There's no way anybody else could find it. It's in a safe I have buried under a bunch of boxes in my linen closet." Raquel didn't want James to find the thick platinum laced wedding band she had purchased for him.

Anna looked at her watch. "We'll have to ditch the pre-wedding photo session. Let's get your stuff and get you in the limo. Then I'll get the bridesmaids to meet us in the limo. Traffic permitting, we should be able to go to your house and still arrive at the church in plenty of time."

Raquel hurried and grabbed her things. She had just told James she wouldn't be returning home. Now she was going to ruin her surprise, but she wasn't about to let James know that, not after he went through so much trouble. Raquel grinned, thinking that James was about to be her husband and he cared enough about her to make sure their first night together as husband and wife would involve a carefully planned surprise. Raquel hated that she had to see it—whatever it was—without James for the first time. But how she loved surprises!

Chapter 14

Several of Raquel's neighbors were outside when she stepped out of the limo. They couldn't help but stare as she walked to her front door, with Anna right behind her, making sure no parts of her gown touched the ground.

Maybe James had the entire house covered with rose petals or maybe just the bedroom. Maybe he had those diamond earrings, which she had been eyeing, placed in a perfect little box and sitting on her pillow. Or perhaps he had gone through the trouble of doing some type of game, like a treasure hunt, where she would go through the house finding clues until she found the ultimate prize.

They only had one night in their home before they were off on their extra long honeymoon. Maybe James had decided that the resort suite was not enough and had splurged on a private condo on the beach, complete with butler service, and he was waiting until the last minute to tell his new bride.

After Raquel opened the door and walked into the foyer, she saw several large suitcases of all shapes and sizes. Raquel smiled. With all the wedding preparations, she didn't have time to pack her clothes beforehand, even though James had insisted. They must be leaving tonight, she reasoned, since James had taken the time to pack her clothes. Perhaps they would spend their first evening as husband and wife on a late-night flight.

She was about to go upstairs and get the ring when she saw an envelope on top of one of the suitcases. She grabbed it. After glancing at her wedding planner, she decided not to read it . . . yet. Anna gave a stern *hurry-up-we-need-to-get-you-to-your-wedding-now* look while simultaneously talking on her cell phone. Raquel walked upstairs, leaving Anna to her phone call.

Raquel walked to her linen closet. The fabric of her dress felt smooth against her skin. She imagined James's reaction the first time he saw her in her magnificent dress. It was going to be priceless.

She rushed and retrieved the ring. She was about to rejoin Anna downstairs when she realized this was the perfect time to take a peek inside the envelope. Raquel took a deep breath and tore the seal on the envelope. Just then, Anna appeared like a mother who had caught her eating a cookie without permission. Raquel put the halfway opened envelope underneath her arm and followed Anna downstairs and back into the limo.

As soon as they were seated, Raquel stuffed the envelope in the compartment right next to her seat. If she read it now, they would expect her to read it out loud. Anna looked at Raquel and her four bridesmaids. "You ladies look absolutely beautiful." She used a sponge to blot Raquel's face. Raquel agreed with Anna, but deep down she felt nobody looked better than she did.

In the limo, it was clear that Raquel didn't really know any of her bridesmaids. They talked to each other, but they barely spoke to her. Since Karen had backed out, all of the bridesmaids consisted of wives and girlfriends of James's friends. These were women she had barely taken the time to get to know. She wanted them in her wedding because they were the props she needed to put on the opulent production she had planned.

Things had gone well. They showed up when she suggested and managed not to get on her nerves, too much. They also put together a really nice shower for her. Raquel found herself wondering what they thought of her.

Of course, they envied her, Raquel decided. Shellie was a doctor who was married to James's friend Luther. The poor thing couldn't have kids, despite years of trying. She also left a lot to be desired in the looks department. Good thing she was a doctor.

Roselyn was petite and beautiful. She was almost too beautiful to be in Raquel's wedding. However, the girl had no curves; she was as straight as a stick—no hips, no thighs, no butt, nothing. On top of that, Roselyn was as dumb as a rock. Everybody knew she had dropped out of high school and couldn't manage to pass the GED tests, despite taking it multiple times. She worked a dead-end job at a parking garage. That's where James's friend Lionel met her five years ago. She'd been working in the boring, dull garage since then.

Carol was a college professor who had never met a doughnut she didn't want to inhale. She had a beautiful face, but that was hard to notice, for her body was consumed by multiple rolls of fat. Things had gotten worse ever since she had twins three years ago. The twins had left a permanent mark on poor Carol; she still looked like she was carrying them.

Charlene was the youngest of the crew and six months pregnant. Raquel was sure the pregnancy was going to cause issues with her dress, but the expert seamstress whom Anna had found didn't have any issues accommodating Charlene's growing stomach. Charlene idolized Raquel. She was currently in beauty school and didn't hide the fact that she wanted to open her own business, just like Raquel. She treated Raquel like a celebrity, sometimes getting so nervous around her that she could barely speak. Raquel enjoyed that very much. She pondered the thought of offering her a job as she looked outside the window of the limo.

Charlene's boyfriend was in a new band. When she suggested they listen to his CD, everyone looked at Raquel for a response. Raquel didn't object. If they were listening to a CD, she didn't have to pretend to be interested in them.

Raquel figured out how to make sure nobody was late for her wedding. She deliberately put the wrong time on the wedding invitations, ensuring that even the late guests were on time.

She had arranged with the hotel where she was having her reception to offer delicious appetizers upon the guests' arrival at the church. Once they walked into the foyer, they were greeted by twenty waiters with trays of sparkling apple cider, stuffed shrimp, crab cakes, and salmon cream cheese rolls. When Anna gave the call, the staff would usher guests into the ceremony site, without them even realizing that the wedding was forty-five minutes late.

Raquel looked at the clock in the limo as they pulled up to the back entrance of the church. Raquel's heart started to race. It was almost time. Anna called her assistant. Everything was set. The groomsmen, James, and the children were all in place. Anna stepped out of the limo, taking the bridesmaids with her. She didn't want to risk anyone seeing Raquel until she was walking down the aisle. She instructed Raquel to stay in the limo.

As soon as Anna and the bridesmaids got out of the car, Raquel checked her makeup. As she was adding more lipstick, she remembered the envelope. She was convincing herself not to open it when she heard a knock on the limo door.

Raquel looked up. It was Karen, looking like her old self. She had ditched the mom jeans and bad weave. She was wearing an emerald green dress and unbelievably high silver stilettos, with a matching handbag. She had a big welcoming smile on her face. Raquel didn't hesitate to open the door.

"Wow, Raquel, you look amazing," Karen said as she peeked inside the limo.

"Thank you, Karen. You look good too. I'm so glad you decided to come."

"You know I thought about it, and we go too far back for that. You have worked your butt off for this day, and I want to be here to support you."

"Thank you, Karen. You don't know how much that means to me."

"Well, let me go. I want to make sure I get a good seat. I can't wait to see the show you are about to put on."

With that, Karen walked away. Raquel really started to get excited. The guests were probably being rushed into the sanctuary now. After that, Anna or someone on her team would line up the bridesmaids.

Raquel needed something to do. She could feel the tears of happiness wanting to flow down her eyes. She would have to go ahead and read the envelope James had left. She would explain it to him later. He would understand. She needed a distraction. She couldn't walk down the aisle with raccoon eyes.

Raquel opened the letter and unfolded the papers inside. The first piece of paper was on letterhead from a place called Emerson Diagnostic Clinic. It had James's name and their address at the top of the page. The middle of the page had a list of tests and a bunch of technical jargon. Raquel skipped to the bottom of the page and read: *In the case of Morris, James is not the father. In the case of Alexis, James is not the father. In the case of James Jr., James is the father.*

The second page was in James's handwriting and it read:

What did it feel like at the altar when you thought I was about to read my vows, only to read the results of the paternity tests? What did it feel like when you saw the two high-definition screens turn to the paternity results letting everybody in the church see the type of woman you really are? What did it feel like when " I'm a Ho" started playing on the sound system? That was good, wasn't it? I paid a lot of money for that. And finally, what did it feel like when I pulled out one single, dead, brittle rose and crumbled it up in your face, signaling the end to our relationship and our fraudulent family right in front of all those people you desperately wanted to impress?

You deserved it. You deserved that and more for what you did to me. Now all I ask is that you get out of my house. Yeah, your name is on the mortgage, but when people find out the type of woman you are, they are going to leave your business in droves. Then when you can't keep up your side of the bargain, I'll be there to buy you out. I already packed up a bunch of your clothes. The sooner you get out of my house, the better. And yes, I did splurge for that condo. Now all I have to decide is who gets to share it with me. Will it be Joan, Pam from your salon, or maybe your girl, Karen? I've always thought she was especially hot. Farewell, Raquel. Good-bye and good riddance.

Raquel heard the limo door open. It was Anna, with a big smile on her face. "I'm so pleased everything has gone flawlessly. Your sweet little flower girl is on her way down the aisle now." Anna reached for Raquel's hand. "It's time to make your entrance, you beautiful bride."

Chapter 15

Raquel stepped out of the limo elegantly, just like she had practiced. Her jeweled peep toe sling backs hugged her feet perfectly as her long train drifted behind her. There were only a few steps from the back entrance to the hallway leading to the elevator. Raquel had given Anna specific orders not to come and get her until Alexis started her trek. After Alexis finished her journey down the aisle, a soloist would start to sing "This Is the Moment," acapella, at the center of the church. Then the ushers would begin to adjust the seventy-five-foot customized aisle runner, slowly. Raquel wanted her guests to have sufficient time to stare at it as they waited for her arrival.

After they had completed the task of rolling it and securing the sides, the soloist, now holding one candle, would start to sing "At Last," accompanied by a pianist. After a few bars, Raquel would come walking down the aisle, alone.

Anna pushed the button on the elevator. While they were waiting, they ran into the florist and her staff. All five of them gasped and began to compliment Raquel all at once.

"Look at her hair all decked out in perfect little roses and jewels."

"Oh, look at her shoes. They look like Cinderella's slippers."

"Her makeup is perfect. I love the bronze and brown. It's so royal!"

Anna smiled, then looked around the room for the security guard. She motioned for him to join them. Raquel had insisted on hiring a security guard after going to a wedding where one of the guests had arrived drunk. She ended up ruining the entire ceremony by talking loudly and often.

Anna was a few steps ahead of Raquel, rambling on and on about how wonderfully everything had come together, when the elevator doors opened. The two of them stepped onto the elevator with the security guard.

As soon as the elevator doors closed, while Anna was still talking and the security guard was staring at her cleavage, Raquel grabbed his gun out of his holster like a pro. She slapped him across the face with the gun before he had a chance to react. Several trickles of blood oozed from one side of his mouth. Anna stood terrified at the opposite corner of the elevator. Raquel had learned how to break someone's arm in a self-defense class. As the elevator approached the second floor, she pushed Anna close to her and twisted her arm until she heard it crack.

When the elevator opened, Anna was lying on one side of the elevator and the security guard was dozing in and out of consciousness on the other. Raquel slipped off her shoes and detached the train on her wedding gown. She took off running, surprised at how fast she could move wearing a heavy dress and weighing in at well over 200 pounds.

Raquel didn't know what she was going to do when she located Karen; all she could focus on was finding her. She was the only one who knew about her sexual relationship with Randall. After she found her, she was going to move on to James. She imagined the two of them working together to destroy, embarrass, and humiliate her. But today was not the day. She vowed to get the last laugh. They wanted to put on a show, and now she was about to give them one.

Raquel stopped running and cocked the gun, seconds before she made it inside the ceremony site.

She didn't notice her guests running or screaming. The terrified looks in their eyes were also easily ignored. She didn't hear Alexis and Morris screaming, "Mama, Mama." She jumped over or shoved whatever was in her way—chairs, people, even the antique gold-plated candelabras she had rented from a specialty shop.

Nobody and nothing was going to stop her. She was like a raging fire consuming everything she touched.

Joan unlocked her condo door, exhausted and confused. She walked her half-asleep son into his room and helped him into bed. She carefully took off his tuxedo while her mind raced. If she had not seen it herself, she would have been sure it was nothing more than an elaborate lie. She tried to piece together what she had seen and what she had heard. She and the other guests had been detained at the church for hours while police and reporters asked what seemed to be an endless barrage of questions.

Joan had arrived moments before the wedding ceremony was to begin. She and all the ladies were given a single red rose as they were escorted into the church.

A pianist was playing classical music as guests admired the beautiful decorations. It looked as if the wedding was taking place in a rose garden. It was fragrant and peaceful. One floral arrangement was more detailed than the next. The roses on the altar stood out from those on the pews and around the church. They had all been dipped in gold and arranged in such a way that it appeared as if they were hanging from midair.

Once the guests had feasted on the beauty of their surroundings, James Sr., the minister, and the grooms-men took their places at the front of the church. Then James Sr.'s mother, Agnes, was escorted down the aisle by Miles. She wore a golden gown with a matching hat. She proudly took her seat in the front row before giving her son a big smile. Miles took his position next to his brother.

Next a quartet of female violinists, garbed in long, flowing gowns, was seated on one side of the church. As soon as they started to play, the first bridesmaid be-gan to walk down the aisle. Three more followed, each wearing a different red gown suitable to her physique. They each carried bouquets of multicolored roses, with the tips dipped in gold. James Jr. and Morris were next; each one was wearing a tux and holding a ring bearer's box.

After that, Alexis appeared. She was escorted down the aisle in an all-white wagon pulled by an usher with white gloves. She wore an embroidered white gown with a train. She methodically tossed rose petals out of the wagon. She seemed not to notice the other people at the wedding. She was only concerned with getting her flowers out of her basket and onto the floor. She was so serious, it was funny; the guests couldn't help but chuckle as she passed by them.

After Alexis made it to the front, there was a rush of movement. The ushers rolled down a custom-made aisle runner. The guests gasped. The aisle runner had been monogrammed with Raquel's and James's ini-tials, along with the date of their wedding. It was hand painted with golden flowers and rich earth tones. It looked as if it had taken months for an artist to make it.

While the ushers were rolling out the aisle runner, the violinists left; then a soloist, with a rich soprano voice, began to sing. The guests looked around in anticipation for the bride's entrance. That's when things got crazy.

Joan put her head in her hands and tried to remember what she had heard from vendors, the police, and the other guests at the wedding. The few people who saw Raquel first said she had looked stunning as she stepped out of the limo and walked along the short hallway leading to the elevator. In hindsight, they said she didn't seem to acknowledge or even notice their admiring words or glances. She was mumbling something to herself. It may have been the same thing over and over again.

Raquel, the wedding planner, and a security guard got into the elevator. Nobody is clear what happened after that, but when the elevator door opened at the second floor, the wedding planner was in tears and her skin had turned a bright red. The security guard was bloody and motionless.

Raquel walked out of the elevator, carrying nothing but the security guard's gun. She stopped for a moment to take off her shoes, then took off running wildly into the sanctuary.

Joan was in the very back row. She was one of the few guests who could see the wedding party before they actually took the aisle. Joan braced herself to see Raquel in a beautiful gown. When she looked up, Raquel did have on a beautiful gown, but she was also running barefoot, with a gun. The other guests in the back row all took off running in different directions. Joan tried to move, but she was too shocked to make her body cooperate.

After the guests in the back row started to run, the other guests, who didn't know why the guests in the back row were running, started to run too. With people

running back and forth in chaos, Raquel ran until she
arrived at the altar. She then proceeded to fire gunshots
in the air. Now everybody, including James, could see
Raquel. He yelled to one of the bridesmaids to take the
children and run, which she did. The rest of the bridesmaids left too. Joan still hadn't moved, and neither had
James, Miles, or the other groomsmen. Since Raquel
was now in the front, and everybody in front of her had
run away, Joan had a clear view of Raquel.

Raquel's eyes scanned the crowd. She was clearly looking for somebody. Most of the people were
hunched down in the perimeter of the room. They
could have run out of the room, but like Joan, they
were too curious to leave. Suddenly James Sr. and
Miles started to walk toward Raquel. Their mother
tried to stop them, but they kept moving. Agnes followed a few steps behind them. Raquel didn't seem
concerned with them. She started walking around the
room, waving the gun in the air. She passed James and
Miles, and hordes of other people, until she found a
lady in an emerald green dress. Eventually Joan found
out this lady's name was Karen, apparently one of
Raquel's former friends. Raquel yanked Karen by her
hair and she hit the floor.

By this time, James had made it to Raquel. He used
his body as a barrier between Raquel and Karen. Miles
tried to take the gun; then Raquel kicked him in the
groin. Raquel turned back around to Karen. James
Sr. was still acting as a barrier. Then gunshots went
off in what seemed to be several different directions.
Everybody, including Joan, started running out of the
church by then.

Some say Raquel became more agitated and shot a
few more warning shots in the air. Some say she aimed
and shot on purpose. Whatever happened, when it was

all over, Miles lay in a pool of blood. Agnes lay on the floor next to him, her pretty golden dress lifted high above her knees.

Joan made herself a cup of tea. There was no way she was going to get to sleep tonight.

Chapter 16

James didn't know his heart could race so fast for so long. His tux was stuck to his body like a wet suit. Everything was a maze of confusion. First there was one doctor, then another doctor, a surgeon, and then a specialist. Next there was a police officer, then a detective—not to mention, the menacing eyes of his family members and friends. They stayed away from him, huddled in their prayer circles in the corner of the hospital's waiting room. James couldn't remember feeling more alone.

His mother's sisters were seated with big black Bibles in their laps. They had been praying out loud, but now they were only holding hands. Tears were flowing from their silent faces. James thought he had wanted them to stop praying, back when they had been praying. He thought all the vocal cries of "Holy Father" and "God Almighty" were making him uneasy. But now that they had stopped, the quietness had brought him no relief.

His mother was dead. James had known before the paramedics got there. He could tell from the way she was lying on the floor. He refused to check her pulse. He didn't want to know if her heart was working or if she was breathing or not.

It was a half hour ago that a beautiful black woman in her thirties had walked up to him and had given him the tragic news. Unlike the other female doctors who walked back and forth throughout the hospital, she seemed particularly concerned about her appearance. She had on a fitted black dress underneath her white coat and had freshly relaxed hair, which reached just below her bra strap. Her hair was the work of an expert colorist, brown with highlights of blond that stuck out between the layers. Her makeup, while tasteful, was overdone and seemed to be more fitting of a makeup-counter girl than a physician. She was the type of woman with whom James would have smiled, flirted, and then left with her phone number. But today he only stared at her as she mouthed the words "I'm sorry, we did all we could do."

James hadn't cried yet for his mother. He was still waiting to hear something about his brother. The minutes turned into hours as James waited to hear word on his brother's condition. It was midnight when the surgeon came in. He was older and self-assured. James tried to read him as he watched the doctor walk closer to him and his family members. The doctor was used to people trying to read him. His face said nothing. The family gathered closer to hear his words. His mother's sisters all got on their knees and bowed their heads.

The doctor said in a low, gentle voice, "During the surgery, we realized Miles's injuries were much more serious than we had initially thought." He said Miles's name like he knew him. He went on. "They couldn't stop the internal bleeding. The team of surgeons tried, but we don't believe Miles will make it through the night. Now is probably the time to go in and say good-bye."

James could feel the walls in the room close in on him. He could barely breathe. What had just happened? His mind raced. Everything had happened so fast. His mother and brother couldn't be dead? Just like that. Wasn't someone about to come in and shout,

"Hey, you just got punk'd"? He must be on some cruel edition of *Candid Camera,* right?

James looked around for the cameras, but all he saw and heard were his mother's sisters wailing and crying bitterly. They wanted to get up so they could walk to Miles's room, but the grief was too strong. There were cousins screaming, uncles quietly weeping, and friends of the family looking at it all and trying to stay strong by rubbing backs and giving long, deep hugs.

This was no little thing. James couldn't shout, "Do over!" "My bad!" or "Psych!" He couldn't run away and start all over again tomorrow. He couldn't walk away from it and deal with it later.

James ran out of the waiting room, out of the hospital, and onto the dark streets. He didn't want to see his brother for the last time. He didn't want to watch him take his last breath. He didn't want to digest the accusing stares his family kept giving him with their tear-stained faces. James couldn't take one more moment of being swallowed up by all those pairs of condemning eyes.

As James walked, he remembered teaching Miles how to ride a bike. He taught him how to tell time, too. Later on, he taught him how to drive and how to tie his first necktie.

When Miles was ten and playing Martin Luther King in a school play, James and Agnes got there early so they could sit in the first row. Their father wasn't there as usual, but Miles didn't seem to care. He delivered his lines with power, clarity, and authority. James got up after Miles had finished speaking and started shouting, "That's my brother. That's my little brother!"

As James walked faster and faster, he allowed himself to cry for the first time that night. He cried and walked, until he couldn't see straight. Then he sat on a bench and cried until he couldn't cry anymore.

Hours later, James walked back to the waiting room. Only his aunt Lorene, his mother's oldest sister, was in the room. She had always been James's favorite aunt. She and her husband had been married for many years, but they had no children of their own. She would dote on James and Miles, often acting as their second mother.

James stood ready for a tongue-lashing, but none came. There was a calmness about Lorene that had not been present the last time he saw her. She stood up when she saw him walk in the waiting room. "I have been waiting for you. Miles . . . well . . . Miles." She wiped tears from her eyes. "We are going to bury them side by side. We are hoping to have the funerals this weekend. Your uncle Carter and aunt Shana are making the arrangements. I'll call you when everything is final."

James took in her words: *We are going to bury them. . . .*

Lorene waited a few moments, then continued speaking. "Your cousin Jackie took Alexis and Morris home with her. But if I were you, I would pick them up as soon as possible. You know how Jackie can be. She will be fine, but as soon as something more entertaining comes up, she will just pop up and leave those kids. Nobody could get a hold of anyone on Raquel's side of the family to take them in.

"I would have taken them myself, but your uncle is old and so am I. We are way past being able to run around after a couple of kids. And you know your aunt Sylvia can barely take care of herself, with her arthritis and all. And aunt Kate already has a houseful, since Randy came home from Iraq and promptly moved his wife and three kids into his mother's one-bedroom apartment."

"Thanks, Aunt Lorene. I'll take care of it."

Lorene started to walk toward the door but changed her mind. "James, what happened? We have all been trying to understand what drove Raquel to do this. With your track record with women, we couldn't help but think it had to be something you did to her." Her voice got uncharacteristically loud. "James, please tell me you didn't have anything to do with this. Please tell me my youngest sister and my nephew were not shot to death over some petty nonsense. Please, James! Please!"

James said nothing.

Lorene gasped, then started to cry. "I need to go. James, maybe you should think about not coming to the funerals."

James knew he would never forget the repulsive look on his aunt's face as she left the waiting room.

Chapter 17

The crystal glass doors at the entrance of the church and the beautifully landscaped cobblestone-lined entryway were two of the many reasons why Raquel imagined herself getting married at the church years before she was ever engaged. She loved the idea of walking hand in hand with James after their wedding and having their friends and family members toss rice as they stood next to sweet-smelling roses and carefully placed daffodils.

A man in a suit spoke to the police officers on both sides of Raquel as they were preparing to walk out the crystal doors. "Peterson, Ramirez, walk straight to the cruiser. Do not talk to the reporters and do not stop. Drop her off at county and meet me at the station. This one is going to be all over the news, and I don't want to have to explain away any goof-ups to the media."

Raquel was walking out of the church, but not to her family and friends throwing rice. Instead, she was greeted by flashing camera lights and reporters. All of her wedding guests had been questioned and told to leave the premises hours ago. She was handcuffed with an officer on each side. Her wedding dress was blood-stained and torn in several places. The biggest hole was in the front, near her stomach, exposing her girdle. The tiny roses that adorned her hair had shifted, causing her carefully done tresses to spike from her head. She had three scratches on her face: one on her left cheek, one underneath her right eye, and the last, about two inches long across her forehead.

The newswoman, bored with the long wait, didn't notice Raquel because she was too busy primping her hair. She used her hands to fluff the ends of her red curls but stopped when her cameraman tapped her on the shoulder. She immediately turned around and ran to Raquel, sticking a microphone in her face. "What happened today? Do you care to make a statement?" Raquel kept moving, trying to stay upright as she watched the beads on her wedding dress fall to the ground, one by one. She wished she could follow them deep into the earth, never to surface again.

The redheaded newswoman now had company. Two other reporters ran out of their news vans, all of them desperately trying to get Raquel to say something. "What happened, miss? Do you care to make a statement? Where did you get the gun?"

The bright lights momentarily blinded Raquel, causing her to trip. She braced herself to hit the ground but never did. The officers held tightly on to her. They walked briskly as they stared straight ahead.

"Did you just snap? Where did you get the gun?" They didn't care or didn't notice that she almost fell. "Why did you do it? Did he cheat on you? What happened today?"

Raquel could see the police cruiser only a few more steps away. She looked around, hoping that somebody, somewhere, would come rescue her. One officer released her and went to the driver's side, while one police officer tightened his grip and escorted her to the backseat. He quickly slammed the door, noticing but not caring that a piece of her dress was hanging out the door.

When Raquel was just a little girl, her mother would leave her alone in a cold, lonely apartment. Raquel used to hum herself to sleep. As long as she was humming, she didn't have to feel the fear and the tears that swelled up in her eyes. The tears never had the chance to fall down her face. The louder she hummed, the braver she became.

As she hummed, she imagined herself not alone in an apartment, but rather surrounded by people who loved her. Her imaginary mother would tuck her in and read her a story. Her imaginary father would stop by her room, once the lights were out. He would refuse to leave until his precious little girl was asleep.

Raquel wasn't allowed to have a pet. But when she was daydreaming, there was always a dog. He was brown and white, and his name was Totter. He loved Raquel as much as she loved him. If she ever had a bad dream, Totter was always there to comfort her.

As Raquel traveled to the police station, even though she hadn't done it for years, she hummed and went to an imaginary place. Instead of being handcuffed in a police car, accompanied by two cops, she was a highly sought-after celebrity named Maggie Fountain. Maggie wasn't on her way to the police station; she was on her way to the Grammy Awards in a limousine. After successfully debuting her first CD, she was the new "it" girl. The past year found her on the cover of *Essence*, *Ebony*, *Newsweek*, and *Rolling Stone*.

The paparazzi were relentless in their pursuit of her. She couldn't go and get a cup of coffee or a burrito from her favorite fast-food restaurant without causing frenzies. As they approached a stoplight, she heard a helicopter hovering right over the car. She giggled and wondered who had rented a helicopter to follow her today. There were reports that she was pregnant, and every magazine and entertainment show wanted to be the first to show her baby bump. She shook her head. There was no baby and therefore no baby bump. She was much too careful for that.

In a few months, she had a movie to film with Taraji P. Henson, Terrence Howard, Mary J. Blige, and Jennifer Hudson. In the fall, she was getting her own talk show and introducing a line of high-end handbags. There was absolutely no time for a baby.

She imagined that a reporter from *Entertainment Tonight* was in the car with her. He was getting an exclusive story on her next project. They laughed and talked like they were old friends until their interview was suddenly interrupted when the car came to a sudden stop.

A waiting officer pulled her out of the patrol car, stepping on her dress in the process. The large gray building looked like a towering mountain to Raquel. There were three times as many reporters now, but they couldn't get close to her. Several dozen police officers held them back behind a thick strip of yellow tape. They yelled out questions and the photographers flashed their cameras. Raquel barely noticed. She was too consumed with what lay ahead as the officer walked next to her and eventually opened the door leading her into the mountain.

Chapter 18

"Welcome to Clarkston County, Miss Raquel," the officer who walked her in said; then he handed her over to the waiting guard. He completed some paperwork and left her to the large dark-skinned guard who sat before her; she had an attitude that Raquel could feel. There were no cameras here, just a frumpy woman behind a desk with a halfway-eaten package of Flamin' Hot Cheetos and a twenty-ounce Coke. Scattered about her desk was a mix of papers; most seemed work related, with the exception of a few tabloid magazines.

Raquel looked up at her, trying her best not to look defeated. Raquel pushed her shoulders back and held up her head. The woman came from behind the desk. "Do you know why you are here?" Raquel nodded. She recalled the officer in the suit explaining her rights before the other two handcuffed her and walked her to the patrol car. She heard him, but she wasn't listening. She nodded when he was finished and he seemed appeased.

"Let me do a quick pat-down and we will start with the paperwork. Do you have any weapons, drugs, syringes? Anything like that?"

"No."

The officer used both of her hands. She moved them past Raquel's arms and shoulders. She slid her hands underneath her arms and then her breasts. She moved down her thighs between her legs and concluded at her ankles.

Raquel closed her eyes and hummed while this was going on. She imagined she was playing a part in a movie where she had to pretend to be arrested. She told herself this was not the most humiliating thing that had happened to her. This was the acting job that would lead to her first Oscar.

"Is she there yet?"

Raquel looked around the room to locate the voice. The female guard retrieved her walkie-talkie from behind the desk.

"Yeah, they just dropped her off." The guard spoke into the intercom. "She's in here, trying to look like she ain't scared as heck." The guard laughed. "Girl, when do you go on break? You gotta come down here and see this for yourself. She looks like a hot mess. Worse than she looked on the news."

Raquel's shoulders deflated and she inspected her dress. She wanted to cry, but she quickly changed her mind. Whatever was about to happen to her, she wouldn't cry.

"Okay, Cinderella, it is time to get booked." Raquel tensed up. "Don't worry, this part is easy," the female guard added.

Raquel answered her basic questions the entire time, wondering what the not-so-easy parts would be.

The guard looked up from her completed paperwork. "That's a pretty dress. Too bad you are going to have to take it off." Raquel remained stoic. Suddenly two officers arrived with five ladies in handcuffs. The guard shook her head in disgust. "It's going to be a busy night. On Saturday night, everybody acts a fool."

The guard turned to the two officers. "I'll be back. Just let me place her in holding." The guard led Raquel out of the booking area and down a hall, where other guards were located. Without words, she was transferred from one guard to another, like she was a piece of trash. The new guard looked at Raquel with compassion, but she was too overwhelmed to absorb it.

"Try not to say anything to anybody," she whispered. "If they ask you a question, answer it. But don't go overboard. I'll come back as soon as I can so you can make your phone call."

Raquel smelled the holding cell before she saw it. There were three women in the cell. Two of them stared into space, with drool hanging from their mouths. They didn't seem to know where they were or who they were. One was standing in her own feces, with vomit covering her shirt. Raquel had never seen a toilet like the one in the cell. It offered almost no privacy. Someone was using it, and her face and chest and legs were exposed. These women were locked in a cage the size of Raquel's master bathroom.

One of the drooling women started scratching feverishly like a dog does when its body is infested with fleas. The thought of being locked up in that small space with those women for an unspecified amount of time had Raquel shaking.

There was no way she could be locked up in there. Raquel let out a scream that could have broken glass. Then she attempted to run from the guard, only to find herself pinned to the floor before she had a chance to move more than a few steps.

"Now, little lady, don't make this harder than it has to be." The guard yanked Raquel off the floor and shoved her in the cell, locked it, and walked off.

Raquel scattered to a corner, mumbling underneath her breath. The drooling women looked like zombies. They had swollen heads, with bulging eyes. She could see the bones in their faces. They looked so skinny, they could wear children's clothes.

Raquel heard the toilet flush. She looked up at the woman walking away from it. She was wearing a pair of cheap high-waisted jeans and an orange T-shirt with matching running shoes. Her hair was freshly relaxed and pulled back in a ponytail. She looked like a soccer mom on her way to a game.

"You know, another outburst like that and you are going to get yourself hurt," the woman said as she walked closer to Raquel. "If that was anybody but Mrs. Penny, you would have been black-and-blue by now."

"I don't belong in here." Raquel glanced at the two drooling women.

"They don't mean no harm. They are just coming off that crack high." The woman laughed. "You act like you never seen a crackhead before."

Raquel shrugged her shoulders. The only drug addicts she had seen had been in the movies. There were rumors that a few of her relatives were addicted to the drug, but none of them looked like this.

The woman's shock faded. "Yeah, these two are pretty bad off. I would say they have been addicts for twenty years or more. You don't look like that overnight." She sighed.

"What happened to your dress?" Raquel shook her head, signaling she didn't want to talk about it. The woman continued talking. "I got caught with some parking tickets. My sister ran them up in my name and didn't tell me. She better be bailing me out right now, or I will hurt her with my bare hands. I spent two years locked up and I promised myself I wouldn't be behind bars again. I better not spend one day locked up in that freaking dormitory."

Raquel struggled to speak. "What dormitory?"

"What dormitory? Girl, are you for real?"

Raquel had a blank expression on her face.

"Okay, let me go slow. This is a holding cell. If you and me don't get bailed out of this joint soon, we are going to end up in jail, or a nicer way of putting it, the dormitory. Most cases you only have to stay overnight, unless, of course, the judge refuses bail. I don't care if it's only one night. I don't want to be anywhere near the place.

"Did you make your phone call yet?" Raquel shook her head. "Did they strip-search you? Did you go to medical? Did you take your mug shot? Get fingerprinted?" Raquel answered no to all of her questions.

"Man, they must really be backed up, or at least are pretending to be. These lazy know-it-all so-called guards get on my last nerves. They need to let you make your phone call so you can get up outta here. What did you do, slash one of your bridesmaids for not staying in step?"

"Phone call or not, Miss Raquel is going to be with us for a while," Mrs. Penny said as she approached the holding cell with a male guard. "Isn't that right, Raquel?"

"Rodgers, you made bail. Let's go," the male guard said. The woman in the orange shirt waved to Raquel before being escorted to freedom.

Raquel watched her disappear and wondered if and when she would ever leave this place. And when she finally was released, would there be anybody to come home to?

Mrs. Penny motioned for her. Raquel took a deep breath thinking, *It must be time for the hard part.*

Chapter 19

The two guards put their hands in Raquel's hair. Her lovely locks, which hadn't known the feel of cheap shampoo for years, were now being invaded by four hands smelling of stale cigarette smoke and coffee. They looked into her mouth, taking their rubber-gloved fingers past her inner jaw and over her teeth. Then they watched as she stripped down to nothing.

Raquel could feel the burning in her eyes that ensured tears were not far behind. She slowly stepped out of her wedding dress and then her lace bra, which only James was supposed to see. A long petticoat was the next item to fall to the floor; after that, her girdle.

Now it was time to step out of her panties. She paused. Had they no shame? Were they really about to do this to her? The two of them didn't waver. They simply stood taller and more demanding. Raquel heard what they were saying through their silence: *"If you don't take them off, we will."*

She tossed them to the floor. The guards came forward. They lifted up her breasts, one by one. They passed her stomach, her thighs, and down to her legs. Raquel breathed a sigh of relief.

The guard heard her and said, "Oh, it's not over, baby girl. Now I need you to turn around and squat."

Raquel couldn't remember feeling so cold or out of place. She turned around, her backside now facing the two women. Right before she was about to bend,

Raquel pleaded with the women. "Please, please, you don't understand. I'm not like this. I'm not supposed to be here."

"Yeah, we know," one of the officers said. "Yesterday, some bougie chick just like you had two crack rocks hidden up there. So stop with the waterworks and squat."

Raquel obeyed, tears falling down her face as the women inspected her.

So much for staying strong. So much for being brave, Raquel thought. Once she started crying, her tears wouldn't stop. She got dressed in jail-issued clothing, took her mug shot, went to medical, and got fingerprinted. Then she was led to a room, where she was allowed to make her phone call.

She called her lawyer, Jesse Lo. He had helped her with the legal work related to the salon. He seemed to be expecting her call. He said the fact that she was being charged and jailed in a small, outlying county was better than having to deal with the system in Houston. However, he didn't expect the judge would let her out on bond. Apparently, the news was reporting that the videographer she had hired to film the wedding had the entire incident on tape. Finally he said he and his associates were going to do everything they could for her, and she needed to hold tight and keep her head up.

After the phone call, the guard handed her linens, shoes, toothpaste, toothbrush, a comb, towel, soap, and her bed assignment in the Clarkston County maximum-security female jail. Raquel felt her knees get weak. She followed the guard closely, trying not to fall. When they approached the door to the dormitory, she could hear a rush of movement; then one said, "Hey, y'all, the 'Killer Bride' is here."

Raquel strained to look at them as they looked at her. It had to be about fifty of them scattered around the large rectangular room. Raquel thought there would be bars separating them. Looking at the intensity in the eyes of some of the women, she wished there were bars. Raquel turned her gaze back to the guard, only now the guard was several feet ahead of her. Raquel rushed to catch up with her. The guard stood at the corner of the room and pointed.

Raquel looked the way the guard was pointing, only to see a glass-enclosed room with several showerheads and a dingy tile floor. Raquel gasped. There was a pregnant lady showering. She was methodically scrubbing her body as if the entire dorm, plus the surrounding guards, couldn't see her. It was all too much. Raquel's knees buckled underneath her, causing her supplies to fall to the floor. Within seconds, Raquel's body made the same trip.

Chapter 20

Raquel listened as the woman next to her snored. She wondered how long it took her to learn to sleep so soundly in a place like this. She couldn't fathom how she would ever get any rest, although there was relief, now that it was lights-out. Nobody was poking at her body, yelling in her face, or staring at her naked body. She could quietly cry in the darkness. She turned on her stomach and buried her head in the pillow.

She envisioned a woman running in a wedding gown. The woman ran faster than she knew her feet could carry her. She ran until she found Karen. James appeared, then some other men. The woman in the wedding gown got angry and tried to fight them off. She decided they needed to be taken care of by the weapon she had in her hand. Raquel opened her eyes. She couldn't be reminded of the next scene. She held on tightly to the pillow. The woman in the wedding gown wasn't just *any* woman. Raquel was the woman in the wedding gown.

Raquel shook her head from side to side. How could she and the woman in the wedding gown be the same woman? She was a beloved mother and a successful entrepreneur. But now what was she? What would her future be like? Who would help her now?

At least three nights a week, Raquel made it home to tuck her children into bed. This was the most relaxing part of the day. Morris claimed he was too old to get into the Jacuzzi bathtub with her, filled with sweet-smelling bubbles and aromatherapy oil, but Alexis loved it. She would giggle as she blew the suds around the tub. After she became tired of that, she would sing whatever song she was learning in day care.

"'Sweet little birdie, fly fly fly. Sweet little birdie, fly, fly fly, all the way to the sky, sky, sky.'" Without fail, she would cry when Raquel removed her from the bathtub. One time, she decided to run. She was wet and slippery and slipped right out of Raquel's hand. Raquel caught her right before she was about to run downstairs. Who was going to give baths to her baby now and make sure she didn't slip and fall on the stairs?

Raquel felt like all four walls in the dormitory were sucking the breath out of her. She needed to think straight and she needed to do it now. She needed money and lots of it. A good lawyer might be able to get her released. If only she hadn't insisted on having that $7,000 wedding dress, or those overpriced wedding shoes, a private makeup session, or the luxury bridal suite.

Raquel had overspent on the wedding in many ways. At the last minute, she had decided to splurge on steak and lobster for the reception. Originally they had decided on chicken marsala, because it was one of the cheaper dishes, but still delicious and elegant. She had allowed James to convince her that this was the best thing when they were doing the food tasting. But when she went to make the final deposit, she changed the entire menu. Her wedding was going to be over-the-top in every way. She couldn't serve chicken. Every wedding had chicken, in some form. But that one change added an additional twenty-five dollars to each plate, causing Raquel to do what she promised James she would not. She removed $7,500 from their savings account.

She had planned to work extra hard after the wedding and replace the money before James had time to figure it out. Raquel wanted to slap herself. How in the world did she think she was going to be able to replace the money before James noticed?

She did the math in her head. Among their three accounts and the money she had stashed to the side, she had less than a couple of thousand dollars.

Raquel allowed her mind to roam where she hadn't allowed it to go before. She had been charged with murdering two people. Raquel stuffed her face into the pillow. There was nothing she could say that was going to make this right. She couldn't undo this. It was over. Her life as she knew it was over. There was no more James. There were no more children. Her business was a distant memory.

This place that reeked of urine, covered up by perfume-laden cleanser, would be her home. These people whom she didn't even want to touch would become her friends.

Raquel knew that many of the women in the beds around her were mothers, just like her. She remembered seeing the photo necklaces some of them wore around their necks, with pictures of their children. Would Alexis and Morris be something she just wore around her neck?

Chapter 21

On a normal day, the cabdriver's constant chattering into his cell phone would have annoyed James. But James barely noticed. There was too much racing through his mind. After talking to the staff at the hospital for the last time, he saw several officers waiting to talk to him. They asked a few more questions. James told all of them about his plan. There was a part of him that wished he had actually committed crimes. Going to jail right now seemed like it was justified. With more than a few strange looks, he was released. Apparently, jilting a bride at the altar isn't illegal, just incredibly stupid.

James paid the cabdriver and walked past the sea of reporters hanging outside his hotel. He needed to go to the hotel to get the medication in his suitcase. He had ordered the pills online after the panic attack in his classroom. He sort of hoped someone would be there, waiting for him, but nobody was there. They had so much fun at the bachelor party James paid for an extra night in the suite. He planned to celebrate humiliating Raquel with Miles and his friends.

James' first thought was just to take one pill, but then the pills started speaking to him: *"Go ahead take every pill in the bottle. You have nothing to live for. Nobody is going to miss you. Look what you did. Look what happened. You have nothing to live for. You are worthless. No job. Nothing. You are a sorry excuse for*

*a man. End it now. Right now. Your mother is dead.
Your brother is dead. It is all your fault. How will you
face them? They hate you and everything you represent.*"

James took the pills out of the container. He switched
them back and forth through each of his hands; then he
got a bottle of water out of the minifridge. The house-
keeper would probably be the first to find him. When
she found him, the pills would be lying right next to him.

It seemed so easy, but also hard. He put a handful of
pills in his mouth; then he started to wonder if there
was a place worse than the place he was living in right
now. The last thing he needed was to die and end up
worse than he was right now.

Religion always seemed like a waste of time. But
at that moment, James wanted to study all the major
religions. He wanted to know what they believed and
why. He had once heard a televangelist preach about
reading the Bible for *yourself*. He said if people really
wanted to know what God said, they should find out
for themselves. Those words seemed to make sense to
James that day. But soon after, he forgot all about it.

James had spent his childhood at one church service
after another, but he didn't remember learning much.
There would be a robed man standing behind the pul-
pit and reading from the Bible. The words never made
sense to James. After speaking for a while, the man
would get to dancing and hollering. Soon the church
would be dancing and hollering too. Afterward, they
would sing a song. Sometimes that song would last
thirty minutes. Just as soon as the song seemed to be
over, the organist would start it up again. The people
would get more and more excited with each touch
of the keys. Then it was over. They would shake the
preacher's hand and leave service. People would say
stuff like, "Pastor Fields sure was preaching today."

As a child, James never cared what his pastor was preaching about, but today he wished he could recount one sermon or one Sunday School lesson from the hundreds he had heard. Other than the books of the Bible and the Twenty-third Psalm, he couldn't remember anything.

The moment Joan's face appeared in his head, James dismissed it. He couldn't call her. What would she think of him? He would have to explain the whole thing. But everybody knew that she had changed during the last three years, that she had become some type of Bible teacher. James had seen all her Bible books on her shelf when he was there last time.

James took the pills out of his mouth and scrolled through the numbers in his phone. He dialed and heard her say hello before he had a chance to change his mind.

There was only one night Joan could remember not sleeping at all. She was in labor with James Jr. Now Joan could add one completely new sleepless night to her list. Instead of contractions, it was thoughts of James Sr. that kept her up, hour after hour.

It was seven in the morning when her son walked in her room and said he needed help finding something to wear to Sunday School and church. James Jr. loved church, and the long night he had before was not about to stop him from going. He didn't mention the night before, so neither did Joan. She helped him get dressed, fed him breakfast, and watched the bus leave from a window outside her condo.

Joan had the church bus pick him up. It was originally designed to pick up underprivileged children whose parents didn't have transportation. These days, it was for privileged children with lazy parents. Joan knew she should be embarrassed having her son get picked up by the church bus instead of taking him herself.

It was nine-fifteen now, and Sunday School was about to end and the morning meet-and-greet was about to start. All the members would go around eating muffins, drinking coffee, and socializing for about thirty minutes before the worship service started.

By the time nine-twenty in the morning rolled around, Joan decided she needed to get out of bed permanently. The thought of making a big Sunday dinner brightened her eyes as she made her way to the kitchen. She couldn't remember the last time she had made her famous short ribs and gravy.

As she was making a mental grocery list, she heard her cell phone. She almost didn't go to look at who was calling. Whenever she missed church, an arsenal of people called to check on her. When she saw the call was from James Sr., she picked it up without a moment of hesitation.

"Hello, James."

"Where are you?" It was a low voice that sounded strained.

"Home."

"Can I come over?" he asked.

"I'll be here."

Joan hung up the phone. She looked at her sofa, the television, back to the sofa, then the TV. What did she need to do? The condo looked clean, but who cared about a clean condo at a time like this? Should she cook? Surely, James wouldn't be worried about breakfast, but what if he was?

Joan went to the refrigerator. James always loved her banana cinnamon French toast. She scoured the kitchen for the necessary ingredients. She had bread, eggs, sugar, cinnamon, and even orange juice. As she was looking in the freezer for bacon or sausage, the ice-cold air seemed to bring her to her senses.

Joan slammed the door to the freezer. She grabbed her neck, suddenly feeling the soreness of a weary body that hadn't slept all night. Her eyes were heavy and tender to the touch. Raquel had flipped out in a major way, and now the local news station was reporting that James's mother and brother were both dead. French toast and sausage, no matter how delicious, were not going to fix this.

There was nothing she could do to prepare for James's arrival. She remembered a conversation she had with her pastor. It was a wedding reception and she was sitting at the table with him and several other people. Someone had asked how the McKinneys were doing. They had recently lost both of their parents in a car accident. Pastor Benjy got this sad look in his eyes.

He said he had been with the family, but they barely had spoken. He only sat and cried with them. According to Pastor Benjy, it was vital to allow the bereaved to dictate the visit. Sometimes people wanted to tell funny stories about the sick or deceased. Sometimes they wanted to vent about a doctor they felt had failed them or a system that needed to be changed. The worst were the people who lived with regrets, the apologies that were left unsaid. The grievance that had seemed so huge until they got the call that so-and-so was dead. These were the worst, according to Pastor Benjy. They were the people who wanted to commit suicide and climbed into the casket at the funeral. They were full of regrets, remorse, and plagued by what should or could have been. Joan imagined James climbing into a casket.

***

The man on the CD played a low, melodic tune. James tried to relax and allow the calmness of the music to seep into his spirit, but not even the peaceful sounds of Norman Brown could break through the torment he was carrying around. James needed some relief. He needed to end this pain. But he had to talk to Joan first.

Out of his rearview mirror, he saw flashing lights and heard a siren. His heart started to race as he quickly changed lanes. Did they decide to come after him, after all? When the police cruiser proceeded right past him, it occurred to him that he wasn't on the freeway.

James looked left, then right. "What was I thinking?"

When he looked up at the street signs and saw he was on Almeda Road, and still en route to Joan's house via a longer route, he was really confused. He didn't remember thinking about the drive to Joan's house. He didn't remember deciding to take the scenic route versus the faster route. Yet, he was only a few short turns away from Joan's condo.

Sweat started to appear on his forehead. Small blotches at first, but then they got bigger and started to drip down his face. James looked around. He wondered if there was anywhere he could buy a bottle of something or even stop for a drink. He remained hopeful until he passed a church with a full parking lot and remembered that liquor stores were closed on Sundays and bars wouldn't be open until evening.

What happens when you die? The question jumped into James's head so fast, it startled him. It could be peaceful and freeing—something like what people call heaven. Maybe nothing happened. Maybe people just died. James could deal with both of these, but then there was the other.

Several years ago, Miles had run into this real paranoid chick. She was beautiful and had a body to match, which was why Miles had put up with her craziness for the two weeks he did. She was a Christian on steroids who needed to be restrained. She was always handing out Gospel tracts to people that could care less. On the weekends and after work, she would go to the malls and parks and hand them out, telling people her story. She said that when she was a teenager, she was addicted to heroin. She had been on the stuff for six months when, she claimed, she overdosed, died, and went to hell. She said she had never been religious and had never been to any type of place of worship, but that experience changed her life.

She said that during her trip to hell, she was falling into darkness for what seemed like hours. Each moment she fell, it got darker and darker; the blackest black she had ever seen. As she dropped, the smell got worse and worse, like flesh decaying. The entire time, she was yelling, with everything that she had, to be saved. Eventually she reached the bottom and felt a force trying to suck her into what she instantly knew was hell.

She knew that once she went in, she would not be able to get out. She was crawling and begging not to go, but she couldn't fight against the force. Just when she was about to be sucked in, Jesus appeared. Then the devil appeared. The two of them started to argue over her soul. The devil claimed she was his, but Jesus insisted He was going to give her another chance because of the prayers of her aunt. Jesus won.

She woke up in her bedroom and never touched heroin again. She didn't need to go to rehab or anything. She was cured instantly, or "delivered," as she put it. She went on to dedicate her life to telling people the Good News of Jesus Christ.

Of course, Miles thought she was like all the other churchgoing women he knew, full of hot air—a Christian on Sunday, but a sexual freak the rest of the week. But despite his efforts, he never was able to get to first base. He kicked her to the curb, but James never forgot her story.

James pulled up to the light on Allum Street. He was the first car waiting at the red light. He heard a car behind him screech on his breaks in an attempt to stop. Before he knew it, the speeding car had pushed him into oncoming traffic. James looked up and saw an eighteen-wheeler racing toward him. There was nothing he could do. The eighteen-wheeler was coming too close and coming too fast. James was about to die. He cried out, "Jesus, help me!" The 18-wheeler stopped inches from his car.

When James realized he was alive, he dropped his head to the steering wheel and began to cry. He only stopped sobbing when the truck driver started banging on his car window. James looked up and rolled down the window.

"Young man, I don't know what God has planned for you, but it must be something big." He had tears in his eyes. His entire body was shaking and big drops of sweat were on his forehead. "I can't explain how I was able to stop. It was like somebody else started driving. I just knew you were dead! I knew you were dead! I just knew it!"

Dozens of people were outside their cars, shaking their heads and talking hysterically into their cell phones. None of the crowd could believe what they had just seen. James knew it was only a matter of time before the police showed up. The truck driver was still in the middle of the street, pacing back and forth. James pushed on his gas pedal and drove off. Joan and the answers he needed were only a few blocks away.

Chapter 22

Joan opened the door and immediately gasped. She expected him to look bad, but not dead. He stepped through the door, and past her. Each step seemed more painful than the last.

She had a flashback of the last time she had seen him in her condo. He was lively and confident. This man before her now was heavy with pain; it seemed like it was consuming him more and more each minute. He put his hands on his face. Joan quietly walked closer to him. She hadn't seen him cry before. If he was crying now, she wanted to see it up close.

During the time she had been with James, he hardly showed any emotion. The angrier she got, the quieter he became. She shouted and cursed, and he calmly spoke. Even in the midst of unexpected circumstances, James never seemed to sweat. She hated him for it. She felt so misunderstood. James thought she was an overworked drama queen that needed to chill, and she thought he was a zombie that needed to react.

She sat on the sofa next to him. Those were tears falling from his face. James was quiet as he wept. Joan's first reaction was to reach out to him. But then in a voice filled with torment, James said, "It was all my fault, Joan. Everything was all my fault."

Joan's eyes got wider and she reached in closer to James. He began to weep bitterly and his breathing became strained. Joan rushed to the bathroom and retrieved a box of tissues. When she came back, James was on the floor in a fetal position, rocking himself back and forth.

Joan rushed and knelt before him. She handed him a tissue. He took it, but he didn't wipe his face. He was trying to say something, but he was too overcome to speak. Joan rubbed his back as he continued to cry and rock.

"Momma, I'm sorry. Momma, I'm sorry," James began to whisper over and over again. James turned his body and was now on his back. He stopped rocking and closed his eyes tightly. Joan watched as his chest went up and down as he breathed.

He pulled Joan's face to his. "I might as well have shot them both. I might as well have pulled the trigger. I might as well be the one in jail." Joan didn't move, even though the grip James had on her was tight and uncomfortable.

James took a deep breath and let her go. "Joan, I'm sick. I have been sick for a long time. I'm not right, Joan."

Joan tried to hide her shock. James's words matched his description.

"I got fired from my job because I was running after somebody's wife." James Sr. stared at the ceiling. "Maybe that's why this all made sense to me."

"What all made sense?" Joan asked.

"I had the kids tested. Miles had the kids tested for me. Alexis and Morris—they belong to another man."

Joan's mouth dropped open.

"I just found out a couple of weeks ago. I wanted Raquel to pay for what she did to me. That's why I planned to leave her at the altar. But then all of this happened."

James wept bitterly. Joan went to the bathroom and wet several towels with warm water. She returned and began to compress them on James's face and neck. James looked like he was going to start hyperventilating at any moment. After several minutes, his breathing returned to normal.

He took off the towel Joan had on his eyes. "I know this is going to sound funny coming from me, but I need to know what you think about something." James hesitated for a moment. "What happens when you die?"

Joan's eyes gravitated toward the clock. Church was over. It was just time for the after-service fellowship to begin. Joan always brought the cookies. She wondered who was bringing the cookies today.

James voiced the question he had asked Joan in his head. "Joan, am I making you uncomfortable?"

"Oh no, James, of course not."

"I mean, you do have a lot of Bibles and other things around this place. I thought religion was important to you."

Joan shifted back and forth. "What was the question again?"

"What happens when you die? You know, heaven and hell. Who gets to go where, and why?"

Still, Joan said nothing.

"Okay, forget it." James's voice dropped. "I guess there's just not any hope for me, huh?"

"No, James. It's just that . . . Why do you want to know?"

"I'm thinking of killing myself later on today."

Joan laughed; then she realized James was dead serious. "Why?"

"Joan, don't you understand? Don't you see? I'm not fit to live, and I'm too scared to die. I need some answers, and I need them now."

"But why do you want to die, James?"

"Let's see. My mother and brother are dead because of me. Raquel is in jail, probably for a long time, because of me. Alexis and Morris belong to another man. I still can't get my head around that. A few days after I found out, I started having panic attacks. Now I'm popping pills. I lost my constable job. I feel like I'm walking on eggshells and everything is caving in on me. I'm a sorry excuse for a man. I don't want James Jr. to be anything like me. So that's why I want to die. Everything, Joan, everything. I just don't want to be here anymore!" James shouted.

"I just want my life to be over. I don't want to be in this pain anymore." James dropped to the floor again and started writhing like he was in pain. He was on all fours, rocking and crying.

Joan wanted to be somewhere else, talking to somebody else. She had never seen James like this. She had never seen anyone like this. She needed some help, but the only person she knew to call was her pastor. She was too embarrassed to call him, after the last conversation she had with his wife, Minister Makita.

James took a break from grimacing and pulled a large bottle of pills from his pocket. "I need you to tell me why I shouldn't take these pills and kill myself right now."

With that, Joan picked up her cell phone to dial her pastor's personal cell phone number. She was one of the few church members to have it. Pastor Benjy gave it to her when she was working on a speaking project with him. She was careful not to pass it around or abuse it. When she needed to speak to him about most matters, she went through the church secretary, just like everybody else.

"Hello, Pastor, it's me, Joan."

Chapter 23

Joan sat on the bench outside her condo, twirling her house keys and reading the news on her cell phone. She was doing everything possible to look like everything was fine in her world. Pastor Benjy left church and came directly to her condo to talk to James. He was up there now. Joan wanted to be sure she was outside to meet James Jr. when the church bus dropped him off. There was no way she could risk letting her son see his father this way.

Pastor Benjy didn't say anything the first few moments after he arrived to meet James. He simply sat on the sofa next to him, closed his eyes and bowed his head. If another man had sat this close to James, he would have been offended.

James couldn't help but smell Pastor Benjy's cologne, see his gold watch, his expensive glasses, and his freshly pressed suit. James still had on his tuxedo jacket, pants and shirt; each was badly stained. His feet were covered with flip-flops. He couldn't remember taking off the leather loafers he had purchased especially for the wedding.

All of a sudden, James wanted to bathe, shave, change his clothes, and put a few eyedrops in each eye. That's what his mother always said: "Look your best and nobody will suspect the hell you got buried up inside." His mom was always good like that. She made sure she never looked like she was trapped in a loveless

marriage and that Saturday nights were spent ironing
her Sunday dress, rolling her hair, prepping for Sunday
dinner, and wondering which woman her husband was
with this time.

Pastor Benjy bolted off the sofa urgently. He looked
around like he had forgotten something important.
He had that protruding stomach over his belt that was
common for men his age. The idea of walking around
with a spare tire around his waist was what kept James
in the gym five days out of the week. The chiseled six-
pack of his teenage years was gone, but not by much.

"Do you want something to eat?" Pastor Benjy asked.

James started to laugh low at first, and then it hit a
midway point. Before he knew it, he was chuckling and
howling uncontrollably, like he was at a comedy show.

Pastor Benjy looked surprised initially, but then he
reared back, grabbed his stomach, and burst out laughing too. He laughed until his stomach hurt and tears
were running down his face.

After an unspecified time—James couldn't tell how
much time went by—his laughing dwindled down to silence. Pastor Benjy got the cue late and stopped laughing a few awkward moments after James.

James's eyes aimlessly wandered around the room,
trying to remember what had brought on the outburst.
He was waiting for something magical or profound to
come out of Pastor Benjy's mouth, not "Do you want
something to eat?" Here he was thinking Pastor Benjy
was somehow going to make it okay, but nothing was
ever going to be okay again. He was laughing instead of
crying. He heard the pills rattling in his pocket.

"I hear your stomach growling. Let me find you
something to eat." At once, Pastor Benjy walked to
Joan's refrigerator, looked around, then started pulling out items, one by one. James watched Pastor Benjy

place bread in the toaster, wait for it to brown, then layer it with mayonnaise, cheese, and smoked turkey.

Then Pastor Benjy cut the crust off the bread and sliced the sandwich in two equal parts. He handed it to James, who had left the sofa and was now seated on a bar stool in the kitchen.

James saw that he would be eating alone, since Pastor Benjy started to clean up after making only one sandwich. James still hadn't bit into the sandwich after Pastor Benjy had put everything away. He couldn't take his eyes off him.

"Aren't you going to eat?" Pastor Benjy asked.

James bit into the sandwich.

Pastor Benjy looked at his watch, then said, "James, there's a story in the Bible about a crippled man who has been sitting, waiting for healing, on the side of a pool for thirty-eight long years. Jesus asked him a question: 'Do you want to be made well?' The man didn't answer him at first. He offered a lot of excuses about why he had been beside the pool for so long. The excuses may have been very valid, but Jesus didn't want to hear any of that. He wanted an answer to his question."

Pastor Benjy's cell phone rang. He looked down at the screen. "Oh, I'm sorry I got to take this. It's my son."

He began to talk into the phone with a much softer voice. "Hey, I hate I missed your call. I called back but got your voice mail. I see. Well . . . you know how I feel about that house. I'll support you whatever you decide. Okay, do that. Think about it for a few days. Don't be in a rush to sign. I'll be in prayer for you. All right, son. We'll talk about it then. Love you. Kiss the girls and Nicole for me."

Pastor Benjy hung up the phone. "I'm sorry. My boy is about to buy his first house. You've got to be careful."

James nodded blankly and his mind wandered to the gentle way Pastor Benjy dealt with his obviously grown son. He bit into his lunch again and tried to remember if his father had ever made him a sandwich.

"I only talked to Joan a few moments, but I learned a lot about you. I know you despise Christians. I know that you believe that you know me and what I represent. I know that you are suicidal. I know that your brother and mother were just killed and you have a part in it. I know that you love women and sex, and both have gotten you into trouble many times. I know that you are in pain and you desperately want it to end. I know that this is the defining moment in your life. I know that the God of this universe sent me to you to ask this question.

"James, this is a 'yes or no' question." Pastor Benjy paused, then continued. "It is the same question Jesus asked the man who had been sitting by that pool and waiting for healing for thirty-eight long years. It was a 'yes or no' question then, it is a 'yes or no' question now.

"Today, a team of men and I are going on a three-week-long mission trip. I have been planning this trip for months. This morning, one of my men canceled, due to a family emergency. When I realized that God was opening the door for somebody to come instead of him, I began to pray. All morning and all afternoon long, I've been looking for God to show me who to take. After I talked to Joan about you, hours before we are set to leave, I knew it was you.

"I'm not going to promise you that Jesus is going to come into your heart and you are going to feel all fuzzy and warm inside. I've been in ministry too long to lie to you like that. All I ask is that you come on this trip with me. But only if you can answer yes to this question: James, do you want to be made well?"

James hesitated a moment, trying to find words to describe what he was feeling. "I respect and appreciate that you came here to see me today. I want to be honest with you. I don't know what I want to do next. A few days ago, the last person I wanted to talk to was somebody with 'Pastor' in front of his name."

"And now?" asked Pastor Benjy.

"Now I feel like I've been hijacked from my life. I don't know if I want to be made well, or if I want to just sit by the pool and die a slow, cruel death. One minute, I'm glad that I'm alive, and the next minute, I wish I were dead. I just need somebody to talk to, somebody that knows about these things."

"Most men I meet aren't very good at talking and expressing what they are really feeling," Pastor Benjy said. "They are good at talking about cars, sports, work, and women, but not their feelings."

"Most men didn't just find out that two of their three children belong to another man, that the woman they were about to get married to is the biggest liar ever, and that their mother and brother are dead. Most men aren't looking for reasons not to kill themselves."

"This is true," Pastor Benjy said. "What you said is good enough for me. Get your stuff and let's go."

The thought of getting out of town sounded like a miracle to James. His aunt made it clear she didn't want him at the funerals. James didn't mind not going; he did not want to cause his family more pain. With all that had happened, he couldn't dream of going on what would have been his honeymoon.

He wasn't sure how he felt about Pastor Benjy or this mission trip. However, James was positive he needed to get away, clear his head, and escape into something different. Who knew? Maybe he could find a whole new life and never come back to Houston again.

Chapter 24

Raquel's burdened body sat at the edge of the steel chair as she looked into the eyes of her attorney. The last thing she needed was more bad news. At her bail hearing that morning, the judge had refused her request to get out on bail due to the seriousness of her crimes.

This was her first time meeting with Hector Jimenez, the criminal defense attorney Jesse Lo had recommended. He had spent most of his adult life building a successful track record. He gained notoriety when he got charges dismissed from a local politician accused of setting his business on fire for the insurance money. Jesse assured her Hector was the best defense attorney money could buy.

Hector was trying to convince Raquel she needed to take her chances and go to trial with a plea of temporary insanity, when his cell phone rang. Whoever was at the other end of the phone was doing all the talking while Hector nodded. At one point, he started nervously stacking and restacking the same documents.

When he hung up the call, he started pressing buttons on his cell phone. He was intensely watching some sort of video. Instantly Raquel believed it was the video captured at the ceremony site.

"Like I said, Raquel, you need to take the deal," Hector said matter-of-factly.

Raquel didn't bother to tell him that he had said no such thing until he saw the video. Hector picked at his beard, got out of his chair, and paced the floor. He reminded Raquel of the lawyers on TV. "I know ten years sounds like a long time. But honestly, considering what happened—and the fact that it is on tape—well, miss, it's really a wonderful deal."

Raquel felt like she had stepped into the middle of the conversation. He went on: "You don't have a choice, Raquel. You don't want to go to trial. With the videographer's tape and the media hype, you could get much worse. In ten years, you will still be young. You can have some kind of life. Look, Raquel, there is no way they are letting you walk. Two people are dead. If this thing goes to trial, you might end up doing thirty or more years. Not to mention . . ."

Not to mention Raquel wouldn't be able to afford to have Hector's high-priced law firm handle a lengthy trial. He agreed to take her on initially, only as a favor to Jesse Lo. His powerful name was what caused the prosecution to offer her the plea deal in the first place. If they caught on that she couldn't afford his firm, they would certainly be going for extended time.

He shuffled his papers and scanned them over again, like some new information was suddenly going to appear. "You have two days to decide. I'll be back then with the paperwork."

Raquel nodded. Hector walked out, and a few moments later, Jesse walked in.

"You knew, didn't you?" Raquel asked.

Jesse looked down.

"You knew they would offer me a deal if Hector was on our team." Raquel whispered, "Thank you," and then started to cry.

The two of them had nothing but a business relationship, but she could tell Jesse wanted to reach over and give her a hug. He had three children of his own, so he knew what ten years in jail meant for Raquel. She could see the tears in the corner of his eyes when he said, "We need to talk about the kids."

He opened and closed his briefcase slowly. "What about their biological father?"

"They have never met him, and besides, he is a loser. He doesn't know they are his, and that's how I want it to be. He has nothing to offer them."

"What about your mother?"

"She didn't want me and she doesn't want them."

"What about the relative that has them now?" Jesse looked down at his paperwork. "Yes, James's cousin Jackie."

"I talked to her this morning. She definitely does not want them in a long-term arrangement. She barely wants them now."

"What about James Sr.?"

Raquel was crying so hard by now, she couldn't see. "I have tried to get a hold of him, but he will not answer the phone."

"Is there a friend, somebody that I can call that will at least agree to temporary custody until we can find James?" Jesse pleaded.

Raquel sat motionless.

"What about your friend . . . the one I used to always see you with?"

"Karen? She has her own problems now, and besides, she is living with her parents and she's never been the motherly type. And let's not forget what I did to her at the ceremony. I'm so glad she's okay."

"Okay . . . well, let's keep thinking. Come on, Raquel, trust me, you don't want your kids as wards of the state. They will end up in foster care. Most foster parents are great, but some of them . . .? And remember, there is no guarantee that they will be able to stay together. And you have put so much work into them by sending them to the finest schools and programs. You don't want to waste all of that. Come on, Raquel, give me a name, a number, something. There has to be somebody you can trust with your kids."

"There isn't!" Raquel stood up and shouted.

Jesse grabbed her hand gently. "There has to be. I can see it on your face." Jesse stood next to her. "Raquel, this is not the time to let your pride get in the way. These are your children that we are talking about." They both sat down.

Raquel couldn't say it, so she wrote it down. She printed, *Joan Dallas*. Underneath it, she printed Joan's cell phone number. Raquel had memorized it after finding it repeatedly on James's cell phone.

Jesse grabbed his notepad. "Who is this?"

"James Jr.'s mother."

"Is she a good mother?"

Raquel paused for a moment. "Yes."

"What does she do?"

"She owns that new bakery everybody is talking about, Happy Endings."

"Where does she live?"

"Those yellow condos near the stadium downtown."

"I see, a business owner who lives downtown in an exclusive complex. This should be easy to approve, provided she agrees. So the two of you get along okay?"

"She hates my guts."

Jesse's voice went up several notches. "Do you think she will do it?"

"I have no idea."

"Should I call her now?"

Raquel grabbed the pad from Jesse. "I'll have to do it."

"Okay, but you don't have time to waste."

Chapter 25

There was a phrase James's mother used to say when things came together in a way she couldn't explain. Like the time his aunt Lorene lost her job one morning, and then that same afternoon, when she should have been working, she ran into someone looking to hire her for a more lucrative position. Or the time James's cousin Tania was short on cash, with a bad tooth that needed to be pulled immediately. She went to her mailbox and there was a $500 electricity refund check in the mail. Unbeknownst to her, they had been overcharging her for years. He could almost hear his mother's voice whisper the popular saying "The Lord works in mysterious ways."

Since James was planning to leave after the mock wedding, he had his bags packed and his passport in tow. He showered and changed his clothes at Joan's house, while Pastor Benjy made a few calls. Now, less than two hours later, James was seated in the back of a chartered plane headed to Mexico.

He knew one of the phone calls Pastor Benjy had made was to the police. He wanted to be sure James was no longer needed for questioning and could leave the country. James also worried one of the good little church people might not want him around and Pastor Benjy would be forced to rescind the invitation at the last minute, but none of that had happened.

The text from James's next-door neighbor said that their entire street had been inundated by reporters. He kept getting calls from Raquel, but he wasn't ready to talk to her yet. James was glad he was going somewhere where nobody could find him.

Pastor Benjy and eight other men were in the back of the plane having some type of meeting. James was too exhausted to care what the meeting was about. He put his seat back and closed his eyes.

"Hello, I'm Kenneth Harrison." The man held out his hand with a big, fake smile. The annoying voice coming out of his mouth reminded James of those obtrusive telemarketers who called his house like a long-lost best friend. "Pastor wanted me to come and introduce myself, and brief you on what we will be doing once we get to our destination."

James nodded his head and gave him a sort-of handshake.

"About fifty of the men from our church use their vacation time to make this trip every year. Most will stay about two weeks. The men on staff, including myself, will stay longer. You can leave whenever you are ready. Let me know and I'll get the church secretary to make the arrangements.

"Each team is made up of two men, one American man and one Mexican pastor. The two of us are set to be with Pastor Gonzales. We are the only team of three. You will simply shadow what we do. You will not have to speak or anything." Kenneth took the empty seat next to James and buckled himself in. "Pastor Gonzales is a real visionary. I met him a while ago on my first trip to Mexico. Pastor Benjy helped him plant the church he pastors. Each time we visit Mexico, we have a different mission. The theme of this trip is meeting people where they are, in prisons and on the streets. We will go to various locations throughout Mexico."

The word "we" caught James's attention. What did Kenneth Harrison mean about "we"?

Kenneth continued talking. "You will also have your share of downtime. Pastor B told me you needed some time to just chill and think. I can certainly understand that. This trip came at the perfect time, just what I need to get refocused." Kenneth lost his professional tone and started whispering to himself, "She was looking so good yesterday."

"Excuse me," James said. He thought he heard the good little church boy mention a woman.

"Yeah, I'm sorry, man." Kenneth's voice was casual and relaxed now. "My girlfriend, I dropped off some stuff over at her place yesterday. Let's just say, I really need this trip. She opened the door, looking all laid-back and sexy. A brotha wanted to just . . . God was with me, because I know I would have tried something if her daughter hadn't been there. Yes, all these days and nights of celibacy are starting to show. I thought it was getting easier, once I actually found the woman God wanted for me. But, man, now I feel like a horny teenager." He bowed his head like he was embarrassed.

"My devotion and prayer life used to be so fruitful," he continued. "I could get up at four-thirty in the morning and easily go until it was time for work. Now I get up and all I want to think about is *her*. I walk around the house and wonder what she is doing. Oh, man, I'm sorry I'm babbling like I'm crazy. It's just that sometimes it is easier to talk to strangers about things like this." Kenneth looked around the plane. "Everybody around here expects for me to be so perfect."

"I see." James hoped Kenneth was finished talking. He hated when men talked too much.

"Do you?" Kenneth asked. "Everything was so simple when I was a new Christian; those were the good old days. Before I was Kenneth Harrison, the worship leader at Miller Street Church. I was just Kenny, sitting in the back pew, soaking up as much as I could. No agenda, no protocol, just Jesus. That's what it is going to be like in Mexico, at least most of the time."

Somebody called Kenneth from the front of the plane. Desperate for rest, with eyes that felt more like weights, James exhaled in relief. His tense muscles went limp and he drifted off to sleep, as if yesterday were only a dream.

Chapter 26

A trip to her favorite mall bookstore didn't give Joan the rush she had anticipated. In her unbelieving days, she used to run to the store after work for the latest erotic masterpiece. Since she hadn't been to the store in a while, she didn't realize it had changed owners. Instead of the latest spicy novel, it housed children's books, with a few handmade wooden toys scattered around.

The drama with James Sr. and Minister Makita had her needing an escape. Church, Bible Study, and work—week to week, and month to month—had gotten old, real old. She checked her phone as she walked out of the store and through the mall. Of course, there were messages from Tisha, Lila, and Janet. Joan didn't have the energy to talk to them. All they wanted to do was go back and forth to church, and Joan was not in the mood.

She remembered she needed to buy James Jr. a new shirt and headed to Suit Palace. When she saw one of her old boyfriends, Darren, trying on one of his signature Italian suits, she knew she should have walked out of the store; instead, she walked right up to him and said hello.

Darren didn't remind her of how she had brushed him off the last time they saw each other. He only took her cell phone and programmed his number into it, telling her to give him a call so they could catch up.

Joan got close enough to smell his cologne. Just as she remembered, Darren smelled divine. She practically skipped away.

Two hours was all Joan could wait before she heard Darren's sexy voice again. "Hey, lady," he answered.

"What's up? You busy?" Joan asked, and then held her breath for the answer.

"Just driving to the airport to pick up my cousin. He's in town for the weekend. Why don't you grab a friend and meet us for dinner tonight. I would love to see you again, spend some quality time together."

Joan drew a blank. "I don't know if I could get a friend on such short notice."

"What about Tisha or Lila?"

"Oh, no . . . that wouldn't work." It was obvious she hadn't talked to him in a while.

"Come on, Joan, there has to be somebody you can call. Meet us at Anthony's at seven-thirty tonight."

Joan hung up the phone. No, there really wasn't anyone else she could call. There was no way Tisha would be anywhere near Darren, and Lila was practically married. All Joan had were church friends, and they wouldn't understand why she needed this night out. A classmate was having a sleepover birthday party and James Jr. wouldn't be back until the next day.

Suddenly Joan remembered the woman who had just moved across the hall from her, Sonya. She was some type of corporate trainer. They would talk briefly in the morning when they were both working out in the gym in their complex. The woman was new in town and had asked Joan about the hot spots. Of course, Joan couldn't answer her. Ever since she became a Christian, she had stopped hanging out. But tonight she was about to get her party on.

Joan went and tapped on Sonya's door.

"Hey, Joan, come in. It's about time you came over to welcome me to the neighborhood." She laughed.

"I'm so sorry. I kinda been caught up with work and stuff." Joan walked in and her mouth dropped. "Oh my, you have beautifully decorated your condo." Everything was red and black.

"You like?" Sonya grinned. "I wanted a sexy vibe to my place. I was a little worried right after I painted the walls. I thought I might have taken my theme a little too far. But it turned out hot!

"You want some ginger tea? I was just about to make a cup for myself." Sonya started to prepare the tea. All of her appliances, including her stove, were a bright shiny red. Even the tiled floor was red and black.

"Of course, it's good to meet a fellow tea drinker." Joan sank into the red leather sofa. Sonya's entire mantel was covered with high-end red and black stilettos. She had them mounted and on display, like works of art. "I wish I had the nerve to be this daring," Joan said.

"The way I see it, you only live once, and I'm not living my life for anybody but myself." Sonya handed Joan the tea in a cup with a red base and a black handle.

"I like the sound of that." Joan took a sip. "Oh my, this is delicious."

"You like? I fell in love with this tea in Thailand. The gentleman I was living with drank it every morning and every evening." Sonya paused. "I know what you are thinking: 'What was a black girl doing in Thailand?' Well, let's see. . . . I was going to school, drinking tea, and screwing as many fine Thai men as I could find." Sonya burst out laughing.

Joan didn't see what was so funny, but she started laughing too.

"What I wouldn't do for a good lay," Sonya went on. "Since I've been in Houston, all I have been meeting are straight losers. I don't mind dating a married man, but come on, you need to be able to afford to have something on the side. These fools want something extra and can barely afford what they already got at home. I'm sorry, I'm not a buffet, burger, buffalo wing kinda girl. If they don't take reservations, don't have a wine list or a valet, then you need to keep moving."

Joan saw a bag from what used to be one of her favorite clothing stores lying on Sonya's chaise. "I used to shop there all the time. Let me see what you got."

"Oh, you are going to love this." Sonya pulled out a gold knee-length dress, matching stilettos and a clutch.

"Oh, this is too cute," Joan said, putting the dress next to her body.

"You think this is cute? I went to the mall last weekend and had one of the most successful shopping experiences of my life. Come . . . follow me to my closet. Everything I purchased was heavenly."

While Joan looked through Sonya's extensive closet, she learned about her world travels, her boarding-school education, and the men in her life. She preferred them older, highly educated, and rich.

When Sonya realized she and Joan were the same size, she insisted Joan try on several different outfits. Joan hesitated at first, but when Sonya showed her the cutest little black dress, she stripped down and put it on. The dress was tight, short, and cut low. Joan knew it wasn't an appropriate dress for a single, modest Christian lady. She turned around in front of Sonya's full-length mirror. The dress fit flawlessly. If Sonya said yes, Darren was going to love her in this. Joan casually mentioned how her friend needed a date for his out-of-town cousin.

When Sonya found out they were meeting at one of Houston's famous and most expensive eateries, she was not only willing to go, but very excited. She changed into her new gold dress and Joan wore the black one. They helped each other with their makeup and accessories before jumping into Sonya's black Corvette.

Joan couldn't remember the last time she felt this giddy with excitement. It was time to have fun; there would be no rules, and no one looking over her shoulder. It was her time to be single, sexy, and free. Driving down the Richmond Strip, with all of the other people heading for a night out, was blissful. Everybody was smiling, honking their horns, music blasting, all dressed to perfection. She ran her hands through her hair. The night was full of scrumptious possibilities.

At every stoplight, Sonya and Joan had the men giving them second and third looks. When they pulled up to the valet and proceeded to get out of the car, everything stopped. Joan imagined this must have been what it felt like to be a star on opening night. The valet was so entranced, he couldn't move. The two couples waiting for their cars couldn't stop staring either. The doorman hurried to open the door to the restaurant. Sonya and Joan pretended not to notice it all. They just kept gabbing as they followed the host to their table. It looked like they had been friends for years.

Darren and his cousin Sean looked good enough to eat. Joan had met Sean only once years ago when a bunch of them went skiing. When they got close to the table, Darren and Sean stood up. Joan pointed to the seat next to Sean. Sonya looked over at Joan with an impressed look on her face. Sean was just as handsome and as well built as Darren.

Soon after they were seated and the introductions were completed, Sonya eyed the menu and then looked at Sean.

"Why are you looking at me like that?" Sean asked, grinning.

Sonya batted her eyes. "I'm thinking of ordering the lobster."

"Hmm . . . you know what that means, don't you?"

"Oh . . . I do. I'm just wondering if I want to go there. I did just get my hair done and I'm singing a solo in church tomorrow. It is not a good time to sweat out my hair."

Sean got up from the table and walked around it. Then he opened his gray suit so she could see how fit he was. He sat back in his seat. "You want to touch me? Trust me, baby, there is nothing soft on me."

Sonya looked him up and down; she grabbed his hands, then glanced down at his feet and turned back to the menu.

The waiter came to take their orders. Sonya let out a huge laugh; then she ordered the lobster. As soon as they finished eating, Sonya and Sean left, leaving Darren and Joan at the table.

"That was interesting," Darren said.

Joan sighed, and said, "To say the least." The entire time Sean and Sonya were at the table, Joan wished they would leave so she could be alone with Darren. Now that she had Darren all to herself, she was starting to feel uncomfortable because their table was so quiet.

"It's good to see you." Darren broke the silence.

"Likewise."

The waiter put a chocolate soufflé in between them. "Why did you call me back tonight? I really didn't think you were going to call," Darren said as he put his spoon in the dessert.

"That makes sense—"Joan avoided his eyes, "considering how things went the last time we were together." Their spoons tapped together in the soufflé. They both decided not to discuss the incident any further.

Back then, Joan was so sure that the next time she had sex would be on her wedding night. Now Joan wasn't sure of anything, besides the fact that Darren looked finer tonight than he had this morning. Joan had been having flashbacks all day of their many sexual escapades.

They finished their dessert. Darren paid the bill and then looked at Joan as they were leaving the restaurant. "Now, what?" Joan didn't know what to say. Darren answered for her. "How about a walk in the park across the street?"

That sounded perfect. Joan was glad she kept a pair of flats in her handbag; stilettos were not made for long walks. There were several couples walking hand in hand. Joan wanted to be one of them, but Darren kept his distance. For a long time, they didn't speak; eventually Darren stopped at a bench and sat down. For the first time tonight, Joan could see that something was bothering him.

"What's up, Darren? Back in the day, you would have been all over me. Now you are practically acting like a monk." Joan expected Darren to say something funny and change the subject. She had dated Darren for a while, but he never let things go too deep. So when he started telling her what was bothering him, she turned away so he couldn't see the shock on her face.

"My mom's addicted to prescription drugs. My dad is cheating on her with a woman half his age. My brother and his girlfriend had a baby boy last month. The first day his girlfriend returned to work, she had a car accident and was killed. Did I tell you that I was supposed to graduate from college?"

"Yeah."

"I lied. I have been in school long enough to have five degrees, but I don't have one. My dad is fed up with me. He is cutting me off at the end of the year. He will no longer pay for education or my expenses."

Joan was about to speak.

"No, wait—there's more. I have daughters, six-month-old twin girls, Chiya and Madelyn." Darren handed Joan his phone. There was a picture of two cute, chubby, bald baby girls.

Joan couldn't help but smile. "This must be at least one bright spot."

"It should be. . . ."

"But?"

"But when my father cuts me off, I won't even be able to buy them a pack of diapers. Last month, their mother called me saying she needed some formula. I had already spent my entire allowance for the month. I had to borrow the money from a friend. I'm a grown man who gets an allowance from his parents. I don't have anything to show for the three decades I've been on this planet."

"Are you and their mother together?"

"I don't know, Joan. Things were going fine between us, but when the babies came, well, everything changed. She wants *me* to take care of them, not my father. She wants us to get a house and be a family. I can't take care of myself. Ever since I got out of high school, I've been having a good time. Life has been one big extended party."

"And now?" Joan asked.

"The party is over. In reality, the party has been over. Things stopped being fun long before all this happened. A guy I used to go to grade school with caught up with me one day in the store. It was early in the morning, about four o'clock. I was in the checkout line with a pack of condoms. He was buying Children's Tylenol.

"He invited me to his house the next weekend. I had no intention of going at first, but for some reason, I went. We all sat around the table; it was me, his wife, and their two girls. He sells insurance and lives across the street from our old elementary school.

"After dinner, we got to talking and he invited me to church. That's what happened to you, isn't it? That's why you kicked me out of your room that day, because of your relationship with Jesus, right? You notice, I never called you after that. I respect that."

Joan nodded her head. "I see."

"So many girls I know spend Saturday night screaming some dude's name and Sunday morning screaming Jesus' name. I'm glad you are not one of those girls. Well, that night at his church, I almost walked to the front. I know a lot of people do it, but I have no intention of having one foot in the world and one foot in the church. I'm too scared of God to play with Him.

"Saying no to me that night, even though you had that desire, I never forgot that. I would be with other women and remember you. No disrespect, but I know how much you enjoyed sex. So if you love Him enough to say no, well, that must be some kind of love.

"I guess that was the first time I realized that people who call themselves Christians aren't all the same. I know lots of people who go to church, but they all do the same things I do, or worse. You know what my friend told me? He said, 'Being in the garage doesn't make something a car, and being in church doesn't make someone a Christian.'

"He gave me a Bible and I've been reading it. I didn't realize Bibles came in other versions. I got an NIV. Have you ever heard of it?"

Joan didn't bother telling him that the New International Version was one of the most popular versions of the Bible. She just nodded.

"There's this big men's conference at the stadium downtown. My friend wants me to come with him."

"You should go."

"Thank you, I needed to hear that coming from you. Joan, I got two questions for you. Why are you dressed like that, and why are you hanging around with a woman like Sonya?"

"I don't know, Darren," Joan said quietly. "It made sense at the time. I barely know Sonya." She felt like she had been summoned to the principal's office.

"So you wanted to hook up with me tonight, old-school style?"

"Yeah."

"And now?"

Joan said nothing.

"Joan, I don't know what's going on with you, but let me tell you something. You deserve better than that."

Joan looked confused.

"Okay, let's say we went back to your place and did our thing, just like we used to. Then what? What happens in the morning?" Darren asked.

"You don't understand, Darren. It's been so long. I just need this one night, you know, then maybe I can think straight. You remember when we were in that Chinese restaurant in Charlotte? Do you remember what you did to me underneath the table? It was so spontaneous and so much fun. I want you to do that to me tonight. Only not in public this time, but back at my place."

"Are you listening to me, Joan? What I did to you that night was totally disrespectful."

"Darren, don't make it sound so horrible. I have no regrets. We were just having fun, enjoying life and each other."

"Were you having fun the next day when I just left and didn't bother to tell you where I was going? You called and called me, but I was laying up with some other woman, so I didn't bother to call you back. If I remember correctly, I don't think I called you until two weeks later. Joan, don't make it better than it actually was. I was horrible to you that weekend, and on many other occasions."

"But things are different now."

"Why, Joan? Because this time, you aren't looking for a relationship? All you want is the sex?"

"Exactly, Darren. That's all I want." Joan snapped her fingers. "Now can we please stop talking and walk back to the car and drive to my place? Come on, Darren. I need you tonight. I need to be touched and taken to that place where only you can take me. I need to be held, caressed, and loved like any other woman. I'm human, baby. Don't you understand that?"

"But what about what you said a while back?"

"Forget what I said." Joan grabbed Darren's keys out of his pocket. "Let's do this, Big D."

Darren grabbed Joan's hand, and they slowly strolled back to his car.

Joan tried not to smile too hard. But being this close to Darren made everything in her world better. She was so excited; honestly, she wanted to start singing. When they arrived at her condo, Joan asked Darren to wait on the sofa while she went into the bedroom to freshen up. She wanted to come out wearing a sexy piece of lingerie, but she had thrown all of her pieces away, believing that the next man to see her naked would be her husband, and she would buy all new things for her wedding night.

Without anything special to wear, Joan decided to come out to meet Darren with nothing on at all. Darren apparently was answering a text message when she came in. It took him a few moments to notice she was standing there.

"Wow! Don't I at least get a nightcap first?" he asked.

Joan seductively walked toward him. "Of course, you can have a nightcap, but you are going to have to work for it."

She sat in Darren's lap. Darren quickly pulled her off his lap and onto the sofa. "Just do one thing for me before we get this started."

"Okay, but after that, we are going into the bedroom and you are going to do to me what you did in that restaurant. No questions asked then. . . . You promise?"

"I promise." Darren cleared his throat. "Go get me a Bible."

"Excuse me!"

"Yeah, I need a Bible." Darren started to look at his phone again. "Look up First Corinthians 10:13 and read it to me."

"You got scripture references saved in your phone?" Joan asked with an attitude.

"Will you please just go find a Bible and read that to me?"

Joan didn't move.

"The sooner you move, the sooner we can get on with the night's activities."

Joan realized what Darren was trying to do, but as she reached for a Bible from her bookcase, she vowed it wouldn't stop her. She began to read, "'No temptation has overtaken you except what is common to mankind. And God is faithful, He will not let you be tempted beyond what you can bear.'"

Darren stood up, grabbed Joan's hands, and brought her to him. "My Joan, my delicious Joan. I want you so bad right now, it hurts; but you belong to Jesus Christ and I'm not about to infringe upon His property, however tempting you may be. The next man that gets to enjoy your loveliness will have to go through Him first. I am not worthy. The next man will be your husband and it will be your wedding night." Darren opened the door to let himself out. "Sweet dreams, my queen."

Chapter 27

Joan waited a few moments; then she looked out the window. She wanted to see Darren walk away. He was walking away, only he wasn't alone. Sean was walking with him. Joan got dressed, grabbed a couple of quarts of ice cream, and knocked on Sonya's door. "Hey, Sonya, it's me. I just saw Sean leave."

"I'm coming," Joan heard Sonya say from the other side of the door. Joan waited patiently. It took Sonya too long to get to the door. She reminded herself to get Sonya's phone number so she could call first next time. When Sonya finally answered the door, Joan almost dropped the ice cream.

"What happened?"

Sonya had tears in her eyes. Her face was red and swollen, and she appeared to be hurting all over.

"Help me back to the sofa, please," Sonya insisted.

Joan put the ice cream down and gently walked Sonya back to the sofa. All she had on was her robe. Her once-spotless condo now looked a mess. Joan gasped when she realized it had taken her sore body that long to make the short trip to the door.

"Did Sean do this to you? Let me call the police." Joan ran to pick up the phone.

"No . . . no. Joan, just stop it, please. I'm fine. I just need to rest."

"What do you mean *you are fine?* You can barely walk. We need to call the police and tell them what he did to you."

"Joan, please. What do you want me to tell them? I met this guy for the first time tonight and drove him to my condo with the intent to have sex?" She sighed. "Everything started out great, but then after a few minutes, he began to get rough and eventually started beating and slapping me around."

"But if you told him to stop and he didn't, it is rape!"

"Thank you for caring, Joan, but frankly that's not the thing I'm most worried about."

"What else happened?"

"I always carry my own condoms. I buy the highest-quality products out there and I make a point to put them on whomever I'm with, regardless of what he thinks about it. I have seen too many grown men who don't have a clue on how to use one properly, making them useless and putting me at risk."

Joan nodded.

"So I put the condom on him." Sonya dropped her head. "But at some point, he took it off, without me realizing it. I asked him about it when he was getting dressed, but he just blew me off. I've got a bad feeling about this, Joan. I think he may have given me something on purpose."

Sonya got this faraway look in her eyes. "I remember this HIV-infected lady doing an interview on abstinence. The host kept trying to get her to tell the audience to use condoms. The host didn't seem to like her only speaking about abstinence. Well, the HIV-infected lady finally said something like, 'I'm sorry, perhaps abstinence seems foolish to you, but what seems foolish to me is to trust a piece of latex to guard your life against an incurable disease.'"

Sonya shook her head back and forth. "Now I know what she meant. I thought I could do whatever I wanted, as long as I used a condom, but a condom didn't guard me from this. And just think, Joan, he seemed like such a nice guy."

"Don't be so hard on yourself, Sonya. I've heard that even married men have affairs and give it to their wives. So you could be married and in what you believe to be a monogamous relationship and still get it."

"Joan, I've never met a man who wanted to marry me, so that's not one of my problems, is it?" Frustrated, Sonya said, "Would you please go in that medicine cabinet and get the pills in that plain white bottle?"

Joan rushed to get the pills, along with a glass of water. She handed them to Sonya and asked, "Are these pain pills?"

Sonya smirked. "I guess you could call them that, but I actually call them my I-don't-give-a-care pills." Sonya swallowed two of them without the water. "Because about ten minutes after I take them, I don't care about nothing. You want one?"

"No, thank you." Joan heard a knock at the door.

"Could you get that, please? That's a couple of my friends from work. We are going to pop a few, drink a few, and forget this night ever happened," Sonya stated.

Joan opened the door and two beautifully dressed ladies rushed in to comfort Sonya, one of them carrying a brown bag with several bottles of alcohol.

Joan took this as her cue to leave and closed the door behind her. Once she walked into her condo, she saw the Bible that Darren had made her read. She picked it up and read 1 Corinthians 10:13 out loud. Afterward, she got on her knees next to the sofa and prayed. "Thank you, God, for protecting me. Please forgive me and draw me nearer to you. And, God, please heal Sonya."

Chapter 28

Miles was running so fast, he almost slipped. He knocked on James's bedroom door. "Wake up, it's Christmas! It's Christmas!" Miles was convinced that his letter to Santa went all the way to the North Pole and therefore he and James could expect shiny new bikes as soon as they made it out of their beds and went downstairs to the Christmas tree. James tried to convince him that there was no such thing as Santa, but Miles refused to believe him.

Year after year, young Miles would write letters. Since James refused to write his own, Miles would write James's too. When the gifts on the list didn't show up, Miles didn't get discouraged. He just decided that Santa must have had some great reason and he needed to behave better the next year.

James was ten and Miles was eight on this particular morning. Their dad had been away on a business trip for two weeks. Instead of coming back with the same surly attitude he left with, he came home feeling relaxed and refreshed, so much so that he kept kissing their mother on the cheek and twirling her around while they danced to imaginary music.

James got out of bed that morning, just to prove to Miles that there wasn't a Santa Claus. Before he had the opportunity, he saw two red bicycles underneath the tree. Next to them were two toy train sets and the biggest stack of comic books they had ever seen. James's and Miles's screams woke up their sleeping parents.

They walked into the living room in their bathrobes while holding hands and smiling. It was the perfect Christmas morning, like something out of a made-for-TV movie. Their father played with them, while their mother made cinnamon apple pancakes, pan sausage, scrambled eggs, and hash browns.

"James, do you want another pancake?" his mother asked.

James bolted up, looked around, and then nestled back into the airplane chair underneath him. It was all a dream. A nice stack of his mother's homemade pancakes would be so nice right now, though. A simple "hello" from her would bring joy to his heart. James put his hands over his eyes, daring the tears to follow. It would be nice to hear his mother say something. Anything would be great. But that wasn't happening. He would never hear his mother's or his brother's voice again.

The plane was silent now. All of the men were seated. Most were reading and a few appeared to be sleeping. James was glad they didn't see, or chose to ignore, the tears that he could no longer stop from falling down his face.

Right when he was starting to feel really embarrassed and overwhelmed, he remembered his pills and quickly unlocked his seat belt and went to the restroom. All he needed was one or two to get his mind right, he told himself as he hurried past the other passengers. He splashed water on his face and reached in his pocket for the tiny pills he had placed in a Tylenol bottle as a disguise. He didn't want anyone to know he was taking prescription medication. Only the bottle wasn't there. He retraced his steps. He couldn't remember where he could have lost them. Confused, he walked out of the restroom and sat back in his seat.

Before James could ask Kenneth if he had seen his bottle, Kenneth started to speak. "You remember the story of Adam and Eve in the Bible? There's something there that a lot of people miss. Let me explain. Adam and Eve were running around the Garden of Eden freely, content, without a care in the world. They enjoyed having God around. But what happened after they didn't obey God? They didn't want to be in God's presence. They actually started hiding. Can you imagine? One moment, everything was cool, then they disobeyed, and the next thing you know, they are hiding from the One they enjoyed so much before."

James instinctively knew that Kenneth had his pills. Kenneth was talking in a voice that only James could hear, but he was looking straight ahead.

"We can learn so much from our first parents," Kenneth went on. "There was this girl that lived on my block named Lisa. It was around the time I was fourteen or fifteen. She was what we used to call back then, 'a freak,' meaning she would let the neighborhood boys have their way with her. Despite what everybody else was doing, I decided I wasn't going to be a part of it.

"During the summer, she and I would hang out playing board games and basketball. I was careful not to touch or handle her sexually in any way. The men I knew were always running around and chasing woman after woman. I vowed that I was going to be nothing like them. I was going to be the man who treated women with respect. It was like she was my big sister or something. She seemed to really enjoy our time together, and I'll have to admit, I did too. I don't know. . . . It was like I was doing something important while I was hanging out with her. . . . It was something that seemed to matter.

"One day, my boy Shamar's parents were away on vacation. They left him and his older brother in the house all week. I was there during the day. We really got into a lot of trouble that week. I woke up from a nap one afternoon, and Lisa was there. All the neighborhood boys were running a train on her in Shamar's parents' bed. It must have been at least ten of my friends in line waiting for their turn with her. I heard about Lisa, but that was the first time I had seen her that way. Shocked, I turned to walk away, but then all my boys started tripping about me being scared and stuff. Next thing I know, I was on top of her while they cheered me on, trying hard not to look like this was my first time. When it was all over, I threw the condom in her face, just like I saw the rest of them do."

James looked up at Kenneth, surprised by what he had just said. Kenneth continued to look straight ahead and spoke in a quiet tone. "When I saw her the next day while walking down the street, I didn't even say anything. I couldn't look her in the face. I could barely stand myself. That's when it all started. That's when I stopped trying to be a good boy. That's when I started running from lady to lady. It was like I entered the dark side, and instead of turning myself around and going to the other side, I just kept getting deeper and deeper.

"I mean, I have participated in some stuff." Kenneth's head dropped. "Sometimes I wake up and wonder . . . how exactly did that happen? I mean, what in the world was I thinking for that to make sense?" He turned to James. "Have you ever felt like that?"

James didn't respond.

"In college, the first time I heard about one of my friends participating in a threesome, I was shocked," Kenneth said. "I didn't think I could ever do anything like that. But by graduation, I had slept with so many women, it made sense to try something new and do a couple of women at a time. Before long, what was impossible became routine.

"That's what happens when you start running. We don't confess and turn around. We just keep running deeper and deeper, getting spiritually further and further away from God each day.

"You know what I find intriguing?" Kenneth didn't wait for James to respond. "It's all the different ways people choose to run. For me, it was sex, alcohol, and drugs. For others, it is sports, video games, food, drugs, work, ambition, education, decorating and redecorating their homes, gambling, television, excessively cleaning, or filthiness. Even church work is how some people flee. Whatever it takes so that we don't have to be in God's presence.

"You know what's really funny?" Kenneth again didn't wait for James to answer. "The medical establishment is making a killing off this. They are passing out these pills—these pills that make it so easy to hide, to forget. Now you could keep taking your hiding pills, or you can decide that today will be the last day that you hide.

"Think about it, what has hiding gotten you so far? So, are you ready to try something different?" Kenneth handed James the pills. "Or would you rather keep hiding?"

Chapter 29

All of the men with Pastor Benjy were visibly nervous. The plane had landed. They were in Mexico City, but there was some type of delay with the arrival of the pastors who were set to meet them as soon as they deplaned.

Pastor Benjy seemed the least affected. He instructed the men to gather their things and wait outside. They obeyed at once. James followed behind at a distance. There seemed to be some type of hierarchy in the bunch. Pastor Benjy was at the top, and Kenneth was his right-hand man. The other men followed in line, appearing to be from the oldest to the youngest.

Now that they were outside, James expected the weather in Mexico to be pleasant. On this day, it had to be over ninety degrees, though. Growing up in Houston had prepared him; the heat wasn't unbearable, especially since the air was thankfully free of humidity.

The idle chatter ended when the sun started to descend. One minute, the lights around them in the various businesses were on, and now they were being turned off. The silence ended when a man named Victor was the first to spot the bus. It was hard to tell who was the most excited. The men on the ground were jumping up and down and yelling. The men on the bus were doing the same, only seated.

When the Mexican pastors finally ran off the bus, they each were clearly looking for a specific member of

Pastor Benjy's group. Pastor Gonzales found Kenneth and hugged him, long and hard, like they were brothers who had been lost for years, feared dead, only to return to each other, safe and sound. Kenneth was the first to gain his composure enough to speak.

James was trying to remember if he had ever seen such an outpouring of emotion between men, when Pastor Gonzales attempted to hug him. James took two steps back and extended his hand.

"Let's pray," Pastor Benjy said. The men held hands and formed a big circle. Many of them were weeping happily. James stood near the luggage and several feet away from the circle. There was no way he was about to hold hands with a bunch of men. The fact that people were walking by and gawking at them made it seem even more awkward.

Pastor Benjy looked proudly around the circle. "Thank you, Lord! Thank you, Lord!"

The men joined in. "Thank you, Lord!"

A couple of the Mexican men had to break away, too excited to stand in the circle and be still. James felt that he must be missing something. These men were acting like a bunch of women.

"It's not like me to cry," Pastor Benjy said as he wept, "but when I think about what God used us to do in this city, I just can't help it." Pastor Benjy walked up to one man and then the next. "When we first met José, he was so strung out he couldn't tell us his name. He couldn't have weighed more than a hundred pounds and was living in a cardboard box."

José dropped to his knees.

"Armando was running his neighborhood's brothel. Marco was going to this very airport every day to steal from unsuspecting tourists. Michael was weak and near death because he was taking more drugs than he was selling. This is a group of former pimps, prostitutes, swindlers, drunkards, murderers, fornicators, adulterers, and everything in between. Thanks be to God and His Son, Jesus Christ."

The men cheered and repeated after the pastor. "Thanks be to God and His Son, Jesus Christ!"

"When it became aware to me that it was the Lord's will for me to come to Mexico, I didn't think I could do it. I was already consumed with our church back home, the wife, my children, and, of course, my beloved grandchildren. I was exhausted, as it was.

"When I walked off the plane that first time, I was weary and overwhelmed by the task before me. I had no idea on that first trip that this project in Mexico was going to be the highlight of over fifty years in ministry. I didn't know that each time I left Mexico, I would cry tears of sadness, and each time I would return, I would cry tears of happiness."

Pastor Benjy bowed his head and closed his eyes. The men did the same. "Thank you, Lord, for bringing this group together once again. Thank you, Lord, for a place where men can worship freely. Thank you, Lord, for the amazing friendships, like none we have ever known.

"Because of the unconditional love you have for us, we can be men who freely cry at the sight of the ocean, worship with our hands held high, kiss our sons and our daughters, drop to our knees and pray, and dance if we want to. Oh, how we love you, our Master, our King, our Savior, our Help, our Salvation, our Sufficiency, our Rock, our Redeemer, our Lord."

With that, the men detached hands and started with the hugging again. James started pacing back and forth around the luggage. This ongoing public display of affection was annoying him. After several more minutes, the men started to get into separate taxis, two by two. Eventually everyone had gone, except for Kenneth and Pastor Gonzales.

"Hey, man," Kenneth said, looking at James, "I'm sorry to keep you waiting. It's just that, well . . . I love this man." Kenneth started to walk to the bus that had carried the Mexican pastors to the airport. Kenneth shoved their luggage into the back. "I know it is kind of weird." He paused for a moment. "Hey, you know, it's just like Jonathan and David."

"Who?" James asked.

Kenneth looked confused. "You know, King David and Saul's eldest son, Jonathan."

"Oh, yeah . . . in the Bible," James said as they were climbing into the van.

"Yeah, that's the type of love the Mexican pastors and the American ministers have for each other. We have the type of deep friendship that is uncommon among men. We are tied together not by our love of sports, women, sex, or money. We are tied together by our love for Jesus."

"I love this man with a deep love," Pastor Gonzales said, in reference to Kenneth, as he was navigating through traffic. "He risked his life to preach the Gospel to me. I passed from death to life because he cared enough to be there for me. I come from a wealthy family. We have servants and own vast portions of land. I went to the States and got my college degree. While there, I visited several Christian churches. However, each one that I attended made me more confused than the next. Frustrated, I just did what came naturally. I went to the United States a virgin. I came back anything but that. I thought the best thing in the world was sex on top of more sex. And it was so easy in the United States to get it. Several times, women came looking for me. It was fun for a season, but soon I was longing for something simpler. After I graduated, I came back home to work in my father's company, thinking that would make me happy. Then I found myself looking again for peace in women. I convinced the most beautiful woman I had ever seen to agree to marry me. Surely, that would give me the peace I was seeking. I was looking at her during dinner a few days before our wedding and realized, not only did I not love her, but I didn't even like her. I called off the wedding and ran to the airport. I was too ashamed to face my family. I literally did not know where I was going. I just knew that if this was all life had to it, I would rather pass. I was too scared to kill myself, because I didn't know if I would end up worse off than I was, or what. At the airport, I saw a flyer lying on the floor advertising that an American church was in town. I went, and there is where I met my brother here." He nodded toward Kenneth.

Kenneth started in. "The day I got saved, I started reading the Bible and finished four months later. On top of that, I started reading biographies of great Christians. I was on fire and wanted to do something big for God. I talked to my then-pastor about it and he had me teach adult Sunday School. It wasn't what I needed. Most of the people in the class were trying to one-up each other with how much more they knew about the Bible. It was frustrating. I wanted to learn and grow, and they wanted to fight over words.

"The singles at my church decided to go on a cruise," Kenneth continued. "Several churches in the area got together for the cruise. I was excited about having some good clean fun with all my new brothers and sisters in Christ. I had no idea this was nothing more than a major hookup session. There was more sex going on aboard that ship, with so-called Christian singles, than there would have been had it been filled with honey-mooners. I told my old pastor what happened on the cruise and he just blew me off. I was devastated and started looking for a new church."

While they talked, James looked out the window. He had met plenty of people in his past that were Christian hypocrites—which was one reason why he never paid much attention to them. Listening to Kenneth and Pastor Gonzales claim to witness the same things certainly gave him something to think about. He wondered if they were having this conversation for his benefit.

"That search led me to Miller Street Church, where I met Pastor Benjy," Kenneth said. "He asked me to follow him around that first day. He told me his church wasn't perfect, because it was made up of imperfect people. However, he did believe in following the Word of God at all cost, even if it meant disciplining another member.

"After our talk, we went to an apartment complex, door-to-door, sharing the Gospel. Then we went to a nursing home and prayed for the sick. After that, a group of single men met at his house to pray for the strength to be single and celibate in this sinful world. It was like I was finally home! I joined the church, and a few weeks after that, I was taking my first trip to Mexico." Kenneth reached out to Pastor Gonzales. "On that trip, I met Pastor G. Only, he wasn't a pastor then."

"I walked up to him at the end of the service and told him I wanted to know how to be saved," Pastor Gonzales said. "And not only that, I wanted to know what I needed to do after that—"

Now James was sure they were having this conversation for his benefit. He didn't mind. Pastor Gonzales and Kenneth were more like him than he had expected.

"That's exactly how I was feeling at my old church," Kenneth interrupted, "like I started the process, but I was failing to move forward. Yes, it is important to be a Christian, but I just didn't want to be somebody who was calling himself a Christian and not acting the part. Yeah, I wanted to walk the walk and talk the talk. I wanted it all, whatever God had for me. I had been sold out in the world, and now I wanted to be sold out for the Lord.

"Hey, Pastor G," Kenneth said, "you have got to take us to that place that makes that delicious mole."

Pastor Gonzales laughed heartily. "They close early today, which is why I picked up some this morning."

"That's what I'm talking about!" Kenneth said, smiling from ear to ear.

James almost smiled too, until he remembered he didn't have anything to smile about.

Chapter 30

So far, his Mexican trip was going nothing like he had imagined. James thought he was going to some rural area where he would see masses of poor people walking around, looking sick, like the infomercials he would flip past while looking for a game to watch.

James was actually looking forward to sleeping underneath the stars and escaping the busyness of the city. But this looked like a major metropolitan city, and Pastor Gonzales had a large upscale apartment, right in the middle of the action, with a washer and dryer, two and a half baths, and three furnished bedrooms.

James quietly stepped out of his bed and walked to the kitchen, hoping he didn't wake up Kenneth or Pastor Gonzales. The smell of coffee and a dim light let him know he wasn't the only one that couldn't sleep.

"You too?" Pastor Gonzales said solemnly while he poured James a cup of coffee.

James sat across from him at a richly adorned wooden table.

"Thanks for letting me stay here."

"It is my pleasure to help Pastor Benjy. He is a great man of God."

James sipped his coffee. It had to be the best he had ever tasted. "This is very good."

"The best in the world. There are two things I like to spoil myself with: fine coffee and fine food."

James tried to make conversation. "I thought you were about to say women."

"We just met and we know each other so well." Pastor Gonzales smiled. "Yes, my friend, before Jesus, there were three things I spoiled myself with.

"Why are you up, anyway?" Pastor Gonzales asked.

So much for sitting and sipping quietly on his coffee, James thought.

"You go first," James said.

"Tomorrow, our day in the prison, has me concerned. Well, the truth is that I'm a little nervous. I have been reading my scriptures, meditating on the Word, and praying for the last few weeks. I'm still very, very, nervous." Pastor Gonzales stood up from the table. "I keep telling myself it is perfectly normal to be scared. . . . I mean, nervous. I mean, we are going to preach the Word. Even the apostle Paul had a healthy dose of fear. Right?"

James shrugged his shoulders. He didn't know anything about the apostle Paul's fears or anything else. Pastor Gonzales didn't seem to notice. He kept walking from one end of the table to the next.

"I know that Pastor Benjy is familiar with the American prison system, but I'm not sure he understands the Mexico City system. American prisons are high-tech, with trained staff, and highly armed guards. Here, this is just not so. Our guards aren't properly trained; they don't have the weapons they need. Some prisons are run by gangs, and male rape isn't an isolated incident but standard practice.

"Then there's this practice called 'lockup' in the prison where we are going tomorrow. In early afternoon, the prisoners are given their dinner in a small paper bag. After this, they are sent to their cells, big open spaces, where first-time offenders are held captive, right along with seasoned murderers and rapists. By the time the sun goes down, most of the staff has left and the prison is locked up until the morning."

"What? So once the guards lock up, they don't go back in?"

"Exactly, my friend, not until morning. If one of the gangs decides they want to recruit you for the position of 'wifey,' otherwise known as sex slave, there will be no guards to help you. That's why HIV is spreading so quickly."

"Are you serious?" James shook his head. *What have I gotten myself into?*

"Are you going tomorrow?" Pastor G asked.

James didn't answer. He simply poured himself another cup of coffee and went back to his room.

There was a knock at his door. "They are on their way to pick us up," Kenneth said. "Are you coming?"

James was dressed and ready to go. All day, he had been in his bedroom, awaiting this knock. He had thought about completely ignoring the knock; maybe they would just leave him. James hated the thought of appearing weak.

The knock came again, only louder this time.

"James, are you coming or not, man?"

"Yeah, I'll be out in a sec," James answered, wondering what made him say those words.

A few minutes later, he walked out of the bedroom and tried to make eye contact with Pastor Gonzales to see if he was feeling any better about this whole prison trip. Pastor Gonzales avoided his eyes. He was busying himself by stacking and then restacking several boxes full of Bibles.

Kenneth was eating some type of meat stuffed in a corn tortilla. He seemed completely oblivious to the tension in the room. James looked at Pastor Gonzales again. This time, he looked up, but James could tell the conversation they had last night should not be repeated.

There was a knock on the front door; Kenneth rushed to open it, grabbing two boxes filled with Bibles. Pastor Gonzales grabbed the other two, and all three men rushed down the stairs.

There was a van waiting for them. They put the Bibles in the back of the van and joined the others. James sat in the back and tried to take in as much information as he could about what was supposed to happen today.

This would be a united effort. Three of the teams would walk into one of Mexico's toughest prisons. They had tried other locations, but the leaders of those prisons had done everything possible to put obstacles in their way. However, this particular prison had a Christian woman on staff who was instrumental in allowing them to get clearance. She would be meeting them as soon as they walked through the doors.

Pastor Gonzales seemed completely alarmed that a woman was working in a prison guarding men. "Will she be coming in with us?"

Pastor Benjy replied, "No, I told her that wouldn't be necessary. But she actually wanted to come."

Pastor Gonzales still seemed bewildered. James no longer cared about appearing weak. He had to know if Pastor Benjy was aware of the danger. James asked, "Are the prison guards properly armed in this particular prison?"

"No," Pastor Benjy said. "Not only is this prison one of the worst in Mexico, it is also one of the poorest. If something goes wrong, we will not be able to depend on the guards and their guns.

"Also, we might be spending the entire night in the prison," Pastor Benjy added, like it was an unimportant side note. Pastor Gonzales looked like he was going to vomit.

"Why is that?" James tried to sound calm.

"Well, the only way that they would let us go in was if we went in at our own risk. If something goes wrong at some point during the service, the guards might not feel comfortable going in until the morning, when they have a full staff."

"Why didn't we just plan this trip during the morning?" Pastor Gonzales asked.

"After talking with our contact, she suggested that we go in during lockup hours. First, because we could speak with more prisoners at once, and secondly, because going in without a net will get the attention of the prisoners. They will see that we truly believe in the God that we serve. If we had planned the service in the morning, we would have looked scared and unsure of ourselves. We can't be frightened to go where they live and talk to them on their level."

"Pastor Benjy," James said loudly, hoping everyone in the van heard him. "Have you ever heard about what happens in this prison when they are locked up all night?"

"Yes—yes, I have, James. I have been called by God to preach the Gospel to the ends of the earth. These men need to know that Jesus has made a way out of no way for them."

One of the Mexican pastors spoke for the first time. "Prisoners are people too. Perhaps they act like savages because they are treated like savages. We are treating them like men, and we'll be speaking with them, face-to-face, just like you would speak to any man."

James had heard enough. Everything he was hearing was only making him more nervous, anyway. They rode the rest of the way in silence.

When they arrived, they learned their contact was late. Pastor Benjy always looked so cool, but he clearly didn't like having to wait for her. They had just finished praying. They had formed a prayer circle right outside the doors of the prison before they walked in. This time, James hadn't had a problem standing in a circle and holding hands with a bunch of men.

Pastor Benjy must have prayed for fifteen minutes. James hoped he would have prayed for fifteen more. After the prayer, they were escorted to a small room to get briefed by their contact. After that, they would be walking into a large communal cell—as Pastor Benjy put it—"to share the love of Jesus."

Their contact walked into the room, a half hour late, with the grace of a beautiful, exotic butterfly. James couldn't keep his eyes off her. He looked around to see if the other men had noticed this vision of womanly perfection. With the exception of Pastor Benjy, who had stood up to greet the young woman, the other men were looking at the table, doing everything they could to avoid looking at her.

She spoke to Pastor Benjy privately for a minute and then cleared her throat to address the group. She was utterly confused when only James and Pastor Benjy seemed to be listening.

"I'm sorry, Ms. Lara," Pastor Benjy apologized. "It's just that you are a beautiful young woman and our men have made the pact of Job. As Job did, they have made a covenant with their eyes not to look lustfully at women."

"Job 31:1, I know it very well," she said. Ms. Lara seemed impressed.

James was certainly impressed. She was covered from head to toe in her uniform, but that did nothing to hide her shapely figure. James wanted to run his fingers through her long, flowing hair. She looked more like a supermodel than she did a prison worker. James started to feel more comfortable. If she felt safe walking around here, then it must be okay.

"It is with great pleasure that I welcome you to Mexico City," Ms. Lara said. "You have no idea how I, my family, and my church have been praying for this day. As you know, this prison, as well as Mexico City as a whole, is plagued with many serious issues. I believe that God whom we serve is concerned with all of them, from the least to the greatest. I can see by your bravery that you serve the one true God, just as I do.

"I do not take it lightly what you are doing today. I teach English as a second language in prisons throughout Mexico. I know what a dangerous mission this is. I know that you have family members that love you and do not want you in harm's way. Yet, you come. You come because you love Jesus and you love His people."

James found his eyes lingering on her thighs. Pastor Benjy shot him a look. James turned his attention back to her face.

After she finished speaking, they each stood up, one at a time. They formed a single-file line, as if in grade school. The teacher, Pastor Benjy, was ahead of them, walking his class into what could be a death chamber, not a playground for recess.

James thought his heart was going to beat through his chest. He had sweat forming at his temples and sliding down his face. He closed his hands in fists and then opened them again, like boxers do right before they enter the ring. He needed to do something to try to alleviate the tension that was building up inside him. He wanted to jog around in a few circles, but he decided against it.

They walked down a long cement hallway. There were two expressionless armed guards on either side of the mechanical gate. One guard pushed the button to open the gate. It slowly opened from bottom to top. The guard motioned for them to walk in. James hoped the armed guards would follow. However, they both stayed safely outside the gate, along with Ms. Lara.

Pastor Benjy led them past the gate and into the cell. It was worse than James expected. It wasn't enough that there were at least 200 men within inches of them, but they were barely clothed. Plus, the smell was so bad, James couldn't find a word to describe it. There had to be decaying bodies underneath the soil floor. James glanced down for just a second, sure he was going to see maggots.

Looking down for that second caused him to drop a few steps behind the line. He stepped faster, but not too fast. He knew enough not to look scared. After all, just a few weeks ago, he was a seasoned officer of the law in a major city. But he also had a revolver on his hip and a radio to call for armed backup. As much as he hated to admit it, James knew that nothing in his career had prepared him for this.

At this moment, there was a multitude of prisoners that could grab him, squeeze the life out of him, and there wouldn't be anything Pastor Benjy or the guards could do about it. James wished the prisoners would talk or move around or do something—behave like a group of men in suits came around here all the time.

Instead, each of the inmates was quietly standing still as the pastors made their way to the front area. It was clear that this didn't happen every day, and each man wanted to make sure he didn't miss one single part of the show. James felt he was going to faint. The smell was unbearable.

They reached the front. It must have been where they kept the bodies, James concluded, because all of a sudden, a swarm of the biggest flies he had ever seen started to fly past their heads.

Pastor Benjy and Pastor Gonzales, his translator, walked to the makeshift podium. It was nothing more than some cardboard that marked the spot. Pastor Benjy would say a few sentences and then Pastor Gonzales would translate.

"Gentlemen, let me tell you about a man," Pastor Benjy said. "Let's say his name is Sam. Sam committed horrible crimes. What's the worst crime you can think of? Is it murder, rape, molestation? Whatever it is, Sam is standing before a judge having been convicted of the crime. He has been given the death sentence because of the horrific crimes he has committed.

"Right before Sam is to be killed, a man comes forward. This man explains that he wants to take Sam's punishment for him. All Sam has to do is receive it. Sam receives this man's offer and walks out of jail a free man."

The inmates were silent.

"I used that illustration to explain to each of you what Jesus Christ had done on your behalf and on my behalf. Each one of us—all of you, and all of us—is like Sam. We have committed sins that are worthy of us going to hell. The Bible says that all have sinned and have fallen short of the glory of God. 'All' means 'everybody.'

"There is a one hundred percent chance that each one of us is going to die. The only question is where we will go when we leave this earth. There are two destinations. One is heaven, and the other is hell."

Several of the prisoners started nervously shifting
from side to side.

"The Bible says that the wages of sin is death. That
means we all deserve to go to hell because of our sins.
But because God loves us so much, He sent someone to
die in our place. Jesus Christ died and took the punishment for our sins. All we have to do is receive His death
as payment for our sins. When we do this, we get to go
to heaven.

"Now, what if we don't receive His death as payment
for our sins? In that case, we get what we deserve.
Hell—" Pastor Benjy's sermon was interrupted.

"What's that, preacher man?" a man yelled in broken
English from the back of the pack. "I didn't kill anybody. I stole a few things, but not much. So, shouldn't I
go to heaven? I'm not a bad person. I'm not like them."
He pointed to a group of about ten men with wigs,
makeup, and female clothes. "These are the types that
deserve hell," the man said.

"Only you don't have a hell to send them to," Pastor
Benjy replied. "God loves me, you, and them. He sent
His Son to die for all of us. If they repent, turn away
from their sins, and receive Jesus' death as payment
for their sins, they get to go to heaven, just like the rest
of us. As I said, we have all fallen short of the glory of
God. Homosexuality, sex outside of marriage, adultery,
drunkenness, thievery, gossip—all of it is wrong.

"The men that stand with me, we have all lived a
lifestyle full of sin. You name it, and we did it. But we
turned away from that lifestyle and now we follow Jesus." The prisoners were clearly getting agitated and
were no longer listening to Pastor Benjy.

The prisoners dressed like women were whispering
to each other. The prisoner who had spoken out against
them was talking to the men around him. All of a sud-

den, he started patting his chest and yelling something in Spanish.

"It's time to go."

James recognized the pleasing voice coming from the loudspeaker. It was their contact, Ms. Lara. James took a deep breath. Pastor Benjy looked frustrated. It was clear he wasn't ready to go.

Ms. Lara had made it clear that Pastor Benjy would only have a few minutes to speak. If things went well, they could come back. James had already decided Pastor Benjy and his boys would be on their own.

Kenneth and Pastor Gonzales helped Pastor Benjy with his things and they were back in line, only this time leaving the prison cell. They left the boxes of Bibles behind. They hoped the men would pick them up and read them.

James took his place at the very back of the line. He could feel the tension melting with each step. The prisoners watched as they walked away.

Just make it out the gate, James silently told himself, over and over. The guards didn't open the gate until Pastor Benjy was right next to it. The *click,* which signaled the gate was opening, sounded so sweet. James wanted to sing out, only a few more steps to go.

The short-staffed crew felt comfortable opening the gate and letting them out. James was relieved because they did not have to spend the night. Pastor Benjy and most of the men in the front were already safely out of the cell.

"Shut up! Shut up! Liars! Liars!" James heard a group of prisoners running toward him. He instinctively turned to look at them. The guards instantly started to shut the gate. By this time, all of the men were safe— except for James. He was only inches from the gate, confident he could make it out on time.

Suddenly two of the prisoners, not a part of the running mob, pushed James down. He landed on the ground. He was certain there was no way he could get up and make it through the gate before it closed.

Kenneth made an attempt to crawl underneath the closing gate. He prayed he would be able to reach James and pull him out in time.

Chapter 31

Kenneth watched the gate close, with James inside. "Why are you pulling me? Why are you pulling me?" Kenneth yelled at the guard. "I almost had him."

The guard said nothing. He continued to pull Kenneth aggressively to the meeting room, where they had initially met Ms. Lara. He used his gun to motion to Pastor Benjy and the other men that they were to follow him as well.

Once they reached the room, the guard released Kenneth. Ms. Lara walked in; there were tears in her eyes. The guard whispered something to her that only she could hear. Ms. Lara put her head down and spoke loud enough for everyone in the room to hear her. "When it became obvious that you were not going to reach James, the guard felt he had no choice but to pull you to safety and quickly get all of you away from the cell."

"He didn't give me a chance!" Kenneth was so loud that Ms. Lara and the guard took a step back. "You have guns. You can open that gate and get him, if you want to." Pastor Gonzales put his hands over his face and quietly sobbed. Pastor Benjy went to a corner and started calling a number on his cell phone.

Kenneth turned around and looked at the men who had come with them. They were all standing huddled together. Frustrated, Kenneth said, "It would have been nice to have gotten some help." Kenneth waited for a reaction. They looked at the floor. They looked at their shoes. A few of them looked at each other. None of them looked at Kenneth.

Ms. Lara spoke to the guard in Spanish. She turned to Kenneth. "I'm sorry. The gate will not be opened until the morning." Ms. Lara and the guard walked out of the room.

Kenneth walked back and forth in the tiny room, repeatedly, until Pastor Benjy hung up the phone.

"Did you get somebody to make them open the gate?" Kenneth asked hopefully.

"No." Pastor Benjy shook his head.

"What are we going to do?" Kenneth asked.

"We are going to pray."

"We prayed that we would all make it out of the cell safely, but God didn't answer our prayer," Kenneth replied.

"I know you are upset," Pastor Benjy said as he looked around the room. "We are all upset. But getting angry isn't going to accomplish anything."

Kenneth appeared to calm down.

Pastor Benjy pulled a small Bible out of his pocket. He sat down and motioned for the men to do the same. They quickly sat down and opened their Bibles. Pastor Benjy had taught the men always to pack a small Bible.

"Now I want all of you young men to listen to this old man." Pastor Benjy settled into his seat. "There are going to be many times in your life, especially after you get married and start to raise your families, that you aren't going to know what to do. These are times when you will pray, but God won't seem to be listening.

"You are going to have a decision to make. Do you get mad and give up? Do you run away? Or do you stand on the promises of God? Somebody find and read Romans 8:28."

One of the men read, "'And we know that in all things God works for the good of those who love Him, who have been called according to His purposes.'"

"What does 'all' mean?" Pastor Benjy asked.

"All!" the men shouted. Pastor Benjy often asked this question.

"So even in our heartache, even in our distress, and right in the midst of our confusion," Pastor Benjy said, "God is working some things out for our good, right?"

"No, Pastor," the men replied.

"God is working a few things for our good?" Pastor Benjy questioned.

"No, Pastor," the men said. "God is working all things for our good!"

"Somebody find and read Psalm 30:5."

"'Weeping may stay for the night but rejoicing comes in the morning.'" Pastor Gonzales stood up and said this proudly, with tears staining his face.

"Somebody tell me what Jesus said in Mark 10:27," Pastor Benjy continued.

Kenneth said, "'With man this is impossible, but not with God, all things are possible with God.'"

"I was on the phone with Mother Jacquelyn," Pastor Benjy said. "The prayer chain has started and it will continue until the gate opens in the morning."

Mother Jacquelyn was seventy-five years old and a founding member of Miller Street Church. She was known for the prayer chain she started twenty-five years ago. First the person who needed prayer would call Mother Jacquelyn and dictate his or her prayer request. Mother Jacquelyn would hang up the phone and immediately pray. After that, she would call the next person in her prayer chain. That person would hang up the phone and pray; then he would call the next person in the prayer chain. Before the prayer chain was completed, over one thousand people, covering six continents, would have prayed for the same request.

The guard returned to the room. Ms. Lara was behind him. He said something in Spanish and she translated. "All of you might as well leave and return in the morning. At six o'clock, we will have a full staff and we will go into the cell at that point." She looked as if she didn't want to say the next sentence. Her voice cracked as she said, "We will have an ambulance waiting, just in case . . . you know, just in case." She could not finish her thought.

Ms. Lara put her hand on Pastor Benjy's hand. "I'm so sorry. None of this would have happened if I hadn't insisted you come. I feel terrible. What if they kill him?"

"What does James 5:16 say about prayer?" Pastor Benjy asked Ms. Lara.

She replied, "'The prayer of a righteous person is powerful and effective.'"

"We will be praying all night," Pastor Benjy said as he got down on his knees. The other men did the same. It was going to be a long night.

Chapter 32

Morning after morning, Joan was waking up and feeling more confused than the next. She felt unstable, like a building without a foundation. One moment, she was sure she wanted to forget this whole celibacy thing; the next minute, she wanted to embrace it. Then there was this whole fiasco with James Sr. and Raquel, the episode with Darren, her conversation with Minister Makita, Sonya, Sean, Tisha, and Marcus. Her mother had taken James Jr. to spend a few weeks on the beach in Galveston. Joan was glad for the reprieve. She needed time to refocus, or focus, or simply stop feeling like she was a leaf blowing in the wind.

The woman she wanted to be and the woman she was seemed as if they would never connect. Every time she finally thought she had it together, one of her ducks would get out of the row. She heard her cell phone ring. She expected it to be the bakery manager at the coffee shop. Since Joan was failing to come to work, the manager had been working for days without a break. Joan had promised to go in that afternoon. Instead of Karla's number, she saw her friend Janet's cell phone number flashing on her screen.

The last thing Joan wanted to hear was Janet's voice. Ever since Janet had gotten married, Joan didn't really feel comfortable around her, alone. Janet was constantly inviting her over to her new home, and Joan was constantly making up excuses. Surely, a visit to Janet's home would stir up a whole other degree of jealousy Joan didn't have the energy to deal with. So every time they met for a girl's lunch or a shopping spree, they did so without going near Janet's place.

Since she had several missed calls from Janet, Joan picked up the phone. She didn't need Janet and her baby bump knocking on her door. "Hey, Janet, I have been meaning to call." Joan wished she wasn't able to lie so easily.

"Hey, lady, how are you? I was starting to get worried."

"I'm fine. Just been a little busy, you know."

"I understand. It gets that way sometimes."

Joan hated her for being so darn understanding. Was it so hard to yell at her for being so inconsiderate and selfish?

"Please come and help me put this nursery together. I'm really starting to regret not finding out the sex of the baby. I can't get a color scheme that would work for a boy or a girl. I went out and purchased all these sample paint colors and I can't see any of them working. You are the one person I know with a natural sense of style, so you've got to come help your girl out."

Joan desperately wanted to lie her way out of this situation. She had a built-in excuse: she needed to go to the bakery.

Janet would have no idea she wasn't due at the shop until that afternoon, giving her plenty of time to stop by her place and still make it to work on time. Instead, she said, "Sure, would right now work?"

She could feel Janet's enthusiasm through the phone. "Yes! Of course now would work. Oh, Joan, I didn't think you would have time to come by so soon."

It was official; Joan was a very bad friend. She needed to get Janet's address, since she had never bothered to write it down; and she couldn't remember where it was located, since she hadn't driven there since the house-warming a few years ago. In perfect Janet fashion, she gave it to her without sounding the least bit upset.

Joan hung up the phone. She closed her eyes and picked up her journal:

I'm the friend that is so happy for you when you receive your degree that I arrive at the commencement early, so I can sit in the front row and clap really loudly when you make your walk across the stage. I'm the friend that purchases you a new designer outfit when you finally lose that last twenty pounds. I'm the friend that prays for you night and day when you want a new job or a promotion. But what I really want to be is the friend that is deliriously happy for you when your left hand adorns an engagement ring. Will I ever be that type of friend?

Joan closed her journal and stepped out of her bed. An hour later, the gated community and the beautifully landscaped streets greeted Joan as she arrived in Janet's neighborhood. There was a playground and a water park, even a place for the kids to ride horses after school. As Joan drove, she imagined she was driving through her own neighborhood on her way home to meet her husband and family.

Janet's husband, Jerome, answered the door; he had a big welcoming smile on his face. Joan smiled back at Janet's husband. She liked the way the word "husband" sounded. Joan remembered him being kind of short and chubby, but today he looked striking in his three-piece suit.

"Janet will be right down. I swear, ever since she has been expecting, she has to go pee every five minutes." He laughed heartily.

At the housewarming party, they had yet to begin to decorate and furnish the home, but Joan could see now that it was complete, with dark wooden floors and high-end leather furniture. The walls were painted a peaceful shade of light green. Over the fireplace hung a large portrait of the two of them on their wedding day. They were on a beautiful beach, looking into each other's eyes while each clutched a white Bible. It was an absolutely breathtaking photo: husband, wife, and God. Joan couldn't take her eyes off it. It wasn't merely a picture, but a snapshot of a passionate love story.

She forgot Jerome was around, until she heard him walk over to the staircase and yell, "Joan's here. Are you okay? You need me to come up there?"

Joan peeled her eyes from the picture, hoping Jerome had not noticed her reaction to it.

"No, I'm coming!" Janet yelled.

"Okay . . . well, I'm leaving. I don't want to be late. I'll call you when I get there." Jerome turned apologetically to Joan. "I'm sorry to leave you down here by yourself. But I have a meeting I have got to get to. Janet should be down momentarily."

Joan watched him leave. His cologne still lingered in the air, even after she heard him drive off.

The circular living room would have been perfect for book club discussions and Bible Study meetings. But Janet had not hosted one in the three years she had been married. Suddenly Joan realized she wasn't the only one who avoided Janet's place. Tisha and Lila did the same.

They had never discussed it, but Janet's home was a reminder of what they didn't have and what they might never have. Joan looked around and sighed. *So this is what "happily ever after" looks like.*

When Janet arrived downstairs, with a huge welcoming smile on her face, Joan walked up to her, grabbed her hand, and said, "I'm sorry."

"Sorry for what?" Janet stepped back and looked around the room to see if she had missed something.

"I'm sorry for being jealous of you when you got married. I'm sorry for lying and avoiding conversations with you. I'm sorry that I had to ask you for your address today, because I haven't bothered to come by."

Janet clutched her light blue sundress and walked to the sofa. She put her hands on her face and started to cry.

Joan went on speaking. "Minister Makita didn't allow me into the Wife Preparation class. She said I had a long way to go before I became anybody's wife. I got so angry with her that I stopped going to church and even attempted to have sex with an old friend I used to date. Thankfully, it didn't go down, but let's just say, my life has been really interesting lately."

Janet looked up. "I've missed you. I've missed all of you. I'm so thankful for my godly husband, but I hate that it cost me my friends. My entire marriage has been so bittersweet. I even thought that maybe it was all in my head, that I was just imagining that the three of you were avoiding me."

"No, it wasn't your imagination. My pastor always says that the true sign of jealousy is how you react when someone gets what you want. If you bought yourself a brand-new Range Rover or took a fabulous vacation, it would be easy for me to be happy for you, because I don't desire those things." Joan looked around the room. "I want this. I want it so badly, it is blinding me."

"So I guess telling you that everything happens in God's timing will not work."

"No, none of that. I'm familiar with all those scriptures and I'm not going to lie to myself anymore. I'm tired of waiting for a husband. I want one *now*. I'm tired of not being touched and not knowing if I ever will be again. Those women at church scare me. I don't want to be one of them, old and with nothing to clutch but a Bible. I'm not going to pretend like I'm okay with it, because I'm not. I hate it! If that makes me an immature Christian, then so be it. From now on, I'm all about the truth. Am I wrong? Yes, I am. However, I'm going to go back to church and get back into my Word. One day, maybe I won't feel this way. But right now, it is what it is."

Janet nodded her head. "I can respect that."

Joan clapped her hands together. "Now that we have the hard stuff out of the way, let's get started with this nursery. How about a black-and-white zebra theme?"

"What?" Janet frowned.

"Yes, let's do something modern, nothing babyish. I'm talking painting one wall black and leaving the rest white. Getting a black crib, but getting the rest of the furniture white, and we need a pop of color for the accessories. . . . Hmmm, maybe apple green!"

Joan grabbed Janet's hand as they headed upstairs to the nursery. Joan smiled. She was feeling better already.

Chapter 33

There was complete silence in the room. It was six in the morning, time to open the gate. Pastor Benjy and the other men had closed their Bibles. All of them, except Pastor Gonzales, were in their seats, with their eyes closed and their heads bowed. Throughout the night, the men and Ms. Lara had prayed in various positions. They spent some time on their knees. Then they switched to standing. They held hands, sang, and even walked around the room. But Pastor Gonzales never left his knees.

Pastor Benjy asked the guards if he could be near the gate when they opened it. They denied his request and instructed him to stay in the meeting room until further notice. Right after that, Ms. Lara left, explaining she would get back to Pastor Benjy as soon as she could.

Thirty minutes later, they had not heard anything. Quietly Pastor Benjy started to sing "It Is Well with My Soul" by Horatio Spafford. As a teenager, he had heard the story about the conditions in which the song was written, and from that moment, it had become one of the pastor's favorites. Horatio Spafford was a Christian businessman who lost his four daughters in a shipwreck. Shortly after learning of their fate, he sat down and wrote a hymn that didn't focus on his grief but rather on the fact that one day he would see Jesus, face-to-face.

The song reminded Pastor Benjy that one day all of the pain that is experienced on earth would be gone in an instant. When he was facing something difficult, he would think about Horatio Spafford and the powerful lyrics to that song.

Pastor Benjy recalled singing the song in the waiting room at the age of twenty-five when he lost his first child to a miscarriage. He sang it again four years later when his only brother was killed in a car accident. When he and Minister Makita watched their first church burn down because of an electrical problem, they sang it to each other.

Through the years, Pastor Benjy had seen more grief than he could have imagined. When parents discovered that their wayward child was dead, he was one of the first people to be summoned. He couldn't recount how many times he had heard one of the members of his church mouth the painful words "I have cancer."

Each week was filled with new baby blessings, anniversary celebrations, and a myriad of other praise reports. Each week was also filled with heart attacks, strokes, and emergency surgeries. Pastor Benjy had seen miraculous healings, but he was also there when the healing didn't come. He had spoken at funerals with caskets that didn't hold eighty-year-old men but school-age children.

Pastor Benjy was beginning the third verse when James walked in the room. Kenneth was the first to notice him. He stood up and tried to speak, but he couldn't find the words. Pastor Gonzales was next. He jumped to his feet and tried to move, but his legs felt like lead.

Pastor Benjy was still singing, with his eyes closed and his head bowed, when James tapped him on his shoulder. Startled, Pastor Benjy opened his eyes. It took him a moment to realize that it was James. Once he did, he jumped up and hugged him. Then he put his hands in the air and silently thanked Jesus.

By this time, the rest of the ministers had opened their eyes. They jumped around the room like their favorite player had just made a touchdown to win the Super Bowl in overtime. Soon all the men were hugging each other, and James, while looking at the ceiling and saying, "Thank you, Jesus. We know you didn't have to do it, but you did!"

James seemed confused by the excitement. He shrugged his shoulders repeatedly, trying to understand why Pastor Benjy and the rest of the men felt the need to act this way.

It was a full fifteen minutes before things started to calm down. Pastor Gonzales was the first person to notice the expression on James's face. He got the men to be quiet; then he asked James to sit down. "So what happened? How did God rescue you?" Pastor Gonzales asked.

"What?" James looked around the room at the smiling faces. "Rescued?" James shook his head back and forth. "Why would I need rescuing?"

Ms. Lara walked in the room, with a bright smile on her face. James looked at her, and then looked back at Pastor Benjy and the other men.

"You didn't tell them?" James questioned.

"We didn't tell them what?" Ms. Lara asked.

James was starting to think everybody in the room had gone crazy. Frustrated, he said, "That you had three armed guards in the cell all night to protect me."

Ms. Lara started to walk backward. Her mouth dropped.

Pastor Gonzales walked up to Ms. Lara. "Did you have armed guards in the cell the entire time?"

"Of course not," she shot back. "There were no guards in that cell last night. We couldn't pay anybody to go into that cell last night."

James got out of his seat. "Well, who were the men with guns that stood over me last night? They told me everything was going to be okay. I just needed to go to sleep and wait until the morning." James looked at the assembled men for an answer. They looked back at him blankly.

Ms. Lara took the seat James had been sitting in. "A few years ago, I was in a car accident with my two nieces," she said. "We were sideswiped on a one-way road. The other driver kept going. I was fine, but both of my nieces were bleeding and screaming.

"I got the first one out of the car. When I went back to get the other girl, she was already out. A man was standing next to the car with her in his arms. He was wiping her tears and talking to her calmly. He comforted her, while I comforted my other niece. Eventually the paramedics came. I turned around to thank him, but he was gone. There wasn't a trace of him. There was no way he could have walked off that quickly or even driven away, for that matter."

"My sister was the primary care provider for my father in his last days," Kenneth said. "Both of his legs were pretty bad off and he had to have a wheelchair to get long distances. Every morning, my sister would pick up the wheelchair and put it in the car without a second thought. Well, after my dad passed, we decided to sell the house.

"My sister went to pick up the wheelchair and put it in the moving truck, only it was too heavy," Kenneth continued. "I told her to roll it into the moving van, but she wouldn't listen. She kept trying to pick it up, like she had so many days prior, but she couldn't do it at all."

Ms. Lara smiled and said, "God gave her supernatural strength to pick up that chair. But after your dad passed, she didn't need it anymore."

"Yes, and God sent an angel to help you and your nieces after the car accident," Kenneth said. "When the paramedics came, the angel left."

"James, where are the armed men now that protected you all night?" Ms. Lara asked.

James scratched his head. "I don't know. One of them woke me up this morning and told me they were about to open the gate. He walked me up to the gate, but there was so much going on by that point." James struggled to remember all the details. "When I thought to turn around and thank them, the gate was closed. I looked around, but I didn't see them."

The men started jumping up and down and praising God all over again. James watched them, but he couldn't say another word. He was too overwhelmed by what he just heard.

Did God really send angels to protect me last night?

Chapter 34

Joan knocked on Minister Makita's closed door. She knew that Makita kept her door opened, unless she had someone in her office. But Joan got up the nerve to come to see her and apologize, and she wasn't leaving until she had the opportunity.

Makita looked somber when she opened the door. Joan instantly wanted to turn around, but Makita grabbed her hand and pulled her inside, quickly locking the door behind them.

Joan saw a familiar-looking silhouette of a woman from the back facing Makita's desk.

"Look who just arrived!" Makita sat behind her desk.

The woman turned around. It was Tisha.

Joan had been avoiding Tisha for almost a month. It felt weird to be looking at her, especially since Joan could see the tears in her eyes.

"I'm glad you are here. Now I can tell the both of you the bad news together," Tisha said.

"Why do I feel like I should be scared?" Joan sat in the seat next to Tisha.

"Well, I'll just spit it out." Tisha paused. "I had sex with Marcus." She exhaled deeply. "No, that was a lie. I have been having sex with Marcus for the last week."

Joan looked puzzled. "What? Is this some kind of a joke, Tisha? Okay . . . it's funny. . . funny." Joan let out a laugh. "Girl, why do you feel the need to get my blood pressure up? I'm too old for you to be playing with me like this."

Makita said nothing.

Tisha's voice started to crack. "No, Joan, this isn't one of my jokes."

"But it wasn't that long ago that he came over and you kicked him out," Joan said.

"What a difference a little time makes," Tisha responded. "Well, a few weeks after that happened, I stopped off at the Home Place to get some stuff for my new apartment. You know, blinds, curtains, pictures, and a bookshelf. Right when I was trying to figure out how I was going to get everything out of the car, Marcus drove up and offered to help. I thought about it briefly. It felt kinda stupid to refuse his help when I clearly needed it."

Tisha started fidgeting back and forth in her seat. "Well, he kept complimenting me and telling me how proud he was of me for finally getting my stuff together, paying my own bills, and getting a stable job. The things I never did while we were together.

"As soon as we walked into the apartment, he started putting up my blinds and curtains, and then nailing pictures to the wall. When he was done with that, he put the bookcase together. It took him a few hours to do what would have taken me a few weeks to accomplish."

Joan aimlessly looked around Makita's office. She still didn't fully believe Tisha.

"Joan, it felt so good to have a man around. Girl, until I had him there, walking around, breathing, looking into my eyes, I just didn't know how much I missed that."

Joan nodded in agreement and looked at Makita. Joan couldn't read what Makita was thinking.

"Well, he left around eight and called me on the phone at ten that night," Tisha continued. "He told me how good it was to see me and that he wanted to be friends, not enemies. We stayed on the phone for hours. Mostly, I just listened to him talk about his business and all the interesting things that occur when he's traveling.

"When I hung up the phone that night, I knew I was in trouble. I couldn't stop thinking about him the whole night. The next morning when I left for work, there was a bouquet of yellow roses on my doorstep. When I walked downstairs to my car, I saw a card on my windshield. He wanted to know if I would meet him at Geneva's pizzeria for lunch. That used to be our favorite pizza spot." Tisha's hands started to tremble.

"I met him at the restaurant. When we walked in, the owner recognized us, and for whatever reason, she assumed we were married by now. I waited for Marcus to correct her, but when he didn't, neither did I. The following day, he picked me up after work. He said he had something he wanted to show me. An hour later, we arrived at a lakefront cottage in Conroe—"

Joan interrupted Tisha. "Is that where it happened?"

Tisha hesitated, and then took a deep breath. "We walked around the lake. We laughed. We played cards and dominoes, just like we used to. The whole time, I was getting calls from Lila, and from some other ladies from the church. I just ignored them. I told myself, I wasn't going to allow anything to happen. I was only enjoying some time with a male friend."

Makita rolled her eyes.

"About nine at night, we were sitting on the porch, overlooking the lake, when a boat pulled up. I was having so much fun, I hadn't realized I had missed dinner. He told me we were going to have dinner on the boat. By this time, I could hear the Spirit screaming at me not to get on that boat.

"But get on the boat, I did. At the bottom, there was a single beautifully decorated table. We were the only people on the boat, with the exception of a few workers. We sat down and the waitress brought us the most delicious seafood dinner." Tisha got a faraway look in her eyes.

"Afterward, she led us to the upstairs area. There was what looked like a hotel room up there. It had walls for privacy, but there was no ceiling, unless, of course, you count the sky and stars. Did you know you could see stars in Conroe?"

Joan and Makita didn't answer.

"Had you even talked about going to a room before you arrived upstairs?" Joan asked.

"Not once," Tisha said. "He never even alluded to sex. I guess that's why I felt so comfortable. Well, the lady showed us all the amenities in the room; then she left, saying, 'I'll see you in the morning.'"

"So what did you do, Tisha? He certainly went all out."

"When he reached for me, I didn't resist. We rocked as the boat rocked all night long. It was so intense, so passionate. It was like I was breathing for the first time."

Joan felt uneasy. She wished Tisha had left out that last sentence.

"The next morning, while we were in the midst of another session, his blaring cell phone interrupted us. He looked at the number, jumped out of my arms, and went to the bathroom so he could talk. He might as well have stayed, because I heard every word he said." Tisha sighed. "The next thing I know, the boat is docking and he is rushing me back to the car."

"What happened?" Joan asked.

"He was having so much fun with me that he didn't get the text from his girlfriend that said she was coming home a day early from her trip and he needed to pick her up from the airport."

"Tisha, I'm so sorry."

"Wait, I'm not finished. I didn't hear from him until the day after, when he arrived back at my place. Joan, I was mad, devastated, hurt, and confused. But you know what? I slept with him again, and a few days later, he came by and I did it again. I knew he wasn't telling me the truth about her. I knew they were more than just friends. I knew that things were going nowhere with us, but I just couldn't help myself. I craved his touch. Even if . . ."

"Even if what?" Joan asked.

"Even if I knew it was a lie. Even if I knew I was going to get my heart broken. Even if I knew he was going to walk out of my bedroom and into her bedroom." Tisha turned to look at Makita, who still had a blank expression on her face. "It's like you always say, 'Queen for the night, and a slave for life.'"

Tisha was crying now. "I feel so hurt and hollow inside." Makita grabbed Tisha's hand from across the desk and handed her a box of tissues. "This is what God was trying to keep me from. Not just diseases and unplanned pregnancies, but the emotional pain of giving myself so deeply to another person. It was just sex to him, but it was so much more for me." Tisha paused. "Minister Makita, does God still love me?"

"Of course, He does."

"But why? I went and gave myself away like that, and disregarded His Word so easily. I was so quick to give Marcus all of me, even though he offered me nothing in return.

"Minister Makita, I want Joan to do the class I was supposed to teach next week. How can I get in front of the singles in the state I'm in?"

Joan grabbed Tisha's other hand and looked at Makita. Makita nodded, and then Joan said, "Because we serve a forgiving God. Remember 1 John 1:9? 'If we confess our sins, God is faithful and just to forgive us.'" Then Joan turned to Makita. "I've already spoken to God, but now I'm here to speak with you. Please forgive me for my selfishness, pride, and plain ugly attitude. You were right. I am jealous of Lila and Kenneth, and of any woman who marries a godly man. I understand why you didn't allow me in the marriage class, and I hope your offer to meet with me privately still stands—"

"Wait a minute," Tisha interrupted. "You didn't get into the wife preparation class? How is that possible?"

Joan was about to speak, but Makita cut her off. "Joan didn't get into the wife preparation class until today. She just told me everything I needed to hear."

"Oh . . . okay," Tisha said. "But who's going to coordinate the singles meeting next week? We have had so many people RSVP. I think it is going to be the biggest singles event ever. But there's no way I'm standing in front of them, looking and feeling like a hypocrite."

"What is the meeting about?" Joan asked.

Tisha handed Joan a bunch of index cards. "Well, if you would come to church, you would know," she said as she patted Joan on the leg, and smiled.

Joan looked embarrassed but smiled back.

"Well, you know how when we have our singles meeting, the same things come up over and over. But it's like we just don't get to the real root of the issues," Tisha stated.

"Yeah, I know exactly what you mean," Joan responded. "It's like everybody is afraid to talk about the real issues."

"Exactly. We are all trying to pretend like we have it together," Tisha said. "Well, I heard about this church. I believe it is called New Faith. Well, somebody came up with the idea of getting all the singles to place questions anonymously in a box. What would they ask in church if nobody knew they had asked it? I think we should try it at our church."

"Oh my," Joan said as she thumbed through the cards. "This is going to be a singles meeting like no other. I've never heard anybody talk about this in church. Tisha, there's no way you can't continue with this meeting. This meeting is what I need, and I know it's what a lot of other singles need. I'm so sick and tired of pretending."

"I'll do it on one condition," Tisha said.

"What's that?"

"I'll do it if my best friend is right beside me."

Joan looked at Minister Makita and saw that wide smile she so desperately missed. "Tisha, I would be honored to stand with you," Joan replied.

Chapter 35

Joan and Tisha glanced at one another repeatedly as they added more and more chairs into the largest meeting room at their church. Miller Street Church was a megachurch, with a congregation of thousands, but most of them only came on Sunday mornings. Ministry meetings and Bible Study, held during the week, only averaged about a hundred to 200 people. Singles meetings were the worst, only averaging between forty and sixty people, most of whom were women.

Joan and Tisha were thoroughly encouraged when one hundred people—half of them men—signed up for their singles event the week before it started. They had the janitors put out twenty-five extra chairs, just in case people who hadn't registered beforehand wanted to come.

"Do you see how many people are in here?" Tisha asked.

"Yes, I can't believe it." Joan looked around the room. "I knew we had a lot of singles in this church, I just never thought there would be so many of them in here."

Minister Makita rushed into the room with the head janitor. She was breathing hard as she said, "Ladies, looks like we are going to have to move this meeting into the sanctuary."

"What?" Joan and Tisha responded in unison.

"Apparently, you two haven't looked outside," the janitor said. "The line to get in practically reaches the front door of the church. The parking lot is almost at its capacity. There's no way we are going to be able to get everybody in this room."

"We have to inform the rest of the staff," Makita said. "I will see y'all in the sanctuary."

Tisha and Joan rushed to the entrance and peeked through the blinds so they could see outside. Their mouths dropped open. The staff at the registration desk looked overwhelmed. It was church policy to get everybody's name and information before allowing them into a church event. It was a way of finding out what ministries were most effective for the church body.

Tisha shook her head back and forth. "I guess we aren't the only ones that are tired of business as usual."

"Hmm, this line is shocking," Joan said. "Here I was thinking I was the only one that needed this information, but it looks like every single in the church needs to know."

"I knew that flyer you made was going to get people in here, Joan." Tisha started to quote the flyer, "'Join us for an evening of the truth, the whole truth, and nothing but the truth. Singles, it's time to take the mask off. No question is taboo. There is no subject we will not explore. If you want to keep pretending like everything is okay, stay home, but if you are ready to go deep, we will see you there.'"

Tisha looked startled all of a sudden. "I know what happened!"

"What?"

"I sent a copy of the flyer to that guy on the radio, Harris Mann. He came to Bible Study months and months ago. I recognized him as new to our church, so I went and introduced myself."

"Sorry, I'm not familiar with him," Joan said. "I don't listen to radio like I used to. So which Christian station is he on?"

"That's just it, Joan. He's not a Christian DJ! He's a secular DJ. I recognized him from our nights in the club. You remember, he had that deep Barry White voice? He's been on WBTH for at least fifteen years."

"Wow! Now I know who you are talking about, 'Horny Harris.' He used to do all the best parties back in the day. He's still on the air?"

"Yes, and more popular than ever. Well, that day he was here, I sensed he was going through something. I gave him a Bible and a few books and prayed with him. He seemed really grateful. He handed me his card and told me if I ever needed anything to shoot him an e-mail.

"Well, I did. I asked him to read the flyer on air." Tisha laughed. "Of course, I didn't think he would, or even could. It's not like we paid for advertising or anything."

Joan looked through the blinds again. The church's staff was directing people into the sanctuary. "Yep, there's no other way to explain this. Horny Harris, I mean Harris Mann, must have announced it on air," Joan remarked.

"Why is it that God keeps blowing my mind?" Tisha asked.

Joan shrugged her shoulders. "I guess because He's God. Let's make our way to the sanctuary; I can't wait to see what He is going to do next."

The meeting started a full hour late, not because they were not ready or because the praise team hadn't shown up on time as usual, but because it took that long to find everybody a seat. The janitors estimated there were at least 10,000 people in the sanctuary, just like a typical Sunday morning service. Singles had traveled from all over the city.

Tisha rose to the microphone. "Thank you so much for attending this event. We thank God for each of you. We would also like to thank Pastor Benjy and his fearless wife, Minister Makita. Joan, will you please introduce our panel."

"Thank you, Tisha. Over the last several weeks, we have had a container outside of our church. We asked singles to write questions they have always wanted to know but were afraid to ask. We felt by their writing the questions anonymously, we would get questions that have never been asked before in church."

Joan quickly introduced the panelists, made up of both male and female ministers. She didn't bother to read their bios aloud, because they were printed on the program each person was handed when he or she walked into the sanctuary. The panelists included Mimi Jefferson, Erin Lambert, Julian Broussard, and Cecil Montgomery.

Tisha handed Joan a big black box. Joan held the box up so everyone could see it. "All of the questions have been placed in this box." Joan reached in and grabbed the first question. "'When dating someone, how far is too far . . . kissing, touching, cuddling, etc.?'"

The congregation gasped. The panelists looked around at each other; even they seemed surprised by the question. Joan looked through her notes, and then said, "How about having Ms. Erin Lambert answer this one."

Ms. Lambert shook her head. "I'll answer it, but I can guarantee you will not like my answer. First of all, let's be clear. The Bible doesn't specifically mention kissing, or cuddling or dating, for that matter. It does however mention sexual immorality. As a matter of fact, First

Corinthians 6:18 tells us to flee sexual immorality. That means run fast and move away!" She stopped and looked around the room. "I would say, you shouldn't kiss, touch, or cuddle during the dating process."

The singles looked confused. They started talking to each other.

Tisha got up. "If you want to respond to the panelists, you need to step to the microphone. If you notice, we have one at the end of each aisle."

One lady with snakeskin sandals and a matching purse couldn't get to the mic fast enough. "Hi, thank y'all for coming. My name is Shawna. I just could not stay in my seat. Is that really realistic? I mean, seriously. Don't get me wrong—I love the Lord. I want to please Him, but that is just downright unreasonable."

"Let me put it to you like this," Ms. Lambert said calmly. "Since this is all about being real, let's get real. How many of you have made up your mind not to have sex only to end up having sex? You don't have to raise your hands. I'll raise mine for us all."

Tisha gently wiped the sweat that was starting to form on her forehead.

"When you start touching, you will start kissing, and now you are kissing and touching," Ms. Lambert chronicled. "Where does kissing and touching lead to? Right, more kissing and touching. Now, where is all of that kissing and touching going to lead to? It might not be the first time it happens, or the third or the fourth, but eventually it will lead . . ." She stopped and waited for the answer.

A male panelist said, chuckling, "Straight to the bedroom!"

"So who does that?" Shawna asked. "I mean, there are people out there who get married and they have never made out before? Come on!"

"Yes," a slender lady in a lavender sundress said, smiling. "Hello, I'm Cynthia." She was standing at the microphone opposite Shawna. "That's what me and my fiancé are doing right now. I'm not trying to say that it is easy. In order to keep our minds right, we fast one day each week, pray before and after our dates, and memorize scripture together. We also don't spend very much time alone. We usually meet at restaurants, coffee shops, or bookstores.

"This is my first relationship since becoming a Christian, and I must say this is the best relationship so far," Cynthia continued. "It is so good to know that my fiancé can't wait to see me, even though he knows our dates will not end up with sex. It's like we have a deeper level of intimacy. We really get to talk and get to know each other."

Shawna shifted her handbag from one side to the other. "Oh, sweetie, please. If he isn't having sex with you, he's having sex with somebody." The congregation laughed.

"Actually, I'm not." The attendees focused their attention on the tall man who was now standing next to Cynthia. He nodded to the panelist. "Good evening, I'm Chris, Cynthia's fiancé." He turned and looked around at the people seated close to him. "You know, I am getting really tired of people assuming that we men aren't capable of controlling ourselves. Women say they are abstinent due to their relationship with the Lord and people believe them. But when men say it, then people start laughing." Chris got loud. "Can somebody please tell me what's funny?"

Nobody said a word.

"Here we are in a place full of so-called Christians and the fact that a brother is trying to live right is funny," Chris went on. "Is it so unbelievable that if God can be trusted to escort us from heaven to earth, that He can be trusted to give us the strength to control ourselves?

"I wasn't always a Christian and didn't always conduct myself in a Christlike manner. But now I'm a changed man. It would be nice to get some love from my so-called brothers and sisters in Christ."

"You talk a good game, but please! I'm not buying it," Shawna said. "Every man I know can barely go three days without it. What makes you any different?"

"Four years ago, on December twenty-fourth, I decided to follow Christ," Chris said plainly.

Shawna paused. She appeared to be waiting for the rest of Chris's response. When she realized he was finished, she said, "And?"

Chris answered her, using only scriptures. "Philippians 4:13, 'I can do everything through Christ, who gives me strength.' Isaiah 40:29, 'He gives strength to the weary and increases the power of the weak.' Second Corinthians 12:9, '"My grace is sufficient for you, for my power is made perfect in weakness. Therefore I will boast all the more gladly about my weaknesses, so that Christ's power may rest on me."

Chris looked directly at Shawna and said, "Either God can give me the strength to do what He has called me to do, or He is a liar. Which one is it?"

Shawna took her seat.

Chapter 36

"We have run out of time. I'm so sorry we didn't get the opportunity to answer all of your questions," Joan said into the microphone.

"But what about the rest of the questions?"

Joan couldn't tell who had asked the question, but it seemed to be the sentiment of the entire congregation. Joan looked at Makita, who was seated in the first row.

Minister Makita stood up and walked to the podium. "I see this Q and A session is something we need to have regularly. I am going to get with the Singles Ministry leaders and come up with a schedule. Joan, how many do we have left?"

Joan turned the box upside down. "Four, 'Are singles allowed to read erotica or watch pornography?' 'What does the Bible say about masturbation?' 'My clock is ticking, should I have children without a husband?' 'I'm young and healthy. What does God expect me to do with my sexual urges?'"

"Those are great questions," Makita said. "However, the Drama Ministry is hosting their annual conference starting tomorrow morning. People have come from all over the country and we have to allow time for our staff to get the sanctuary ready for them." Makita looked puzzled. She looked up at the panelists.

Tisha stood to the microphone. "Do any of our panelists have any ideas?"

Mimi Jefferson stood up. "I would be more than happy to get with the other panelists and post our answers to the rest of the questions on my Web site, tonight, www.mimijefferson.com."

Tisha, Joan, and Minister Makita looked relieved. "So until we can meet again, check out www.mimijefferson.com to get answers to the rest of the questions," Tisha said.

The singles started to walk out of the sanctuary. A few of them stopped to talk to Tisha and Joan. "Oh, my gosh! Oh, my gosh! Please tell me this isn't the last event we are going to have like this," gushed a twenty-something woman in a tank top and skinny jeans. "It was so informative, so real, just so what I needed. You feel me?"

"I'm so going to that Web site. I want to know what God has to say about masturbation," one lady whispered in Tisha's ear.

"It was so much information to take in," said a young pregnant woman. "I need to read my notes over and over again and study the scriptures they talked about. My hands couldn't write notes fast enough."

The three women walked off, chatting about the event. Tisha turned to give Joan a high five, when she heard a man's voice.

"What up?"

Joan and Tisha looked up and Harris Mann was walking toward them. He had dropped his hip-hop attire and was wearing a pair of black slacks with a white shirt and tie. He was also carrying a Bible and a notebook.

Tisha smiled. "Joan, this is Harris. Harris . . . Joan." Joan and Harris shook hands. "Thank you, Harris. When I sent you that e-mail, I had no idea you would actually read it on air. I hope you didn't get in trouble."

"Trouble, no trouble at all. Besides, after I read it, I quit."

Tisha and Joan looked puzzled.

"Yeah." Harris shook his head. "That's a young man's game. I just couldn't do it anymore. It was getting harder and harder to play that music and live that lifestyle." He turned toward Tisha. "You know that night I came here a while back? Well, the night before, I was the DJ at a private party. At the end of the night, they brought in these underage strippers. I couldn't believe it. One of those girls looked like she was all of thirteen. When I questioned people about it, they were all nonchalant. Both men and women were in there, dancing, getting all up on the girls. Nobody seemed to notice the strippers were children. It left me sick to my stomach. I've seen it all."

Tisha and Joan looked surprised. Harris went on talking. "Like back in the day, when the men would rub up against women on the dance floor. Then I saw it shift to women getting all up on each other. Later on, the men started dancing with each other like they used to dance with women. All I could say the first time I saw that in the club was . . . what's next? Well, that night with those young girls, I saw what was next, and it got me searching for Jesus."

Harris spoke to Tisha like she was the only person in the room. "Thank you again for the Bible you gave me. I read all the Gospels, just like you suggested. Now I'm reading Acts."

"You are so welcome," Tisha said. "I can't believe you quit your job."

"What are you going to do now?" Joan asked.

"Nothing, at least for a while. My mom didn't teach me about Jesus, but she did teach me how to save money. So for now, I'm good. I just want to chill and focus on being a better man. I saw they are having a men's conference coming up soon."

"Yeah. It's always a huge success," Joan said. She could tell by the way Harris looked back at her that he wanted a moment alone with Tisha. "Y'all know what? I need to find Minister Makita. I have to ask her a question." Joan tiptoed away.

Harris moved in closer to Tisha. "You know what? You make me want to get married, buy a house in the suburbs, have a couple of kids, all while working at some corny job . . . like selling lawn mowers."

"What?" Tisha laughed.

"Okay . . . maybe that didn't come out right. What I'm trying to say is . . . can I take you to dinner?"

Tisha was about to open her mouth to answer him, but Harris stopped her and said, "Wait a minute, let me be clear on one thing. I'm not trying to be your friend; I'm trying to be your man. I know pretty girls like you are always trying to make a brotha your friend. But if that's all you want, then let me walk away. I know I'm nothing like Pastor Benjy or any of those Christian brothers I see around here, but I'm willing to learn and respect your body and your boundaries. I want to do this thing right, just as much as you do. Okay? Now you can answer."

Chapter 37

For the last five minutes, Raquel had been sitting alone at a table and staring at her breakfast. "Hello," the squeaky voice said. Raquel looked up quickly, wondering how a child got stuck in jail with her. The dark-haired woman looked and sounded like a twelve-year-old girl. She sat across from Raquel in the prison cafeteria.

Noticing Raquel's startled expression, the woman said, "Hi, I'm Sheila, and by the way, I'm twenty-one. I just have a baby face, I guess." She giggled. "You should try to eat your food. I know it's hard to believe, but breakfast is the best meal of the day."

Raquel was starting to get irritated by her presence. She had been in the place for over three weeks. She knew this meal of lumpy grits, cold but overcooked sausage, and runny eggs was as good as it got. She had been too involved in her thoughts to be concerned with food.

She was certain someone from her life would have shown up by now, offering some type of help. She wasn't surprised that James wasn't answering her phone calls. But she thought her mom might be concerned with her one and only child being locked in a jail. Maybe even a client or two. They always treated Raquel like she was a part of the family, inviting her and the kids to birthday parties and other family gatherings. Did it matter that she never showed up?

James's cousin told her she had two more weeks to find somebody to keep the kids. She talked to Raquel like she was some sort of child, calling her "stupid" and "selfish." Raquel just listened. What could she say to the woman who was keeping her kids with no financial assistance whatsoever from her?

Her attorneys were already working to sell her business. But it would take time, maybe months, before she found a buyer. James had emptied the accounts, and even the secret stash she kept hidden from him was gone. Apparently, James knew about her little secret.

She could attempt to sell the house, once she talked to James, but the housing market dropped right after they signed the dotted line. It would be next to impossible for them to make a profit. For the first time in years, Raquel was broke, and she didn't know what to do about it.

"I have some phone cards and cell phones," Shelia said. "Actually, I have a lot of phone cards and cell phones." Each day the inmates lined up to make phone calls on one phone. The problem was, the line was usually long. If the person whom the inmate was calling didn't answer, she had to go to the back of the line and start the process over again. Then there was the fact that they had no privacy. Everybody could hear every detail of the conversation. A cell phone and phone cards solved those problems.

However, as far as she knew, cell phones were not allowed. On cue, Sheila said, "If you agree to work with me, I'll tell you where you can go to make your calls, and the guards will not bother you."

"So what do you want?" Raquel asked.

"I can tell you are new here. I want soap, magazines, cigarettes, and, most important, food that I can actually eat. I want to load up on stuff at the commissary.

That's what everybody wants around here. The news-people said you were some kind of big entrepreneur before you got locked up. So when your people come by with your money, make sure I get some too, and I'll keep you supplied with all the talk time you need."

That deal sounded good. The only problem was, Raquel didn't have those people. Last week, on *Dana Dillard Live,* a local morning talk show, she saw several of her relatives giving live interviews. A few of them made up stories about coming to visit her and how she was doing well, despite the circumstances. The few women who were watching TV turned to look at her sympathetically. Each knew she hadn't had any visitors beyond her attorneys. Raquel kept waiting for one of the guards to call her name during the two hours they were allowed to have visitors, but none came.

Raquel kept avoiding the fact that she was running out of time. She couldn't put it off any longer. She needed to talk to Joan, and soon. Raquel looked the young woman up and down and instantly switched into the saleswoman she used to be years ago. What worked in front of grocery stores just might work in here. "You have an even bigger problem than your need for soap and magazines."

"What might that be, Killer Bride?" Shelia said with an attitude. "Sounds to me like you are the one with the problem. I'm getting out of here in a few months. The newspeople say you are going to be here a long, long time."

Raquel pretended like she didn't hear her. "Do you have any idea how beautiful you could be with that thick, wild hair of yours? Yes, your cornrows are fabulous, and on somebody else, they would look perfect. With your round face, large eyes, and narrow cheek-bones, though, they are making you look plain." Raquel learned a long time ago that each woman, regardless of how beautiful or intelligent, was always looking to be more attractive. If someone wanted to make it in the beauty business, they had to use this fact to their advantage.

"You say you will be stepping out of here in a little while. How about stepping out while looking like a million bucks? Why don't you let me give you a makeover for the phone and cards. I can do wonders with a little heat. You think you could find me a blow-dryer and hot comb and some kind of oil?"

Shelia looked like she wanted to be offended, but she was intrigued about the idea of having a makeover. "I'll see what I can do," then she moved to another table.

Later in the day, when all of the inmates were sitting around watching TV, Shelia came up to Raquel with a box full of all kinds of hair stuff, curling irons of various sizes, cutting shears, gels, and sprays. Raquel was shocked; some of the stuff was high-end, like the supplies she used in her shop.

"How did you get these?" Raquel picked up the cutting shears and curling iron. "Isn't some of this stuff illegal in here?"

"You see the two guards over there. Don't look up."

Raquel nodded.

"They collected all this stuff for me." Sheila paused. "You need to remember something about prison life, Raquel. Everything you buy on the outside can be bought on the inside." She gave Raquel a devious look. "Remember that, just in case you need a little something special to get your mind off things or maybe just to fall asleep. Miss Sheila can hook you up. I may be young, but I'm resourceful."

Raquel took a deep breath and went to work with her newly acquired supplies. Everybody, including the guards, couldn't wait to see what she was going to do with Sheila's dull, dry hair. The curling irons and cutting shears were going to make the trendy precision cut, which Raquel had in mind for Sheila, into a reality.

"Ping! Ping! Shoo!" That's what Raquel always said when she handed her clients a mirror after she completed one of her masterful hairstyles. Just as she had anticipated, everyone was mesmerized by her skills.

Sheila pulled her hands through her soft, shiny hair. "Oh, wow! It's beautiful. I mean . . . gosh . . . I look like a model or something."

Sheila motioned for Raquel to follow her. They went to a room the size of the bathroom. There Sheila handed Raquel a cell phone and some phone cards. "Don't worry," Sheila said. "Nobody will bother you. I'm sexing one of the head guards in this very room, at least once a week. All these guards know not to bother me in here. Just as long as you stay with me, you will be fine. Go on, dial the number you need."

Raquel felt like she was going to faint at any moment. Her mouth was dry and her hands were shaking. This was the part when she needed to dial Joan's number. Raquel recalled one more time everyone she knew who might be able to take care of her kids. She tugged at her hair and brushed lint off her clothes.

She had to do it. She knew her mother didn't want the kids. She knew her aunts didn't want them. The women she worked with hated her. Of course, they had their reasons; Raquel hadn't been the kindest boss. Then there was Karen, but she couldn't be on the list either.

Raquel could tell Sheila was starting to get annoyed. She went through the facts again. She wanted to cry, but there was no time for tears. She had to be strong for her children. She dialed the number.

"Hello, this is Joan Dallas." She sounded like she was answering her work number instead of a cell phone.

"Hi, Joan, it is Raquel." Raquel bit her bottom lip. She was sure Joan was going to hang up the phone.

"Excuse me? Is this some kind of joke?"

"Yeah, I know I'm the last person you expected to hear from today."

"You got that right."

Raquel didn't hear any condemnation in her voice, despite the blunt words. "Joan, I need you to come and see me tomorrow. I need to talk to you about something important."

"What would that be?" Joan sounded slightly irritated.

"Visiting hours start at eleven and end at one. Please come see me. What I need to say to you, I need to say face-to-face. I guess you know where I am." Raquel started to cry. She didn't know what she was going to do if Joan refused to come. "Will you come?"

Chapter 38

Joan was reading and journaling from 1 Corinthians 13 at her kitchen table. She had promised herself that the very next time she started to feel fed up with the single life, she wasn't going to go shopping, sit around feeling sorry for herself, surf the Internet, or find something good to eat. She was going to head straight to God's Word.

It was Tisha and her new friend, Harris, who had her meditating on the scriptures all evening. The last few times she had spoken to Tisha, every other sentence started with Harris's name:

"Harris is almost finished reading the entire Bible, even though he just started. . . . Harris and I pray at the beginning and end of each of our dates. . . . Harris likes sushi. . . . Harris is so funny."

Harris . . . Harris . . . Harris!

Joan wanted to call Tisha and tell her about the unexpected call she had received that afternoon. However, she knew Tisha would find a way to insert Harris into the discussion. Joan was determined to be happy for Tisha, but she had reached her quota of "Harris" sentences for the day.

She thought about calling Minister Makita or Janet, but instead she went back to the scriptures. When she first became a Christian, she was constantly memorizing scripture that she would write on index cards. She couldn't remember the last time she had done that. She found an old discarded, blank batch in her nightstand and began to write and say out loud, *"'Love is patient, love is kind. It does not envy, it does not boast, it is not proud. It is not rude, it is not self-seeking, it is not easily angered, it keeps no record of wrongs. Love does not delight in evil but rejoices with the truth. It always protects, always trusts, always hopes, always perseveres. Love never fails.'"*

Joan recited these words, over and over, until that next day, when she was face-to-face with the woman who had been her enemy for as long as she could remember.

Raquel looked at Joan from head to toe. She wasn't the cutest, but she certainly was working everything she had. She had on a sundress that stopped just below her knees, and her hair was so bouncy and light, it would have been blowing in the wind, if they had been outside.

Her handbag and jewelry looked so unique, it had to be handmade. She showed off her curvaceous legs with a pair of strappy high-heeled sandals. Everything fit together perfectly. Her ensemble of greens, yellows, and browns looked like it had been put together by an expert stylist.

Raquel was in an orange jumpsuit. Her hair was rolled back in a tight bun. Her face was naked of makeup and her eyes looked the way they had since the day she walked into prison—tearstained, highlighted by dark circles.

Raquel thought about the last time they had been together. "I'm sorry about the way I treated you at Cyclone." Then Raquel remembered all the threatening phone calls she had made to Joan, and all the angry voice mails she had left on her cell phone. And finally there was the time, years ago, when she and Joan came to blows with James in between them.

They were both silent for a while, meditating on their past altercations and the years they had spent in love with the same man. They were sitting across from each other. The only thing that separated them was a plain black table.

The question left Raquel's mouth before she realized it: "Do you still love him, Joan?"

"I don't know. Sometimes I'm absolutely certain that I'm completely out of love with him. I can go days, months, without really thinking about him. Other days . . . well, other days are different."

"I see." Raquel folded her arms around her chest.

"The one thing that I'm absolutely certain of is that I do lust after him," Joan continued. "I don't like being single and celibate. As a matter of fact, it really sucks. As of recently, I have decided that I'm no longer going to be one of those people that sit around and say how saved and satisfied they are. I am not going to be satisfied until I'm married and having a lot of mind-blowing sex."

Raquel was intrigued by Joan's response. It seemed as if she was walking into a discussion Joan was already having with herself. "What if God doesn't send you a husband?" she asked.

"If that's God's will for me, fine, but I'm not going to pretend like I'm happy about it," Joan said. "I'm not that mature—maybe one day, but I'm not anywhere near that point yet."

Joan folded her arms in the same way that Raquel had. "Do you love him?" she asked.

Raquel looked at her brightly colored jumpsuit and the cold gray surroundings of the meeting room. "Look at what I did, Joan. Isn't it obvious how much I love him?"

"I'm not sure if what we feel for him is love or worship."

Raquel looked at her, confused. "I've never heard those two words compared."

"Up until last night, I'm not sure I would have compared the two," Joan said. "You know, no man could get to me the way James could. I was happy when he was acting right. I was sad when he decided to start tripping. I could be having a good day, but one wrong word from him and I would lose my footing. 'Is he going to call today? Is he going to lie to me today? Who is he with? Where is he going?' It was a constant roller coaster."

Raquel said matter-of-factly, "Should one person have that much control over another human being?"

"Do you know what the First Commandment is?"

Raquel thought a minute, and was surprised when she realized she actually did know the answer to Joan's question. Watching those religious movies around the holidays had taught her something. "It's about loving the Lord with all your heart, mind, and soul." Raquel sank down in her seat and silently recited the words back to herself.

"So my problem is that I was worshipping James instead of Jesus," Raquel said as she gave Joan a fake smile. "And all I have to do is start to worship Jesus, and everything will be okay, right?"

"Wrong!" Joan shook her head. "It's not easy to switch loyalties, at least not for me. Part of me just wants to find a two-hundred-fifty-pound all-muscle personal trainer and have my way with him."

Raquel laughed. "So what's stopping you from running to the gym for that personal trainer?"

"You know when I was at my happiest . . . ?" Joan suddenly stopped speaking.

"Go on and talk." Raquel knew Joan stopped because she didn't want to hurt her feelings. "You are speaking of the time when you, James, and James Jr. were all living together in the same house."

"Yes. I thought everything was finally going to fall into place, that I was finally going to have my peace. But it still wasn't enough. There was this nagging, gnawing thing that wouldn't go away." Joan paused a few moments and then asked, "Do you know what I'm talking about, Raquel?"

"That's why I wanted to get married to James," Raquel said. "I thought when we were all legal and everything . . . well, it would go away."

"Well, that's the answer to your question," Joan said. "That void . . . incompleteness, that's what's been keeping me from that personal trainer. I know that he would only be a temporary high. It will be fun for the moment, but after it goes away, then I will have to find something else to make it go away again.

"Some days, I'm completely filled with the Spirit and enjoying every moment of God's presence," Joan continued. "The last thing on my mind is a man. And other days, I'm so frustrated, I could cry. On those days, it is the hardest thing I have ever done.

"The only thing I have going for me is knowing that my soul is saved and that I'm not going to the hell I deserve to go to." Joan put both of her hands in the air. "There will be a day when there are no more tears, no more pain, and no more sorrow."

"I don't want to be one of those that find Jesus in jail," Raquel said. "You know the type, 'My whole world was in chaos until this missionary came to my jail and told me about Jesus. I know that He has washed all my sins away. Now my whole life has changed since I let Jesus into my heart. These bars don't bother me because one day I know I'm going to be free with him in heaven. Hallelujah and praise God!'" Raquel mocked.

"I don't think it's funny that people find Jesus in jail," Joan said. "People in a crisis situation can't help themselves, so that's the only time they are open to it. My pastor says you can't find an atheist in an emergency room or on the front lines of a war. When things get that bad, everybody is ready to pray to Jesus."

"Why don't you think there are any atheists in the emergency room?" Raquel asked.

"I guess on your deathbed, it doesn't seem so unlikely that an all-powerful Savior came to the world to save you from your sins. You no longer are filled with pride about what happens in the afterlife, knowing you will be there in a hot second."

"I'm going to be in jail a long time, at least ten years."

Joan tried to hide her disbelief. "I would say that's a crisis situation."

"But I still would be surprised if I ended up being a Christian."

"After today, I don't think anything would surprise me," Joan said. "I mean, how long have we been talking and you still haven't asked me to keep your kids."

Raquel pushed her seat away from the table in shock.

"Your attorney called me this morning and explained the situation. We have a hearing with a judge to grant me emergency custody. If everything goes well, the social worker could drop them off at my place as early as next week."

Raquel started to cry. "I can't believe you would do this for me."

"Well, of course, I was shocked. I'm still shocked," Joan said. "But I'm not looking at the world the way I used to. I want to get married to a man who loves Jesus so much, he wouldn't dare touch me until our wedding night. I want more kids. I want to sit around the table and eat fabulous family dinners, followed by prayer sessions. I want it all, the two-story black-and-white house, with two golden retrievers in the backyard in a beautiful neighborhood with top-notch schools. Not to mention great sex, and godly friends to endure the storms of life together. In other words, a life filled with passion, purpose, and laughter."

"But until then?" Raquel asked.

"Until then, and if 'then' never happens, I want whatever God wants."

"You believe God wants you to keep my kids for me?"

Joan paused and looked up to the ceiling. "Yes, I have peace about it. Me and you? We aren't enemies, we were just suffering from the same disease. We made a man our god and suffered the consequences."

"You know, most of the women in this prison are here because of something they did to a man or because of a man, or right alongside a man." Raquel pushed her chair back to the table. "Joan, I don't want my baby girl to grow up anything like me or the women serving time with me.

"And on top of that," Raquel continued, "I don't want her living her life through other people's eyes, like I did. I want her to get the First Commandment right. Caring what other people think, trying to manipulate their impression of me, and making a man my god is what got me here.

"I was so desperate to get their approval that I lost it, and now . . ." Raquel stopped and slowly let the words flow from her mouth for the first time. "I shot two people . . . dead. It wasn't an accident. The gun didn't just go off in the tussle. I fired and shot. And you know why? Because my gods had failed me. I was worshipping the wrong people and the wrong things. They hurt me, left me, and treated me badly, and I retaliated in anger. Those gods can't be trusted. Tell me, Joan, the God you serve, can He be trusted?"

"With all of your heart, your mind, and your soul." Joan stood up to leave.

She gave Raquel a small bag filled with a leather study Bible and a journal. "No pressure. I understand you have a lot of free time on your hands."

Chapter 39

James had spent the last three weeks in Mexico watching Pastor Benjy, Kenneth, and the other men minister to the inmates in the prison. He stayed in the background, listening and taking notes.

The night James spent in the prison changed the negative atmosphere. The guards reported that the inmates rarely had fights anymore. They read their Bibles daily and eagerly waited for Pastor Benjy and his crew to present their lessons each day. The guards were so impressed with the inmates, even they became interested in learning more about the Bible too. Pastor Gonzales volunteered to come on the weekends and teach them separately.

Each evening, after the men spent the day ministering, they would prepare dinner together. Then they would play basketball, video games, or dominoes. James would spend most of his time on the sidelines, barely touching his food and making excuses not to play the games.

Pastor Benjy asked James if he wanted to discuss the night he spent in the prison any further. James declined. Pastor Benjy told him if he ever wanted to talk, he was available. That's how all the men dealt with James. They never pressured him; they just let him know the door was open if he ever felt like walking through it.

James tried really hard not to like them. After all, he spent his life not liking Christians. He told himself they must be a bunch of uneducated idiots, but he found out all of the leaders on the ministry team had advanced degrees and professional positions. Then he decided they must all be homosexuals; but after watching them around women, and listening to them talk about women, he realized that didn't fit either.

Kenneth often found a way to insert Lila's name into the conversation. Everyone was starting to tease him about it, but instead of getting defensive, Kenneth would simply keep talking. He explained he had treated women so badly in his past, he didn't think God would give him a good one again. He told the group he intended on making Lila his wife. Initially he was bothered that Lila had a child, but after getting to know Jasmine, he could see she was not a liability but an asset to be treasured. He often referred to the two of them as "my girls."

Suddenly James had an image of Alexis in his head, not as a little girl, but as a grown woman. She was beautiful, long, and elegant like a ballerina. Then James saw Morris, all grown up and a foot taller than himself. He was in a football uniform, proudly displaying James's last name on the back of his jersey.

Kenneth walked into James's bedroom doorway. Looking at James's surprised expression, he said, "I'm sorry. I didn't mean to interrupt."

James let his forehead fall into his hands; then he squeezed long and hard, like he had a migraine. "No, man, it is no problem. I was just thinking about my kids."

Kenneth started pulling imaginary lint off his suit and casually said, "I never heard you talk about your kids before. How old are they?"

Kenneth and the other men had attempted to get James to open up and talk, but James had refused each time. He didn't want to be their next project. Several times, he had seen them walk up to an inmate, and they would get the inmate talking about something particularly worrisome in his life. Within minutes, they were pushing Jesus down his throat. Sometimes the prisoners would even start crying. At the end of the day, they would talk about how many conversions or potential conversions they had that day.

James knew they were each waiting to have one of those tear-jerking and life-altering conversations with him. James hadn't made up his mind about Jesus. Yeah, this group of guys was different from any of the Christians he had met. Yeah, they seemed authentic and even likable, but he wanted to explore the world's major religions. If there came a point where he did become a Christian, he wouldn't be crying and running to the altar like some weak-minded woman.

Not telling their ages, James stood up and looked at Kenneth, eye to eye. "What brings you around? I thought we were just chilling today. Did something change?"

"No, no, I was just going to pick up some groceries for dinner tonight. I wanted to do something special, since we are leaving in the morning. I heard you telling Pastor G you were some sort of grill master." James recalled the conversation. Pastor Gonzales was trying to get him to talk. James was careful to keep the conversation related to food.

Kenneth went on with his pitch. "Besides, you barely eat what we cook. I was thinking we could pick up something more to your liking. . . . So you wanna ride?"

"It's not that complicated. I'm just not a big fan of Mexican food," James lied. He had barely been eating and playing games with them because, as the days went by, he was starting to like them. If he had started sharing meals and playing games, he might have let his guard down.

James went on, "I'm more of a meat-and-potatoes kind of guy."

"You aren't the only one. I could use a nice New York strip myself, along with a roasted sweet potato and a spinach salad, with cherry tomatoes and goat cheese, tossed in a simple lemon vinaigrette," Kenneth admitted.

James perked up. He hadn't had a good steak in months. "I'm in. I'll go with you. I have a rub I put on all my steaks that will make you sing. I just hope I can find all the ingredients at the store."

James saw the smile spread on Kenneth's face and immediately wished he hadn't let his emotions show. He would have to be extra diligent to make sure he didn't share anything more with Kenneth, no matter how much he pried.

His kids were his business. *His* kids? This was the first time since learning Alexis and Morris were not his that he thought of them as his kids. James could feel the peace flowing through his body. Morris and Alexis were not liabilities, but treasured gifts.

They were barely out of the parking garage before Kenneth attempted to get James talking. "What are your plans when we get back to the States?" Kenneth asked.

"I have no clue."

"You know the thing that really jumpstarted my spiritual growth was when I decided to write letters to all of the women in my life that I had done dirty," Kenneth offered. "Pastor Benjy did an entire series on honoring the women in our lives. It made me realize that I had some wrongs I needed to make right. It really helped me deal with my past. So how about writing letters to Joan and Raquel?"

James was surprised to hear their names. Kenneth and the other men never appeared to know his story, and he never mentioned it to them. He also never bothered to tell Kenneth he'd known his girlfriend, since she and Joan had been close friends for years.

"I'm surprised to hear their names come out of your mouth," James stated.

"We have been praying for you, asking God to give you wisdom about what to do when you get back."

"Thanks, I appreciate that."

"We have a position available at the church. It's a security position. Pastor asked me if I thought you might be interested."

James's voice got higher. "Churches need security?"

"You ever heard the saying, 'The devil comes to church every Sunday'? Well, it's true. There are people who come to worship and fellowship with other believers, but there are also people who come to steal anything that is not nailed down. You would be working closely with several other men in the church. By the way, Pastor Benjy encourages everybody on staff to come to church and Bible Study regularly. So, are you interested?"

James was shocked. Pastor Benjy was really going out of his way to help him. He felt himself want to cry, but he wasn't about to let one tear fall. He simply said, "Yes, I'm interested."

"Cool. I'll let him know."

The entire time he was in Mexico, he had tried not to think about what was happening back home. Both Raquel and Joan had called him repeatedly, but he refused to answer the phone. He just didn't have words to explain everything that was going through his mind, and he didn't want to risk saying something he didn't mean. But with letters, maybe he could get his point across. He tried to imagine what the first conversations would be like when he arrived home.

Before long, he knew Kenneth was right. He definitely needed to write letters.

Chapter 40

Raquel closed the Bible that Joan had given her, and for the first time in her life, she stared at the sky, the clouds, the birds, and listened for the wind. Each day, the inmates were allowed one hour to exercise outside. For the last few days, Raquel had used this time to read her Bible and think. She sat on the concrete pavement, while the other inmates used this time to gather in small groups.

Raquel had just finished reading:

The heavens declare the glory of God, the skies proclaim the work of his hands. Day after day they pour forth speech; night after night they display knowledge.

Psalm 19 was quickly becoming her favorite.

She closed her eyes and pondered a God so big that He spoke and the world appeared. Within seconds, she started to feel fuzzy all over, like she was getting one big invisible hug.

"You have a visitor."

Raquel stood up and looked at the guard suspiciously. There was no need for her attorney to visit her. "Are you coming or what? You need to hurry up. Visiting hours are almost over."

Raquel followed the guard, wondering who would be there waiting when she arrived. Her visitor stood up when she walked into the room. He had clearly lost weight, and his beard, which was always perfectly shaved, was overgrown. But his eyes—those sleepy eyes that she had fallen in love with back in the eleventh grade—were bright and welcoming.

He reached his hands out to her. She willingly accepted his embrace. She put her hands around his waist and sank her head deep into his chest and cried. He cried too. He tried to speak; then she tried to speak, but the words couldn't break through the constant tears.

The guard came and broke them up. She reluctantly let him go. They were only allowed to hug at the beginning and end of the visit. They took their seats across from each other.

"I almost didn't get in here. Apparently, visiting hours are almost over." James tapped his foot nervously.

"James, there is something I need to tell you."

"Me too. Actually, it's something I wrote." James pulled the letter from his pocket and gave it to Raquel.

She looked at it first. "You want me to read it now?"

"Please go ahead."

Raquel started to read the letter silently:

Raquel,

I'm sorry. I'm sorry for every lie I ever told you. I'm sorry for the horrible way I treated you. I'm sorry for cheating on you. I'm sorry for not being the man you deserved.

I have learned that I can't expect forgiveness unless I, too, forgive. Please forgive me, Raquel, and, in turn, I promise to forgive you. Instead of dwelling on the past, I'm moving forward. No more part-time fatherhood for me. I'm going to get our children around positive people who not only claim to be Christians, but are living according to the Bible.

I'm going to make sure they know all about you; how hard you worked for them, the gentle way you took care of them. How in spite of your busy career, you made sure their needs were met.

I will bring them to visit you often and I'll make sure they always know who their mother is. I'll never allow them to hear anyone speak negatively concerning you. They will hear words of forgiveness and grace.

I know this is going to sound crazy coming from me, but I have found some comfort in Christianity. No, no, no, I'm not turning into some "no drinking, no dancing, no fun" Bible thumper. But a little while ago, I was ready to kill myself, and I had the pills to prove it.

But now that I have been reading the scriptures and hanging out with some authentic brothers, I don't find myself dwelling on taking my life. This hope is coming from somewhere. Just between me and you, I believe it's coming from Jesus.

This road isn't going to be easy for us. We have both made choices that we are going to have to live with for the rest of our lives. However, I'm going to be encouraged, and I want you to be encouraged too.

I learned a scripture this morning. "Weeping may endure for a night, but joy is coming in the morning." The morning is coming, Raquel!

I found the necklace Morris made for you on the first day of kindergarten. I want you to wear it. It's in a circle. In a circle, there is no ending and no beginning. I want you to remember that you are loved with a deep, enduring, everlasting, no-ending type of love.

James

They talked a few more moments; then James put the necklace around her neck. After a quick hug, the guard led her away.

***

Joan popped a bag of popcorn and logged on to her favorite social networking site. It was one in the morning, and even though she was exhausted, she couldn't sleep. She had too much on her mind.

She spent the entire day getting ready for Alexis and Morris to arrive the next day. Her spare bedroom was all decked out with a princess bedroom set for Alexis. Joan didn't know if James Jr. was more excited about sharing his bedroom with his big brother, Morris, or the new bunk beds she had purchased.

Then there was the phone call she received from Harris. Although he wasn't going to propose to Tisha for several months, he wanted to get prepared to purchase an engagement ring. Harris needed to make sure he could afford to get Tisha exactly what she wanted. It took Joan only a few moments to text Harris a link to a Web site with a picture of Tisha's dream ring. It was something the best friends had discussed many times. Harris ended the call by asking Joan not to tell Tisha. Joan was happy for Tisha, but she was sad for herself.

She typed her password on her laptop and waited for her page to come up. Darren had posted a picture of himself getting baptized, while his little girls and their mother looked on. Janet posted pictures of her newborn baby boy. Joan laughed out loud. There were at least seventy of them. The first-time parents had documented every detail of his birth.

Joan was looking for photo paper to print out pictures of Janet's baby, when she noticed a letter somebody must have slipped underneath the front door. As soon as she opened it, she recognized James's handwriting:

Joan,

I know it seems weird getting a letter from me. I've been so distant lately. I'm sorry for so many reasons. I'm sorry for the lies, the other women, for not being the man you needed me to be. I'm sorry for all the confusion, strife, and tension I brought into your life. Please forgive me; I didn't know what I was doing. I was trying so hard to act like a man, but I only ended up acting like a fool.

You know you have affected me more than any other woman I have ever met. I admire the way you never allowed me to knock you off your feet. You never lost yourself. Deep down, I always knew you were too much woman for me to handle.

You proved it to me so many times, just like the last time we were together. Your body was screaming "yes," but you refused to obey it and kicked me out.

It was Jesus, wasn't it? That's how you overcame temptation. I have met a lot of women, people in general, who claim to be Christians. You are the only one I'm completely sure about. You are the real deal, and I want you to know that kicking me out that day was the best thing you could have done for me. You let me know that God was real, and even though I chose to ignore it at the time, it was a life-changing moment for me.

That's why when I was contemplating killing myself, I couldn't get to you fast enough. I could see that God had changed you, that you knew Him intimately and could tell me something about Him.

Thanks for introducing me to Pastor Benjy. I don't have words to describe what the last few weeks have been like. But I'll say this, instead of wanting to kill myself, I want to grow and learn.

While my mistakes are many, I know that I can be a blessing to the world. (Well . . . maybe.)

I knew women were powerful, but I really had no idea how much so. A woman who is serving God in word and action is impossible to ignore. The world would be a better place if women realized they have the power to influence men to straighten up and act right.

I was on the crooked path, but God used you to lead me to the straight path, and I will be eternally grateful. I wanted you to read this letter before I saw you. I talked to Raquel and she told me what you agreed to do. I'm in awe of you, Joan. Now that I'm back, I know there are a lot of decisions that need to be made.

Pastor Benjy offered me a job, and my neighbor across the street has been calling me like crazy. He wants to buy my house; there's something about needing it for his business. I have a funny feeling and sneaky suspicion that everything is going to be okay.

James

Joan went to her bathroom and turned on the water, making it as hot as she could stand it. She stepped into the shower and allowed the water to hit her face. The rushing water made her remember something one of her college professors used to say: "Life isn't about surviving the storm, it's about learning to dance in the rain."

Joan couldn't explain why tears started to fall from her face. She dipped her head into the warm water and smiled. "Lord, I finally learned how to dance."

Reader's Group Guide Questions

1. Joan felt like she couldn't tell her friends about her struggles with sexual temptation. Why do you believe this was so hard for her?

2. Janet was in tears when Joan admitted she was jealous of her marriage to Jerome. Was there anything Janet could have done to reach out to her single friends before three years went by?

3. What should Raquel have done when she found out James knew her secret concerning the children?

4. Joan claimed people are more open to having a relationship with Jesus Christ in a crisis situation. Do you agree with this? Why or why not?

5. Do you know any single Christian men who claim to be abstinent? Do you believe them? What are some of the struggles they may face?

6. What are your thoughts on the conversation Minister Makita had with Joan about the Wife Preparation class? Did Makita go too far? What would you have done if you were Joan? What do you think about the idea of having a Wife Preparation class?

7. James's childhood experiences caused him to be critical of Christianity. How did your childhood influence your relationship with Christ?

8. When Joan agreed to help Raquel, did it surprise you? How so?

9. The event Joan and Tisha hosted featured anonymous questions. How did the anonymous questions influence the event? Would your church be open to an event like this? Why or why not?

10. In the beginning, how did you feel about James, Raquel, and Joan? How did you feel about them at the end of the story?

About the Author

Mimi Jefferson is an author/speaker with a passion for women's ministry. She has spoken to hundreds of women throughout the country. She is a graduate of the College of Biblical Studies, with a B.S. in Christian ministry. Mimi lives in the Houston area with her husband and two children. To contact Mimi for speaking engagements or for book club discussions, go to Mimi-Jefferson.com or e-mail info@mimijefferson.com.

UC HIS GLORY BOOK CLUB!

www.uchisglorybookclub.net

UC His Glory Book Club is the spirit-inspired brain-child of Joylynn Jossel, Author and Acquisitions Editor of Urban Christian, and Kendra Norman-Bellamy, Author for Urban Christian. This is an online book club that hosts authors of Urban Christian. We welcome as members all men and women who have a passion for reading Christian-based fiction.

UC HIS GLORY BOOK CLUB pledges our commitment to provide support, positive feedback, encouragement, and a forum whereby members can openly discuss and review the literary works of Urban Christian authors.

There is no membership fee associated with UC His Glory Book Club; however, we do ask that you support the authors through purchasing, encouraging, providing book reviews, and of course, your prayers. We also ask that you respect our beliefs and follow the guidelines of the book club. We hope to receive your valuable input, opinions, and reviews that build up, rather than tear down our authors.

WHAT WE BELIEVE:

• We believe that Jesus is the Christ, Son of the Living God.

• We believe the Bible is the true, living Word of God.

• We believe all Urban Christian authors should use their God-given writing abilities to honor God and share the message of the written word God has given to each of them uniquely.

• We believe in supporting Urban Christian authors in their literary endeavors by reading, purchasing and sharing their titles with our online community.

• We believe that in everything we do in our literary arena should be done in a manner that will lead to God being glorified and honored.

• We look forward to the online fellowship with you. Please visit us often at *www.uchisglorybookclub.net*.

Many Blessing to You!
Shelia E. Lipsey,
President, UC His Glory Book Club

ORDER FORM
URBAN BOOKS, LLC
78 E. Industry Ct
Deer Park, NY 11729

Name: (please print):_____

Address: _____

City/State: _____

Zip: _____

QTY	TITLES	PRICE
	3:57 A.M Timing Is Everything	$14.95
	A Man's Worth	$14.95
	A Woman's Worth	$14.95
	Abundant Rain	$14.95
	After The Feeling	$14.95
	Amaryllis	$14.95
	An Inconvenient Friend	$14.95
	Battle of Jericho	$14.95
	Be Careful What You Pray For	$14.95
	Beautiful Ugly	$14.95
	Been There Prayed That:	$14.95
	Before Redemption	$14.95

Shipping and handling-add $3.50 for 1st book, then $1.75 for each additional book.

Please send a check payable to:

Urban Books, LLC

Please allow 4-6 weeks for delivery

ORDER FORM
URBAN BOOKS, LLC
78 E. Industry Ct
Deer Park, NY 11729

ne: (please print): _____

Address: _____

City/State: _____

Zip: _____

QTY	TITLES	PRICE

Shipping and handling-add $3.50 for 1st book, then $1.75 for each additional book.

Please send a check payable to:
Urban Books, LLC
Please allow 4-6 weeks for delivery